CHAPTER ONE

POPPY 1.0

Just after I moved into the guesthouse, they buried a dead girl in my yard. That's when my life turned upside down and inside out for the second time. The first time was when the doctors rearranged my colon.

I was thrilled to move into the Topanga Canyon guesthouse, a boho-chic area north of Los Angeles. I knew about Topanga from growing up in the nearby San Fernando Valley. Now, as a struggling, mostly unemployed actress, I was living in a shitty, Hollywood neighborhood. Although it was a cute, little bungalow, the environment was killing me—dirty, filthy, hot, too much traffic, zero fresh air, noisy and people living on the edge. Hollywood was no longer glamorous. And parking was a son of a bitch. Also, at age forty-six, I was done stepping over homeless people. Sorry-not-sorry, and I deserved different and better. Even though many times, I had been on the verge of homeless myself.

The universe spoke when I met Lily Jin at a Hollywood acting workshop. She was exotic-looking and a mixed something. A twenty-two-year-old gal, and a lite-Buddhist, like me. I usually do just enough chanting to keep the demons and gremlins away for the day.

Lily was wearing torn jeans over her long, model-like legs and a midriff exposing a flat, firm tummy. There was not an ounce of fat anywhere.

Oh, to be twenty again and be able to eat, drink, smoke and snort anything. That was several decades behind me. My five-six, lanky frame was getting flabby. Yes, even skinny people can get flabby. I was now in yucky perimenopause, with the last of my overcooked eggs dropping into withering fallopian tubes and heading down through my dried-up hoo-ha. Luckily, at first glance, you can't tell this is happening unless you're airport security staff.

My dirty blonde shoulder length hair only needed a bit of henna to hide the grey and my brown eyes were still bright and youthful. This helped my agent place me in the thirty-five-to-forty-five roles, despite being in my mid-forties.

To date, no surgery, minimal fillers and injectables. However, as I headed towards the half-century mark, I would revisit. In the meantime, I strove to sharpen my acting skills, and let gravity have its way with me.

While in the workshop, Lily and I tried following the acting exercise. As we were pretending to be wounded sheep during an alien invasion, Lily whispered to me, asking if I knew of anyone who wanted to rent her guesthouse. After the workshop, we went to the El Compadre on Sunset to discuss the details. We were served frozen skinny margs, then toasted each other and became

THERE'S A DEAD GIRL IN MY YARD

ANGELA PAGE

MIA ALTIERI

For information regarding permission, please write to:
info@barringerpublishing.com
Barringer Publishing, Naples, Florida
www.barringerpublishing.com

Cover, design and layout by Linda S. Duider
Cape Coral, Florida

ISBN: 978-1-954396-12-8
Library of Congress Cataloging-in-Publication Data
There's a Dead Girl in My Yard
Angela Page and Mia Altieri

Printed in U.S.A.

besties in an instant. When Lily told me that the guesthouse was in Topanga Canyon, I shouted over the mariachi band, "I'll take it, I'll take it, I'll take it!" Even sight unseen and not knowing the price, she had me at "Topanga Canyon."

I had heard about Topanga. It was crawling with the famous and the has-beens who never were. The town was known for its eclectic artists and colorful history, including one of the Manson family murders. During the Hollywood golden age, it was the weekend getaway hotspot for the now-dead stars you can see on the Turner Classic Movie channel. It had changed, but still had some leftover glamour and pricey homes. I was already fantasizing about living among the stars, wearing designer sunglasses and sipping champagne.

Before Lily would show me the property, we had to chant together while we were still drinking at El Compadre. The place was crowded, and the mariachi band was still in high gear. I knew I looked skeptical about chanting.

"Come on, we can do it. Tune the Mexicans out," Lily said as she closed her eyes and chanted.

The waiter came by and made a comment. But I only caught, "*Locas.*" I kept one eye open and one closed while I chanted with Lily.

It felt like a minute, and then she paused. We both instinctually did a pinkie swear. As we exhaled, we vowed to make this living situation work. I was cleared to visit the digs. But the rent Lily was going to charge was under market. So, was there a catch: leaking roof, Peeping Toms, bad plumbing, crawling with critters?

I looked up Lily's house on Google Earth. The main house

looked fabulous, but it didn't give me a good angle of the guesthouse. But I had faith that it was my destiny, especially when I learned about the Tongya tribe. They were the original inhabitants of Topanga and a very spiritual people. The tribe made a concoction with the *Datura* plant that caused visions and other supernatural shit. Organic L, S, fucking D—bring it on.

Those groovy Indians believed in a supreme being who unscrambled chaos. Cool. I could feel living in such a mystical place would give me, literally, spiritual medicine.

The Tongya tribe was so damn woke that going back three hundred years, they had male and female leaders. These natives didn't believe in evil spirits or any sort of hell. "Yes, please," I said aloud, when I read this information. They revered owls and porpoises. Snap, my faves.

I left my dirty, smelly, Hollywood neighborhood and headed to the Pacific Coast Highway. I turned inland and headed up Route 27 and could smell the ocean breeze and see the majestic mountains. The main drag, Topanga Canyon Road, led to a small village with a grocery store, a café, an antique shop, and palm reader signs. "I'm in," I said out loud.

Any serious retail therapy could be done in Woodland Hills, a few miles away.

I arrived at Lily's property at 1611 Bilberry Lane. It had a gate and a camera. Lily buzzed me in, and I parked in front of the main house. As I stepped out of the car, she greeted me in her signature, torn jeans.

"Cool. You made it," Lily said.

"This is heaven!" I exclaimed.

She led me to a stone path around the back of the main house. The guesthouse stood to the right and had its own yard that adjoined a landscaped area near the main house. The guesthouse was perfect. It had a large living and dining area with an open-plan galley kitchen. There was a large bedroom, a walk-in closet and an upscale bathroom, with a shower and a tub. Yeehaw.

It was mostly furnished, which was great as my stuff was Goodwill vintage and deserved to be left at the curb.

Lily opened the walk-in closet, which had clothes, shoes, and handbags.

"Help yourself. I have been meaning to send this stuff to charity," Lily said.

What better charity than the very needy Poppy Shaw? Lily said the clothes weren't her style—too chic and too expensive.

From a large, picture window, I could see the beautifully landscaped yard. I noticed a tree ready to be planted. Lily mumbled something about Jesus the gardener coming to dig a hole, then corrected herself.

"Mexican Heysus, not that dude hanging from the cross."

Lily showed me inside the main house, where she lived. It was magazine-photo-spread ready.

"My mother hopes I get married and raise a family in this house. But my bio clock is on slo-mo," Lily noted.

"You have loads of time, Lily. It's all over for me," I said.

"My Chinese family made an arranged marriage when I was ten."

"What were they thinking?" I chimed in.

Lily frowned and replied, "Duh? At ten, I announced that I

would probably never marry a real guy and had fantasies of sex with a hermaphrodite."

"That was bold," I said without flinching.

"That announcement had me with a shrink for years, until I promised my parents that I would marry a boy and have babies."

"I thought I had troubles when I told my Catholic parents I was dating a Jew," I noted.

Lily said I had to make up my mind soon about renting the guesthouse. She was heading to Japan for a series of modeling jobs and needed to close the deal before she left.

I told Lily I would sign a one-year lease and whipped out my checkbook. Lily looked perplexed and asked, "Wah dat? I only do Venmo or PayPal." There was my age showing. I always tried hard not to mention old TV sitcoms, dead rock stars, TV dinners, and phone booths. But there was my vintage checkbook, shouting out my age like my crow's feet and creased neck. She took my old-school check. She looked at it as if she had not seen one before. I was not even sure she knew what to do with it.

"My mom will come by and tell you she lives here, but she doesn't. Don't pay any attention to her crazy shit. Sending her back to China asap," Lily informed me.

I saluted Lily and said, "Copy that."

I moved in a few days later. Lily got the day wrong and said she didn't expect me so early. She looked nervous and said a memorial service was going to take place that afternoon. They were planting an olive tree to memorialize her friend Dalia, who had just died after a nasty battle with cancer.

"Heysus" and a couple of guys arrived and discussed with

Lily the right spot to plant the tree. The men were awkward in their behavior. Maybe they knew the late Dalia.

Dealing with death makes people act strange.

I heard the front gate buzzer several times and watched as people assembled in the yard near the guesthouse. There was a table in the yard with a champagne bucket and glasses. The tree was in a pot, and there was a hole ready to welcome it.

I busied myself unpacking boxes and suitcases, but I was curious to see what was happening. From my window, I watched the people enter the yard, all dressed up and chatting. Someone popped the champagne and handed out glasses. I watched Lily bring out an urn and hand it to a young man. Another man had a shovel. The people stood around with champagne while Lily placed the urn in the hole; then the young man lifted the tree and put it in with more dirt on top.

I then realized they were probably burying Dalia in my yard under said olive tree—this was the memorial. Holy shit. I saw the damn urn, full of human ashes, being placed in my new yard. Living in a fucking cemetery was not what I had in mind.

A few hours after the burial service, Lily knocked on my door. She was getting ready to leave for the airport.

At this point, I assumed the remains of dead Dalia were in the urn under the olive tree.

But I didn't want to seem like a snooper and Peeping Thomasina, so I said nothing.

"I gave out your number, so you may get a text or two from people asking to come by and see the tree," Lily warned.

"So, I need to let strangers in here to visit the tree?" I asked.

"Hey, you're getting a smokin' deal on this guesthouse," Lily replied. So here was the catch, but I went with the flow.

"How do I know they're legit?" I asked. Lily showed me her phone.

"Adding you to the Dalia FB and WhatsApp fan club groups. These are the legit peeps. If anyone looks sketchy, don't let them in," Lily said.

No sooner had Lily left for the airport in an Uber than I received my first text. It was from Dalia's husband.

Acer: Hi Poppy, it's Acer, Dalia's husband. Can I visit the tree and take the Jag?

Me: Sure, but what Jag?

Acer: In the garage, hope it's still there?

Now, why wasn't this Acer at the memorial service? What Jag? There was no Lily to ask. I texted back that it was OK to come on the weekend. Then I ran out to the garage to look for a car. While I headed to the garage, an older Asian woman emerged from an Uber with luggage. She wore a grey tunic, baggy pants and a red kerchief around her head. She smiled as she walked towards me then looked me up and down intensely. I was being examined and by whom?

"Are you Poppy?" the woman asked. "I'm Lily's mother, Mu Jin. I live here now."

"That's cool. Nice to meet you, Mrs. Mu Jin," I said.

"Just Mu Jin Ju. In Chinese means 'two flowers'—hibiscus and chrysanthemum. My mother says I smelled like one of them when I came out of her body. Can't remember which one."

"Thanks for the fun fact," I responded and couldn't believe

this pure Chinese woman was Lily's mother. She must have sensed my confusion and clarified the situation.

"After I married a Cubano, my mother called me Ba Ba . . ."

I finished her sentence, "Ba Ba black sheep." She added, "He was really brown, not black."

A Cuban father would explain Lily's exotic look, Cuban Chinese. That's also a cuisine, "*comidas chinas.*" I wondered how Mu Jin and Lily ended up in Topanga.

Too early to be a buttinsky.

Mu Jin entered the main house rolling two, large suitcases. It looked like the woman was moving in. I was conflicted about telling Lily and didn't want to be in the position of throwing her mother out.

I went to the garage and only saw Lily's BMW. Where was Dalia's Jag?

I knocked on the front door, hoping Mu Jin would know something. The door was ajar, and as I pushed it open, I saw Mu Jin unpacking a paper house, a car, money, and child figures. Mu Jin spotted me and beckoned me to come in.

"Good, come help. These are for Dalia," she said, handing me a paper car.

"Why does Dalia need these?" I asked.

"Effigies for the afterlife. She needs car, house, money, and children that she never had. Poor girl, so sad." Mu Jin sniffed as she continued unpacking.

"Dalia's husband is taking the Jag. But where is it?" I asked.

"Tell him we sell it already," Mu Jin responded and added, "Don't like him. I think it was fake marriage. Green card."

9

Mu Jin headed to the door to the yard, and I followed her. She set up the effigies around the olive tree and then took out incense sticks. Mu Jin handed me a stick and motioned for me to wave it around the yard.

"We burn a stick for any bad spirit that man brings to that girl," she announced.

I had many questions about Dalia and Acer and who owned the house. But Mu Jin was now kneeling and waving the smoking sticks around the tree. Then she set fire to the effigies, and we watched the burning paper. I became emotional and dabbed my eyes. Mu Jin motioned for me to sit on a bench in front of the tree. She took my hand and felt my pulse.

"Show me tongue," Mu Jin insisted. I reluctantly stuck out my tongue.

Mu Jin nodded and barked, "Hot damp body. No spicy food! You have tummy problems, call me, I fix." Mu Jin handed me her card.

"Mu Jin Ju, PhD. Alfalfa Neuroscience Institute." I pretended not to be surprised.

#olivetree #daliaRIP #doubleflower #instabff #aliensheep #margaritas

CHAPTER TWO

———

POPPY SEED

I always loved my name, Poppy Shaw. There are conflicting stories about why my parents, Palmer and Daisy Shaw, chose it. There's the G-rated version, named for the poppy flower linked to Armistice Day and my dad's birthday. And there's the R-rated version my mom told me during a sangria-fueled afternoon. She had been a young model in Milan and attended an all-night, Euro, drug fest. She snorted some brown powder right off the belly of another model, then asked in Italian, "*Che cosa?*" Wondering what she had just snorted.

"Poppy flower . . . *eroina*," a hot, Italian photographer responded in broken English. As the euphoria hit, she became a dancing poppy flower. She vowed that night to call her first child Poppy, whether it was a boy or a girl.

After Milan, I suppose my mom transitioned from street drugs to alcohol and prescription meds. My parents met at a small college where they were studying for useless degrees. My theory was that it was love when my dad, Palmer, found out that my mom, Daisy, had a mega trust fund. It also helped that Daisy was tall and beautiful. She was probably beauty queen contestant material if it weren't for the substance abuse.

Neither parent had a normal job, and they were always in each other's way, which fueled constant bickering. No kisses, no hugs, and only an occasional pat on the back. All my recollections of their fifty-year marriage were of two people going daily for the jugular.

"Maybe if you sobered up, Daisy, you'd see things my way. The world is collapsing," Palmer said.

"It's your fault I'm not sober. With your every new disaster prediction, I have to increase my meds and alcohol intake," Daisy responded.

My dad, Palmer, was a "red diaper baby," the son of card-carrying commies who were blacklisted journalists during the 1950s. Palmer was good looking—tall, lanky and looked academic. After a few decades as a high school teacher, he went off the deep end and took early retirement. He was a doomsday prepper and had ongoing projects related to catastrophes such as race wars, natural disasters, alien invasion, global financial collapse and nuclear holocaust.

"It's just a matter of time, Poppy," my dad would say as he prepared checklists for each disaster. He made me study the lists and would quiz me on them at dinnertime.

Mom had always hoped one of dad's doomsday gadgets would sell so we could live big. In the meantime, we lived on her family's money. But the trust fund didn't allow us to live in a swanky Los Angeles hood.

Since my birth in 1976, my family lived in a mid-century, one-story, three-bedroom, two-bath, with a garage in Encino, in the San Fernando Valley, north Los Angeles. Encino had its fifteen minutes of fame in an episode of *SpongeBob SquarePants* and the 1992 film, *Encino Man*, about finding a frozen caveman in a backyard.

"My dream was 90210. But we'll have to settle for 91316, kids," Mom would say.

Dad didn't care where we lived as long as he had a garage. A normal family would park cars and recreational vehicles, and store unused shit. Our garage was filled with gadgets and supplies for the apocalypse.

Daisy was so jealous of the time her husband spent in his man cave that she started to throw daggers at his sexuality. When she wasn't needling him about having a gay lover in the garage, she did charity work. She loved "saving" people, but in some cases, she did more harm than good.

One of her charity cases was the Bush family, across the street. The wife, Cherry, was a hoarder. Once, my mother insisted that we do an intervention on my birthday and help them declutter. Instead of having a birthday party, we would give back. I was only ten, but I already had a big mouth.

"The Bush family are all fuckups; leave it alone," I pleaded and added, "Shitty way to spend my birthday, DAISY." When I was angry, I called her by her first name.

Mom paid no attention and dragged me over to the Bushes with large plastic bags.

Cherry Bush answered the door. She was so happy to see us

and even wished me a Happy Birthday. But when she saw our plastic bags and heard Mom's perky, "We came to help you," Cherry freaked out. She clutched her chest, and we had to call 911. As Cherry weighed over four hundred pounds, it took three EMTs to haul her into the ambulance.

It was just a scare, and Cherry needed rest. She returned to her retail habits, judging from the constant deliveries at their house. Cherry recovered in time to crash Daisy's weekly girl parties.

Daisy's girlfriends came over every Friday at three p.m. to watch a *telenovela* and practice their Spanish. I called it "Spanish afternoon."

Amor y Vivir was an over-the-top, Spanish soap opera. The male characters rarely wore shirts. This drove my mom and her lady friends into a frenzy while they fought over the actors and guzzled sangria. Her friends were Petal, a sad divorcee, and Magnolia, a stunning, middle-aged, black ex-model. They would all argue in bad Spanish. I was already three years into Spanish class, so I knew my shit, *mierda*.

"Look at that hot, pool boy. *Caramba, mi* Dios," Magnolia said.

"It's *Dios mio*, Magnolia," I corrected her.

"Is he going after that *perra*, Orquídea?" Magnolia asked.

"*Tu es la perra*," Petal said, then beckoned me to pour her more sangria.

"It's *tu eres la perra*. You're the bitch," I said and topped off Magnolia's glass.

"Love that actress, Violeta Branch, who plays that *perra*, Orquídea. She's married to that hot actor from *Love and Secrets*," my mom noted.

"*Calla-te la boca*, you bitches. Can't fantasize with your blah-blah," Magnolia insisted.

From our living room window, I noticed Cherry waddling across the street, carrying a cake. I alerted the women to the hoarder invasion.

"Hey look, Cherry Bush is coming over."

"Oh shit! I mean *mierda*. Poppy, tell her I'm not home," Daisy said.

"That's ridiculous, our driveway looks like a parking lot. *Cállense, perras*." I ordered the women to be quiet in proper Spanish. I turned down the volume as Orquídea was down to her underwear and about to screw a pool boy. I opened the door as Cherry approached.

"Hi, Cherry. Mom is having a closet-organizing party," I said.

Cherry blanched, handed me the cake, and waddled back across the street.

I headed back to the kitchen and filled my "Marcia" thermos with sangria. I stored the thermos in my *Brady Bunch* lunch box on top of the fridge for school on Monday. Then I guzzled from a freshly made batch on the counter and returned to watch *Amor y Vivir*.

Buzzed at thirteen.

During puberty, I had the usual suicidal fantasies. Didn't really bother me as I thought it was normal to be depressed. My early teen years were harder on Mom than on me. "Poppy, I am going to put you on drugs if you don't snap out of this phase," Mom would say. She hated it when it was my time of the month.

"Better to stay in your room until you stop bleeding. When you are done marking your territory, or when your 'friend' has left, leave all the mess in a plastic bag."

I always wondered what she did with her bloody mess and why she didn't tell me about tampons. It was Cherry Bush, the hoarder, who saved me and handed me a case of Tampax in all sizes. She was in menopause and had no need for them. Snap.

The parental X-ray ended when I was fourteen and Mom ended up pregnant at forty. I assume it was my dad's. But my little brother, Cedar, looked an awful lot like our plumber.

They showered Cedar with their full attention, and I was just fine with that. It kept Daisy and Palmer out of my orbit. He could do no wrong in the eyes of our parents. Cedar was a mischievous boy who got away with murder. He was a rotten student but that didn't stop my parents from dreaming. His California surfer boy looks fueled their fantasies. They encouraged him to apply to Ivy League schools. I confronted them:

"Your son had the lowest SAT score in the school's history. How could you possibly think he's Ivy League material? What about me?" I asked and got no response.

I was really pissed off during Cedar's high school graduation dinner at a fancy restaurant. That's when I started my "Poppy pause." My dad put a set of car keys on Cedar's plate. I was fucking furious. I stood up in the restaurant on a chair.

"That spoiled bastard gets a car for getting a 2.0 average, disorderly conduct arrests, and being caught selling pot to seniors at an assisted living complex."

All the diners watched me as I held my hand up like a

religious fanatic. "Poppy pause, seriously, a car? I had a 3.9 and got a gold-plated pen?"

My dad gestured for me to step down off the chair, and then I was whisked out of the restaurant. As we were leaving, my parents looked embarrassed, but Cedar seemed to take it in stride.

"Great performance, sis. You should be an actress," Cedar said.

Cedar ended up working as a caddy after high school and was a top assisted living dealer until medical marijuana was legalized. Eventually, he found his way to pyramid schemes and producing infomercials. He even unsuccessfully plugged one of dad's doomsday devices.

I took one of dad's doomsday theories of global financial collapse seriously and studied business in college. Even though I was drawn to the arts, having a business degree felt safe. A hundred grand in student loans later, I graduated from college in 1998 and landed my first job as a personal assistant to a Hollywood casting agent. I now realize that I lived vicariously through the talent that paraded daily through the office. I would drool over the hot actors and be green with envy of the gorgeous actresses. No way I could be like them, but I liked being around them. I job hopped for another ten years and had a series of unstable roommates.

Finally, I transitioned to a high-paying, office manager's job for a commercial talent agency in Beverly Hills. My mom was thrilled as I was working in 90210. It sounded glamorous, but the people were generally nasty, backstabbers and addicts. By then,

I realized the actors and actresses were neurotic narcissists. But I wanted to be one of them. I even got a deal on headshots after sleeping with a photographer, but that's as far I went.

I made friends with Oleanna, a Venezuelan from Miami. She worked at the agency in the accounting department. She was also a modeling and acting client. Oleanna was very warm and Latina with hugs and a joyful personality.

We became lunch friends, either eating in the café near the office or in the company cafeteria. She was everything I wasn't: exotic-looking, alluring, and poised. She had olive skin and blue eyes with flowing dark hair to her waist. A solid knockout. There were always men waiting for her downstairs in fancy cars.

I couldn't understand why she didn't do acting full time. She was also a dancer and a vocalist. She had already been cast in a couple of stage plays and commercials and had joined an improv group. I was so jealous that I started dressing and acting like her. I was an Oleanna groupie and attended all her appearances, even when she only had a walk-on part. I took oodles of photos of her and posted them on social media. One of my high school friends sent me a PM and asked if I had joined the other team. I replied it was a "girl crush," but no worries, as I wouldn't be beaver diving anytime soon. I was still way into dicks. There had been a parade of them, but the guys were all losers in the end.

The talent agency merged with a larger one, and there were layoffs. Oleanna was fired before me, as she had no accounting skills but had been the mistress of the now-ex-CFO. I always wondered what she did all day in the office. After a few months, I was also laid off. Oleanna was heading back to Miami, and she invited me to move with her. She had hopes that we would get work as actors.

Why not? I went to Miami to learn Spanish and take acting classes, with hopes of being cast as a token *gringa* in a *telenovela*. As soon as we arrived, Oleanna was getting some walk-on parts while I was taking office temp jobs. We picked a shitty time to start a new life as it was 2009 and smack in the middle of the financial crisis. I didn't have enough money for acting classes, so I continued living vicariously through Oleanna.

Then she fell for a cute, Venezuelan, cruise ship waiter. They spent all their free time screwing loudly. I was happy for them but sad for me. They did invite me in once for a threesome, but I politely declined. Within minutes, a tall, gorgeous blonde showed up at the door. I answered, and she slipped into the bedroom with just a "hi." How long was she waiting in the hallway?

The waiter convinced Oleanna to sign up as cruise ship talent, and they were both locked into nine months at sea. She would be able to show all her acting, dancing, and singing skills on the shipboard shows. I was so bummed she was leaving. Then, to make matters worse, I was physically feeling like shit. Something was wrong.

No one knew what it was, and I feared cancer. My parents begged me to return to California. I had been in Miami for five years but I hadn't learned Spanish yet, so I was determined to stay. My mom threatened to come out to Florida, but I said no and kept them in the dark as to my medical status. I was thirty-five and maybe would never reach forty. I treated my symptoms with prescription meds and was in deep denial for a year until I collapsed one day and was rushed to the hospital.

Luckily, the tumor was benign, but they had to rearrange my colon at Jackson Memorial Hospital in Miami. I swear they left a link on the operating table, as I've never felt the same since. If you looked at the X-rays, my rectum was the shape of a six or a nine, depending on how you looked at it.

The surgery was a few hours and the heavy anesthesia lingered for days. I swore that while I was in the recovery room, someone fiddled with my hospital I.D. bracelet. Then I heard voices. *"It's her alright."* and *"some Colombian is after her."*

In my post-surgery brain fog, I thought some hot Colombian guy wanted me and was concerned about how I looked on the gurney.

I told the nurse and my doctor but they were convinced it was the anesthesia. I was too weak to argue.

My recovery was slow but I was determined to stay in Miami, learn Spanish, and get cast on *Amor y Vivir.* But there was no part for a middle-aged *gringa* on that show or any other.

Then I ran out of money and was evicted from my *casita.* My only choice was to move back to Encino with my parents and start over again. At least, I was in an actor's mecca, and maybe it was for the better.

I endured a year with Daisy and Palmer still bickering.

"I'm telling you, Daisy, it's Tuesday," my dad said.

"And I know for a fact it's Wednesday," Daisy shouted.

"Let's call 911," Palmer suggested.

"No, let's ask Poppy," Daisy said.

As I strategized a game plan to get away from these people,

Dad whispered he had a secret and not to tell my mom. He had patented one of his doomsday gadgets and sold it to a sporting goods company. He offered to fund my living expenses for a year, as I should pursue acting.

"You're still a poppy seed waiting to bloom," my dad said. What a cute thing to say, even though I was almost middle aged.

I moved to Hollywood and put myself out there to be humiliated, both in acting and in more failed relationships. Here I was, almost forty and never been married. Would probably never have kids and end up in assisted living, buying pot from my younger brother, Cedar.

The constant rejection was brutal, and I didn't know a goddamn thing about acting for the first few years. Then Rowan, a famed acting coach, saved my ass. She was the sourpuss nana I never had. They rumored that Rowan had been in silent movies. Some thought she was a vampire and hundreds of years old. Her white hair and saggy jowls pointed to the sunny side of eighty or a lot of gin. Who the fuck cared as she was a GREAT teacher.

At first, I thought she was just taking my money, but an actor assured me she didn't coach everybody. That's what kept me going. Rowan believed in me even when I didn't believe in myself. Once, I asked if I was too old to get acting jobs. She slammed down her cane and shouted, "Never speak like this again. If you're talented, the roles will find you, Poppy."

I landed some voice-over work, commercials, and unpaid indie film roles. I was still nonunion but praying to get into SAG, the Screen Actors Guild. With every audition and job, I was getting closer, then farther away. Some days, I wanted to pack it in and didn't think I was talented, funny, or deserving of the roles I auditioned for. But I carried on.

Nothing else seemed like an option. It was acting or nothing.

Landing in the Topanga guesthouse gave me new energy and a feeling I was on the road to something. No fucking idea what, but it would be big. Never imagined that the "big" would end up with me being consumed and haunted by a dead girl's legacy.

#opium #doomsday #bigcherry #amoryvivir #sangria #orquidea #poolboy

CHAPTER THREE

POPPY PREPARES

WTF? Lily sent me a list of VIP Dalia mourners to visit the tree at my Topanga Canyon guesthouse yard. Who was this Dalia? A head of state, a cult leader? Was she on the path to sainthood, or a sorceress?

I didn't even bother asking Lily if the VIPs had perks or special access. Then came a text from a "Rosita," then a "Sage" who wanted to visit the tree. Holy crap, I hoped dead Dalia's shrine was not becoming a new tourist destination.

I had to focus on my audition and had no time to obsess about the dead girl, Mrs. Yin-Yang Neuroscientist, and the texts from people asking to visit the tree.

Holly, my agent/confidant/therapist, was an old soul in a young body. She was concerned about my upcoming auditions and that I needed a classy look and "none of your *Goodwill* crap." Both casting agents wanted smart, not sloppy or boho. I remembered about Dalia's clothes. I rifled through the closet and realized dead Dalia's designer clothes could make me look like a rich bitch.

The first audition was for a feature film titled, *Henna's Revenge*. After reading the "sides," the scene for the audition, I needed help. I was way out of my comfort zone with the role of a convicted, murderess/psychic, trophy wife. I hadn't been any of these things so had absolutely nothing to draw from personal experience. Maybe I should have watched more of those shitty *Lifetime* movies.

I called my acting coach, Rowan. She'd been a trophy wife to a rich, sick, old man and was a little bit psycho. Murderess maybe, as the dude died under suspicious circumstances, but I don't think she was convicted.

"Hey Rowan, did you get my email with the sides?" I said in a voice mail. A few minutes later, Rowan responded by text.

Rowan: Coaching an A-lister having a meltdown over a lost Oscar. Call you in a few.

Me: Wow, that's a lot to unpack. Did the big star lose an Oscar to another actor, or actually lost the Oscar statuette?

Rowan called and seemed flustered.

"I know you can't tell me who, but can I get a hint?" I asked coyly.

"No way, honey. He OR she would cut my eyeballs out and blacklist me, not sure in which order," Rowan responded.

"Did you read my sides? I don't think I should audition," I remarked.

"Are you crazy? This is a terrific part for you! Gives you a chance to bring out that nasty, vindictive, vengeful feeling," Rowan said.

"Seriously, you see me in this role?" I asked with a quivering voice.

"It's an opportunity for you to explore deep emotions. Think of your parents, your brother," she said.

"Yeah, I hate all three of them," I agreed.

"So, use it for FUCK SAKE. Gotta go. Call me after the audition. And make sure you pronounce the dude's name, like they say, 'BAHSIL.'"

Then she ended the call. What would I do without my bossy-boots babes, Rowan and Holly, to order me around? I'd be a disaster.

I headed to the mirror with my pages, tousled my hair, and put on an angry face as I read aloud:

"BAHSIL, don't bother with the pills. You're a lousy lay with or without them. If I weren't busy, I would kill you. Just go on and disappoint your next trophy wife. Yes, you'll meet someone else, a blonde. I saw it in the cards. But I also saw DEATH!"

As I said the lines, I thought of my parents, my brother, and his new bitch wife. I repeated the lines several times in different voices and while wearing different outfits. Each time, I got angrier.

I went into the closet and pulled out skinny pants and a loose top. I thought a trophy wife would probably wear a perky scarf. Then my eyes turned to Dalia's clothes. They seemed to beckon me. Should I don one of her floppy hats over my short, dirty-blonde bob to hide the gray streaks? Then I spotted a Hermès, black-and-white scarf wrapped around a dress. I grabbed it, put it around my neck, and felt emboldened. Probably cost hundreds.

The audition was in an old, small theater in West Hollywood, the kind with seats that only comfortably fit "little people" and children. We twenty-first century peeps are so much fatter.

I arrived as some of the actresses were leaving and muttering, "That was lame," and "That actor used to be somebody." I asked if they were reading for the role of Henna, the psycho psychic trophy wife. They nodded and informed me that the role of Basil seemed already cast. They said he was a recognizable TV actor, although no one could remember his name or the show he was on.

I said my mantra quietly. "It's not rejection, it's protection. If you don't get the part, the universe is speaking."

In my warped mind, I had already auditioned and bombed.

But the actor playing Basil came up to me and asked, "Don't I know you?"

The director and the assistant looked annoyed, like let's get on with the audition.

"I think we did summer stock in New England?" he asked. I didn't answer but smiled. Summer stock? He must be ancient.

The assistant beckoned me to come on the stage and motioned to "Basil" to read. The actor looked north of sixty, maybe seventy, and may have had some work done. He was slim, wearing tight jeans and a dress shirt. Not bad looking with a full head of salt and pepper hair. He did look familiar but seemed more soap opera than sitcom. He seemed to be off book already, and with gusto, he started us off.

"I know I can't get it up, Henna, but just let me take more of those pills."

I toyed with my scarf, or should I say Dalia's scarf, and circled "Basil," as I do in improv class sometimes. Helps me get it up.

I felt brazen enough to ad lib some of my lines.

"BAHSIL, don't bother with the pills. Not gonna help 'cause you're a lousy lay with or without them. You just don't know what to do with it, soft or hard. There's no excuse at your age or in the twenty-first century to fail at fucking. Watch a movie; ask your friends, the ones still alive. If I weren't busy getting Botox, I would kill you. Just move on and disappoint your next trophy wife. Yes, you'll meet someone else, a blonde, probably one of my airhead friends. I saw it in the cards. But I also saw DEATH!"

I couldn't tell what the director thought as she leafed through the script, wondering if she missed something. I heard the assistant say the word "improv." They thanked me as I stepped off the stage. The actor playing 'BAHSIL' winked at me. Awkward.

I left the theater and texted my agent, Holly, from the street while waiting for my Uber. I told her that I added some lines to the script. Holly texted back.

"How many times have I told you, don't do that shit? Directors hate it especially if they wrote the fucking script."

Well, I probably blew it. I didn't dare text Rowan, my coach, about my "improv" and would only tell her if I got the part. Otherwise, I would risk getting banned from her acting class.

Two minutes before my Uber was due to arrive, the actor playing BAHSIL ran up to me on the street.

"You were terrific! I'm sure you'll get the part!" he announced and added, "By the way, I'm Olmo. I love your scarf. Hermès, right? I bought one for my wife, but she died, but not while wearing the scarf."

Then my Uber arrived, and I jumped in. I heard Olmo shout

as I hopped in the back seat, "See you at rehearsals, Poppy!"

Oh God, he knew my name. I took the scarf off. Now I associated it with Olmo's dead wife. Not wearing Dalia's or any dead people clothes anymore.

I headed home to prepare for another audition for a feminine hygiene commercial. It wasn't clear if we were talking pads, tampons, wipes, or sprays. This one should have been a no-brainer, as I looked like a typical woman stressing over periods. That's what the casting director told me at my last audition. I just made the impression that I took care of my hoo-ha with quality products. This time, I wasn't planning on wearing anything "Dalia."

It turned out that the commercial was for an eco-friendly tampon. God knows what it was made of. Thankfully, I didn't have to try it but pretended I was happy and comfortable with my "eco-tamp" in place. I thought the audition went so well that I put the shoot dates in my calendar.

I put Dalia's husband, Acer, off for a few days, as the Jag hadn't shown up.

Then, mysteriously, a red, Jag convertible appeared one night in the driveway, and I assumed it was Dalia's car.

In the meantime, Rosita, Sage and elderly Miss Twig came to pay their respects to the tree and Dalia. They were all weepy, left notes and flowers. As I was nosy, I read the notes after they were gone. Miss Twig's note was the strangest: "Dalia, you're a double angel, and I'll see you soon." Was Miss Twig at death's door? Rosita's note was just full of hearts and "miss you D." Sage's note had a disturbing sketch of a figure hanging from a tree.

I had to put the Dalia mourner fan club on hold as I had another audition. It was for a role in a TV pilot called *Old Maid*, about four unmarried and childless women, over forty, living together under one roof. The premise was that the women play the card game, Old Maid, every night, and whoever loses has to confess to something awful, cook dinner, or pay for take-out. They get too drunk during the game to go out clubbing.

I wanted to look too hip and cool for the part and searched for my black leather jacket. It was missing, but I spied Dalia's red leather jacket in the closet. I hesitated, as I had sworn I wasn't going to wear her clothes. But of course, the jacket fit and looked fabulous, so I wore it to the audition. I was conflicted about this TV pilot character, as I really didn't want to play my real age and identity—over forty and unmarried.

The audition was very chaotic. They were casting for all the lead women. There were ladies of all varieties in sizes, weights, colors, and gender identification. Most looked way over forty and desperate. It was all too close to home for me.

I made myself believe I was the only skinny, white girl there who really didn't look forty. They brought me in first to read. All the other actresses looked daggers at me as I was escorted in by the assistant. I heard sneers and comments like "Who's she fucking?" and "Who do I have to blow to get this part?"

As soon as I walked into the audition room, the assistant said, "Hot jacket." Then I read a monologue, which was filmed. They also had me read for another character.

Judging from the potpourri of actresses in the hallway, it was clear they had no idea who they were casting and for what role.

"Am I too young for the part?" I asked the casting assistant, hoping to sabotage my chances.

"No, you are perfect. Exiled suburban MYLF," the assistant replied. That did not make me feel any better and made no sense. Was I in the right audition? A MYLF has children and the "Old Maids" were single, desperate, and barren.

I left quickly and was subject to hateful stares from the other girls, although one said she liked my jacket. As I headed outside, my phone dinged with a voice mail:

"Sorry to disturb but got your number from the casting agent. I lied and said I was producing a short film, though not really, but would love to produce a short with you. Poppy, you're so . . . I don't know, anyhow, really like your acting technique, is that Meisner, or Adler? Can we grab coffee sometime? Or a designer water if that's your thing. This is Olmo, remember me? I hope."

Gosh, he sounded like the male version of me. That's just the sort of awkward voice mail I would leave. But he was too old and an actor. I swore I would never date an actor or anyone who could reminisce with my dad.

My phone dinged with a text from Olmo:

"Excuse me, Poppy, again, did you get my voice message? Heard you got the part! So happy to work with you!"

What was he talking about? The guy must be senile.

Oddly, the next text was from Holly.

"Good news but bad news first. No tampon ad but you got the psycho trophy wife and also a callback for Old Maid."

I was kind of shocked and then realized that I was wearing Dalia's clothes for both those auditions where I got the part. Was it possible the clothes had magical qualities?

At home, I took a closer look and examined all the clothes. She had incredibly good taste and bucks to afford all these *haute couture* and fancy-ass labels. Old money, or sugar daddy?

There were new shoes and sandals still in boxes. The shoes were a half-size smaller than my usual size, but the sandals fit. As I pulled out a pair of gorgeous Manolo sandals, I found a Florida driver's license for "Iris Espinoza Ortega" alongside a shiny, silver pistol. This Iris looked a little like Dalia; maybe her sister?

I showed Mu Jin the shoebox and the pistol. She snatched the pistol from my hands, saying, "I take care." But I kept the driver's license.

#ecotampon #creepyoldguy #latinhottie #clothsofthedead #garmentsfromthegrave

CHAPTER FOUR

IRIS 1.0

My *papi*, Eneldo Espinosa III, would tell everyone a bullshit story about how we got to Miami from Cuba on a flimsy boat in 1980. When the boat capsized, he would tearfully tell his cronies, "I carried my little three-year-old Iris to shore and put her little feet on United States sand. Castro can't get us now, *hijos de puta*!"

He emphasized that we both needed at least one dry foot on the sand. This was to ensure that when the Coast Guard approached, we would be granted asylum. He never mentioned my *mami*, Azalea, in this fake story. I just kept my mouth shut, as I knew the truth from Miami relatives and eventually the authorities.

In reality, we were one of the one hundred thirty-five thousand *Marielitos* who arrived in Miami in 1980. It was when Fidel announced, "Everyone who wants to leave can go, but don't come back." Then throngs of Cubans left on boats and barges.

Fidel even opened up the prisons.

Reports indicated that twenty-seven hundred hardened criminals were among the newly arrived Cubans. My *papi*, Eneldo, a handsome *mulato*, could be considered one of them, maybe not "hardened," but certainly a criminal. The move to Miami was a reward for my father, who had opened a critical channel for drug traffic between Cuba and Colombia. He often declared, "This is for a job well done, remember, Iris."

The Colombians convinced the Cubans that his skills were needed in Miami. He could also do double duty and spy on the anti-Castro groups for the Cuban government.

We didn't arrive in a flimsy boat but in a private airplane supplied by a Colombian cartel. We landed at a small airport in the middle of the night and were met by a limousine and chauffeur. Many times, I've pretended to my friends that I had suffered in the camps with the *Marielitos*. Refugee camps in Miami were overcrowded and beset with crime, hunger strikes, and lack of food. By contrast, my family was taken direct to a fancy apartment in Coconut Grove, overlooking Key Biscayne.

In Havana, we lived in a modest house in order not to attract attention and enjoyed some perks. But now, we were in the lap of luxury, in a four-thousand-square-foot, two-story apartment, for just the three of us. We didn't want for anything. Eneldo was a third-generation drug dealer. His father, my *abuelo*, sold weed and coke to a famous mob boss, "Lucky" Luciano. He claimed my great-grandfather, a cigar roller, invented the first blunt in 1920 and made a fortune.

My mother, Azalea, on the other hand, was a third-generation whore. She was blonde and blue-eyed, of Northern Spanish origin, with big tits. Rumor was that she serviced the Cuban communist bosses. Her mother, my *abuelita*, supposedly was simultaneously sleeping with Fidel and members of the visiting Jewish and Italian mobs. My mother joined three generations of her family as a Havana's Tropicana showgirl, with sequins, wigs, spiked heels and Frederick's of Hollywood underwear. As a drug dealer's wife, Azalea toned her style down a tad, but she still liked her bling. They made a handsome couple and referred to themselves in English as "ebony and ivory." They would dance sexy in front of me while the Stevie Wonder song played. Yuk. *Que asco.*

Between my mom's fuck-buddy, commie bureaucrats and Dad's narco pals, they arranged for us to settle in Miami. The cartel wanted my *papi* to run the Miami operation. Eventually we moved to a McMansion with a swimming pool and tennis court.

By the time I was ten, I knew they were up to dirty business. Papi and Mami would say, "Don't answer the door or phone." And "If anyone asks you on the street who you are and who is your daddy, say nothing. Don't even speak to them, especially if they have badges or are gringos in suits. *Silencio, Iris.*"

Cars were often parked in front of or across from our house day and night. You could see men with binoculars and long-lens cameras. Mami would say, "It's the FBI, DEA, DOJ, one of the *D*'s, *m'ija.* They are SO annoying."

But then she would send our maid out with Cuban coffee and expensive Belgian chocolates on silver trays to serve the guys watching our house. They seemed to enjoy the attention. After drinking the coffee, they returned to their binoculars and long-lens cameras.

"Mami, why are they watching us?" I would ask.

"They are nosy, and jealous we live in such a big house," she would answer.

One day in 1991, when I was fourteen, there was a chopper circling above our house. A voice shouted through a megaphone, "Surrender now, Eneldo." I hid under my bed, as I was afraid that they would start shooting. Then the DEA agents and the police burst through the front door and searched the house. Azalea remained on the living room sofa, watching the *telenovela, Amor y Vivir.* She remained calm and nonplussed by the agents overturning furniture, emptying closets, throwing paper around, and looking for any trapdoors to a hiding space. They walked out with a bag of her jewelry. She whispered to me, "The good stuff is up my *concha*," as the agents exited the house.

Meanwhile, Papi escaped to a neighbor's house in a wheelbarrow covered in leaves and cut grass, thanks to the landscaper, Jesus. Another miracle performed by the Son of God. The next time we heard from my father, Eneldo, he was on a tractor on a poppy farm in Colombia. He said he was speaking on a satellite phone belonging to a military official. Azalea and I remained in our house until it was seized by the DOJ. Then we heard that *Papi* had been murdered on the streets of Bogota. Azalea was sad but didn't seem to grieve as much as her girlfriend, another depressed soul and narco widow. The girlfriend convinced my mother to go to an Indian ashram for three months. The three months turned into three years.

Before she left, I was sent to live with the Ortega family, who were distant cousins in Coral Gables. Papi Ortega, as I called him, was literally a larger-than-life character and weighed four hundred pounds. His wife Mami Ortega, complained a lot about his weight and after drinking a few Cuba Libras, reported she hadn't seen his dick in a decade.

Their son, Cardoso, was a year older than me. He was handsome and tall. But we hated each other at first. He would tease me, and I would hide his favorite T-shirts and baseball cards.

"You and your silly girlfriends will get nowhere in life," Cardoso predicted.

"You think your Cuban boyfriends are any different?" I responded and added, "With those baseball caps, and gold chains. *Pendejos* wannabe gang members. Sad."

By the time Cardoso was seventeen, he was able to grow a full moustache. He slicked back his hair every day and walked around the house as the prodigal son. We stopped teasing each other and began fondling each other in my bed. We went skinny-dipping in the pool when his parents weren't home. Cardoso insisted I should stay a virgin until marriage. So, there was no penetration until I begged him. Then he kind of put it half in, then pulled out—I became half a virgin.

"You must preserve your purity," Cardoso said. But I kept reminding him I was technically no longer pure.

I had filled out early, with generous curves stretched out on my five-nine frame. I was considered tall for a Latina, had a mix of black and European features with blue-green eyes. My skin tone was light like my *mami*. I was called "exotic-looking" and could pass for any number of nationalities. I kept my dark hair long and curly. It was my best feature.

Cardoso was already doing sketches of my naked body when I was fifteen. He made me pose on the edge of the pool, the diving board, on the bed, in the shower. There was even a sketch of me washing dishes naked. When his father found the sketches, he quizzed Cardoso and asked, "Who was the model." Cardoso claimed, "Oh, I sketch the *puta* that lives across the street. She poses for free."

"Good, that saves me from taking you to a *puta* to pop your cherry. Just don't knock her up," Papi Ortega warned. The Ortegas were in the import-export business. But that smelled fishy, with middle-of-the-night meetings of dubious-looking armed men.

I later found out that my *papi*, Eneldo, had arranged years ago for the Ortegas to take care of me in case the feds grabbed him and/or Mami. My father handed money to the Ortegas. Later, Cardoso told me it was a million or even two.

The Ortegas were not overly generous in those years when I lived with them. But no complaints: they treated me well. I called the father, Papi O. He said I was the daughter he never had. Mami Ortega was a little distant and doted on her son. I think she thought I was competition, not only for her son's affections but her husband's too.

"If Cardoso won't follow in my footsteps, then maybe you will, *m'ija*. You're smart, and probably absorbed business sense from your *papi*, Eneldo, God rest his soul," Papi O. said at the dinner table and crossed himself.

By seventeen, Cardoso was almost six feet tall. When I wore heels, we were the same height and had similar builds. We already looked like a power couple at the senior prom. I managed to finish high school a year early, so Cardoso and I graduated together in 1994.

Just after high school graduation, my mom returned from India. She had become a devotee of the guru Sai Baba. Gone were the fancy clothes, heels, jewelry, fake eyelashes, and wigs. She was dressed in peasant clothes. Her blonde hair was stringy and unkempt. She wore no makeup, and her unpainted toes stuck out of beat-up sandals. Oddly, she looked younger than forty.

She walked off the plane holding a framed photo of Sai Baba. The guru looked like a black rapper with a 'fro, except he wore a long, orange dress, with flared sleeves.

She brought another souvenir: a young, tall, Indian man. He was tall, square framed and wanted to study in America. With aviators, he could pass for Latino.

"Bakul Indukamal Moshayan, call me Moss," he said meekly when we met.

"He's an orphan with no place to go. What was I going to do?" Azalea said.

"An orphan? He looks like he's in his twenties," I responded in front of Moss.

Moss seemed chill and came to live with us in our new, modest home in Miramar that the Ortegas mysteriously bought for us. They must have used my *papi's* money.

Somehow, Moss managed to enroll at the local community college and began studying accounting as soon as he arrived. I didn't ask any questions.

Azalea, the former whore to communists and sexy showgirl, now appeared asexual. It was hard to believe she was screwing Moss. Additionally, Moss acted a little effeminate, so no way could he be her lover and boy toy. He was so formal around us and acted more like a servant. After a few months, he started to get a little more macho and assertive. But there was no evidence of hoochie-coochie between him and my mom. They seemed short on cash until Moss got a job in the Miami-Dade County accounting office.

Moss cooked, cleaned, and drove me to school and Azalea to the Sai Baba center downtown, where she volunteered. She and Moss were both Sai Baba devotees and would chant Indian *darjans* and *bhajans* most nights and weekends. Very boring.

Their dinner conversation was always peppered with Sai Baba quotes such as "God is not far away, not in hell or heaven, but is always beside you." They would quiz each other on Baba quotes. Moss would start, "What is our duty?" and Azalea would finish the quote, "To be dutiful." I ignored them and had no interest in their guru or their beliefs.

Cardoso couldn't stand the chanting and was convinced they were part of a cult. He alerted me to the possibility they were handing over money to the guru. But they really didn't have much money to give away. I couldn't figure out what they were living on.

Despite Cardoso's distaste for the chanting and guru shit, he was inspired to sketch them.

"They look silly, yet pure and holy," Cardoso whispered as he sketched.

"But are there unholy shenanigans going on at night?" I whispered back.

Moss and Azalea read to each other from Sai Baba's books and books about him. There were titles like *108 Pearls of Wisdom*, *Life Lessons*, and *Eating the Sai Baba Way*, which was pure veggie and no junk food.

Moss did all the cooking, but I got tired of Indian food, so he started preparing Cuban-Indian fusion. Sometimes, it worked, and other times, it was a strange-colored mush, with rice and plantains.

For lack of better ideas for my future, I started community college and took liberal arts classes but never found my groove. The best I could do was working part time in one of Papi Ortega's businesses, a Cuban restaurant, as a hostess.

Cardoso had an internship at a Miami gallery and had access to a studio to continue creating. I teased him about doing the nude models.

"Fuck those skinnies? One finger on them and they would break," claimed Cardoso.

"I'm sure if a model shows up with some flesh on her ass, you'll be on it," I asserted.

Papi O., Señor Ortega, wanted Cardoso to run the family import business, probably drug business. But Papi O. was torn when Cardoso managed to get a full scholarship to study art at the famous Pratt Institute in Brooklyn, New York. I suspected there was some street cred for Señor Ortega to have an artistic son as long as he wasn't a *maricón* or faggot. He suggested that Cardoso could someday do both: paint and sell drugs. Cardoso transformed into a pony-tailed, full bearded artist, despite Papi O's initial objections but finally accepted that it was part of the package.

"Be inspired to paint the flowers and plants that make drugs," Papi O. joked. In fact, Cardoso sold large canvases depicting peasants working in poppy and marijuana fields to narcos to hang in their

Miami mansions.

Although Cardoso was thrilled to study in New York, his heart was in Miami. He planned to absorb the New York art world, then return to Florida and open a gallery. He wanted me to go with him to New York. We would be there for the millennium and celebrate in Times Square.

"That freezer?" I asked.

"We can keep each other warm," Cardoso replied, snuggling up to me.

"You haven't even asked if that fits with my plans," I remarked angrily.

"What plans? I haven't heard you mention a plan. So, I assumed you were still husband shopping," he responded and added, "Joking!"

I loved Cardoso, but he seemed to be frozen in the old world when it came to women. I was on the fence about New York, but I had wanted to spend my life with Cardoso, since I was fifteen. I didn't want to lose him. In order to induce me to join him in New York, Cardoso proposed with a big-ass diamond. I later learned Papi O. gave Cardoso the money to buy the ring from my father's money. So, I basically bought the ring for myself.

I said yes to marrying Cardoso but no to New York. We could stay engaged, and we could visit each other. But when Moss announced he was bringing his nephew, another Sai Baba devotee, to live in the house, that was my cue to pack and leave with Cardoso.

Azalea tearfully begged me to stay.

"Please don't go, *m'ija*. We need you here," Azalea pleaded

Moss was a little less emotional: "If you stay or go, we will always be a happy family, but follow your heart."

Moss's nephew never arrived, so I assumed that it was a ruse by Moss to get me out of the house. As I said my goodbyes, Azalea and Moss looked happy together, like a married couple.

Cardoso and I, now engaged, jumped in his new, red, Toyota Corolla with our belongings and made our way north. He was twenty-three and I was twenty-two as we left Miami and our families of secrets, mysteries, and drama.

Chapter Five

HEALING WITH DALIA

The mourner parade continued at Dalia's burial site. There was no mention of actually when she died on her fan club FB page. The comments begin after the urn was in the ground, in early 2019, when I moved in the Topanga guesthouse.

I found Dalia's website and YouTube channel link and it was as if she was still alive. She still had ten thousand fucking subscribers. I had barely a hundred Facebook friends and a dozen followers on my Insta. I was such a social media loser.

Her "Healing with Dalia" videos started with drums and a voice-over of her reading a poem. Then she appeared on screen, looking intensely at the camera with her shiny, curly, black hair and her gleaming turquoise eyes. She had a mesmerizing Charles Manson gaze that transfixed you. She spoke with a slight unidentifiable accent.

"Hello, my darling viewers. We just hit ten thousand subscribers, and I spent a week learning how to breathe. You must breathe intentionally. We breathe wrongly because we live in a digitally

obsessed and medicated society. It leads to depression and anxiety, which is becoming the number one disability. Breathing correctly can change your life.

"*Breathing properly will increase your compassion, your creative energy, your moneymaking, and yes, your sex life. It's a game changer!*

"*In this video, I'll show you how to breathe properly. How long can you hold your breath? Please don't hold your breath until you bleed from your eyes.*

"*I had a patient who said, 'Breathing saved my life!'*"

I paused the video and followed Dalia's instructions. But I couldn't hold my breath for very long. Then I followed Dalia's breathing exercises and became faint. I started to breathe rapidly. Oh, was I doing it correctly? Now I was panicking. She was so right. I was convinced I was an improper breather, probably the root of all my problems.

Dalia's other videos were inspirational and also health related with titles such as: "*Laugh Away Depression. Sugar is your Enemy. Salt is your Poison. Spiritual Snacks. Spiritual Cocktails. Banish the Emotional Vampires. Sex up your Chakras. Cleanse your Aura with Tea Tree Soap. Happy Hour Liver Cleanse. Make Peace with your Poverty. Love your Sagging Skin. Better Sex on a Bad Hair Day. He's not Worth It. Buy Her that New Car.*"

I so wanted to watch all of these videos and soak in everything Dalia, but each was an hour long. All her videos started with the drums, the poem and ended with her fiery wild look, with those turquoise eyes and arms outstretched. She crossed her heart and in a breathy voice uttered the phrase, "*y siempre con mucho, mucho amor.*" It reminded me of the Miami Cuban drama queens.

Dalia's fans were enthralled with these self-help videos. Scrolling through the comments, there were phrases like: "You saved my life. You saved my marriage. Thanks, Dalia, I was planning a murder-suicide until I watched your 'Banish the Emotional vampires' video. Dear Dalia, thanks to you, I'm sugar and salt free but got very depressed until I watched 'Laugh Away your Depression,' and now I feel great! You're a genius, Dalia, now I love looking at my saggy skin!"

The rave reviews went on and on. Dalia was a guru, healer, change agent, and inspirational guide. I watched the "Cleanse your Aura" video. As expected, my fundamental issue was a dirty aura. I was hoping there was a quick fix, like Tide, Clorox, or liquid jewelry cleaner. But Dalia's solution was long and involved and seemed to be a process that took place over many weeks.

As I studied and followed Dalia's exercises to clean your aura, I remembered Iris Ortega's Driver's License, tucked away in a Manolo shoebox. I took it out and held it up to the screen as Dalia spoke.

Iris could have been Dalia's sister with lighter hair, a bigger nose, and a different-shaped face. I would ask her husband, Acer. He texted me photos of himself. He posed at different locations and in different outfits, and always with a drink in his hand. We had a tentative happy hour meet scheduled in a few weeks. I had to admit I was already fantasizing about him at night with my trusty vibrator, "Bam Bam." Better than thinking about the last boyfriend, the loser drug addict.

I returned to my study of aura cleaning, trying to find a fast track. Honestly, I felt ashamed, walking around with a dirty aura.

Dalia delivered her advice in an authoritative manner.

"Would you go around town with dirty clothes, dirty hair, or shoes caked in mud?"

She paused and answered her online comments.

"Of course not ... the aura is not visible to people but can be felt, and affects your potential success in all walks of life!"

I skipped to a later video called "Healing your Wounds." Dalia looked a lot thinner in this video. Was she already sick?

Just as Dalia was discussing her loveless childhood, there was a FaceTime call from Lily. Her face came on the screen, and she looked like she was dressed as a vampire.

"Hey, Lily. That looks like a fun modeling job," I noted.

"Not a job. I wear this every day now. I get stares all day on the street and in the Tokyo subway. I thought it would be fun to dress like a vampire and scare the shit out of the locals," she responded.

"Is it working?" I asked.

"Not really. The Japanese don't get vampires, not their thing. I'm changing to a zombie geisha," Lily remarked.

"Cool. Hey, I'm getting a lot of visitors to the tree. Kinda annoying," I said.

"Set up a site to make appointments," Lily suggested, and I ignored that.

"Can we do maybe once-a-month group mourning?" I asked.

"Not an option. I thought I was crystal clear that this was part of the deal," Lily noted firmly.

"Part of what deal? I don't remember..." I said before Lily interrupted.

"I know, I'm sorry, you're right. How about I drop the rent by fifty . . . no, a hundred a month?" Lily suggested.

"Seriously? Keep up the mourner parade for a hundred-dollar discount?" I asked.

"OK, two. I think that's fair. Hey, gotta go," Lily responded and ended the call.

I did some quick math, and at minimum wage, this would mean I should spend no more than twelve hours a month organizing in-person, Dalia, memorial visits.

I read through the recent texts, and it was as if Dalia were a holy creature. Comments such as:

"Why was she taken so young? Healed so many." Or *"If I had a Vatican connection, I'd get Dalia fast-tracked to sainthood,"* and *"Did anyone see her in the garden near the tree?"* and another wrote, *"My STD went away after I visited the tree."*

Miracles, healings? Now there were Dalia sightings?

I had to stop reading; it was getting beyond creepy. But I still had nagging questions about Iris Ortega, so I texted Lily.

"I found Iris Ortega's Driver's License, should she get it back? She looks like Dalia's sister."

Lily responded a half hour later.

"No worries. Iris doesn't need it anymore."

Was she dead too? Not driving? Incapacitated? So many questions.

There was a request from the WhatsApp group to celebrate Dalia's birthday at the tree the following week. Would I be OK with that? Cake, balloons, and goody bags?

I needed to get Mu Jin involved so she could help corral the crazies at the Dalia birthday celebration.

"No prob. Can do. Make bean buns," Mu Jin offered.

I wondered if her husband, Acer, would come and noticed he was not part of the WhatsApp or FB groups. I texted Acer about Dalia's birthday.

Acer: "Her birthday isn't for four months. Those people are locos."

Me: "I hear ya."

Acer: "Still on for a drink next month, querida Poppy?"

I texted emojis of a martini and a thumbs-up.

I tried to discourage the faux birthday celebration, but there was an outcry on the Facebook and WhatsApp groups. They arrived early on a Sunday morning, like 8:30 a.m. with balloons and streamers.

I watched out the window as Mu Jin arrived and set out Chinese bean buns. She also burned more incense around the tree. I walked out to help her.

"Crazy people bring bad spirits," Mu Jin said as she waved her burning sticks. How do you celebrate the birthday of the dead? Sunday morning mimosas, apparently. The "birthday mourners" took selfies in front of the tree. They brought food and drink to the yard. They decorated the tree with streamers and balloons.

I put on one of Dalia's long sundresses, as it was an unusually warm morning. I wondered if someone would notice. As they were pouring mimosas, some musicians arrived. They were mostly women dressed like hippies. Except for an accordion-like instrument, it was all drums, big and small. One of the peasant-dressed women came up to me and asked, "Do you drum?" I shook my head.

A young man set up a projector and a screen and had Dalia videos on a loop. In one of the videos, she was wearing the same sundress I had on. I happened to be near the screen when there was a gasp from the crowd. One woman ran over to me and fondled the dress, then knelt and kissed the hem. Holy shit.

The women formed a circle and started drumming, one at a time and then two and three until all of them were creating a fucking racket. For the first ten minutes, it was intoxicating, but when one lady brought out a kiddie xylophone and a wooden spoon, I almost lost it. One of the birthday mourners leaned over to me and said, "This is so healing."

That comment was so annoying I snapped back, "Healing for whom? Too late for Dalia." I took my mimosa, grabbed a bean bun, and headed back to my guesthouse. Then a text came from my agent, Holly; she was at the gate. I totally forgot she was coming over to help me pick out an outfit for a very big audition.

I met Holly at the gate so I could explain the circus in the yard. I noticed she was wearing sweatpants and an oversized top. I hadn't seen her since the last sticks-and-twigs diet.

"I know, don't say it. I'm fat again," Holly said as she stormed through the gate.

"That wasn't my first thought. But that top is good camouflage," I said.

Holly was only thirty and a yo-yo dieter since childhood. Within a year, she could go from a size ten to a twenty. Once, around the holidays, she was on the chunkier side. I proposed she should take the job herself as a mall Santa when she couldn't fill the role with a client. She went on a nasty tirade and almost fired me.

I'd known her for a few years, and we were kinda friends. She was an ex-actress and claimed to have fucked half of Hollywood, even the gay ones, "They can go from giving head to being the head, of the studios."

I escorted Holly down the path and explained about the shenanigans in the yard. "She's buried there, but I'm not supposed to know," I said.

"Isn't that against the law?" Holly asked.

"Never thought about it. Yeah, I could blow the whistle and get out of being the Dalia memorial traffic cop," I replied.

Holly commented on the drumming, "WTF!" Then, as she watched the devoted fans, she lamented that probably no one would do this for her when she died.

I mentioned there was still space in the ground next to Dalia if she wanted to reserve it. We walked past all the fans of the dead to get to the guesthouse. One of the peasant-dressed women handed Holly a tambourine. She took it and started playing. I was horrified, grabbed the tambourine, and handed it to Mu Jin, who followed us to the guesthouse. I introduced Holly as my agent. Mu Jin studied her and made comments. "You help Poppy, she good girl."

"Not good girl. Fed up," I noted.

"They come morning, noon, and night to worship the tree. Poppy gets no sleep." Mu Jin pointed to the dark circles under my eyes.

"Gee, thanks, Mu Jin."

"I know just the surgeon for that," Holly said.

"No operation. Be natural," Mu Jin said, getting weepy.

"I'd be out of a job, lady, if I let all my actor clients BE natural," Holly said.

Holly then put her fingers on my face and pulled back my skin in various places. Mu Jin waved her hand and stepped away. I swatted Holly's hands away from my face.

I showed Holly the guesthouse, and we retreated to the closet. I showed her Dalia's clothes.

"The lady had class," Holly remarked, looking at the labels. "The deal is I have to wear her clothes to get the part."

Holly looked aghast.

"Clothes of the dead? Well, I'm suitably freaked out, girl," Holly said.

"Same," I answered.

Holly left the closet, looked outside the window at the drumming circle, then sat down on the bed and noted, "Girl, you need to get the fuck out of here. This is crazy-ass toxic 101."

That was funny as I had just watched a Dalia video about toxic people and emotional vampires. I showed some of the video to Holly, who shook her head throughout and made a cuckoo gesture with her hand.

"You see, even the dead girl in your yard is telling you to bail," Holly said. I never thought Dalia was speaking to me, but maybe she was.

"There's a reason I'm here, Holly," I said.

Holly did her Southern character: "It's just not right! Playing hostess to the dead. Git yo ass out of here."

"I like it here and it's cheap," I said.

Holly beckoned me to the closet. She rifled through Dalia's clothes, pulling out a tan cashmere sweater.

"If you insist on wearing her clothes, wear this. The show

takes place in a golf club. Need to look like an entitled, suburban, overmedicated wife," Holly said, handing me the garment. Then a scarf landed near my feet. I held it up, and it matched the sweater.

I took a Poppy pause. "Holly, did that just appear, or did you pull that down off a hanger?" Holly shook her head and walked out of the closet to the living area. She waved her arms.

"If you insist on living in this weird-ass place, you're on your own, kid. Now go land that part wearing that woman's sweater," Holly said as she exited.

My phone dinged with a text from the WhatsApp group. It was someone called "R.," with a photo of a smiling, handsome, middle-aged guy.

R. texted that he was coming over within the hour to visit the tree. He wrote he was Romero and Dalia's ex-husband. So, Dalia had an ex? Married before Acer? I texted Lily but had no response.

I checked the VIP list Lily sent me, but Romero wasn't there. I ran out to the yard when I saw Mu Jin. I showed her the text, but she never heard of him.

"You have trouble, we call police," she suggested.

I went back into the closet and pondered on what sexy garment of Dalia's to wear to greet her handsome ex.

#Lilythevampire #zombiegeisha #Whatsappnightmare #Irisdead? #StDalia #Cheaprent #Daliamania #memorialgoodybags #drummigraine #exhubby #cashmere

CHAPTER SIX

—

ROMERO

I chose a pair of tight pants and a silk blouse to meet this Romero, who claimed to be Dalia's ex-husband.

As I waited, Mu Jin tended to the flowerbed in the yard. She disappeared and then returned to the yard from the main house with the incense sticks. I joined her.

"Don't want any evil spirits. This will help," Mu Jin announced as she handed me a burning stick. She muttered in Chinese, waved the burning incense around the tree and then the entire yard.

"This Romero says he's her ex-husband," I said and showed her his photo on WhatsApp. But Mu Jin had never heard of him. I was hoping that Mu Jin would spill some more info. I also asked her about the mention of a sister in one of Dalia's videos. Mu Jin shook her head.

"Her family never visited. Only that bad boy, Acer," Mu Jin said.

The front gate buzzed, and I could see Romero in the camera. He appeared to be in his mid- to late forties. I met him on the pathway and led him around the yard.

He had slicked-back hair and a diamond earring. He wore jeans and an expensive-looking jacket. He didn't say anything, just walked into the garden and immediately approached the tree. Mu Jin looked him up and down, frowning. I introduced her as the owner of the property. Romero shook our hands.

"Romero Robles, nice to meet you. Where is she?" Romero asked and seemed emotional.

Mu Jin led Romero to the tree. He caressed the leaves on the tree, then pressed the dirt around it. He knelt and crossed himself like a good Catholic.

I really wanted to ask him about being married to Dalia. Maybe Romero didn't know about Acer, or vice versa. Mu Jin had no qualms and blurted out, "When you married to her?" She looked him straight in the eye.

"Long time ago. We were very young," Romero responded.

"Where was that?" I asked.

"Miami; we were both from there. Our Cuban parents, dead, I think," Romero said. How could you not know if your parents were dead or not?

Mu Jin then asked him in Spanish, "*Cubanos de la Habana?*"

Romero ignored Mu Jin. How could he not react to a Chinese woman in Topanga Canyon asking him if he was from Havana in Spanish? Weird.

He turned to me and asked what part of the house Dalia had lived in. I pointed to the guesthouse. I led the way, and Mu Jin followed.

Romero entered the guesthouse and looked around as if he were going to buy it. He stopped at a small-framed sketch on the wall of the naked female figure with arms stretched out. I hadn't even noticed the sketch until now. He pointed and said, "I drew that."

As I looked closely, I noticed "Iris" written in small print with the initials "C. O." at the bottom. More goddamn mystery. Is this the Iris of the driving license I found?

"Are you an artist?" I asked meekly.

"In a former life," Romero responded and added, "I took a few pounds off her. She wasn't that skinny. She had more *culo*," then slapped his own ass.

I examined the sketch again. There were little squiggles under the arms, like hair. "Did she not shave under her arms?" I asked.

Romero laughed.

"She was always afraid people would notice. I wanted her natural."

"Judging from her fine taste in clothing, she was a woman who shaved everywhere," I remarked.

Romero gave me a once-over and said, "Did you know her?"

"No, I just moved in," I replied.

"You looking good in her clothes," Mu Jin remarked.

Romero approached me and touched the sleeve of my blouse. He then dropped to his knees and sobbed uncontrollably. Mu Jin and I helped him up, then led him to the sofa. I grabbed a box of tissues and a bottle of vodka. In between snivels, Romero asked for scotch.

"I loved her so much. But she changed," Romero said in between sobs.

I rummaged in my kitchen and found scotch that was left

behind at my Hollywood place by that drug addict, whacko guy I kicked out at three a.m. Before that, I caught the dude going through my jewelry box in his underwear.

I poured Romero a drink. He sat silently sipping and staring at his sketch on the wall. Then he put his feet up on the sofa like he owned the joint. Mu Jin positioned herself on a small ottoman nearby. She stared at Romero.

"Show tongue," Mu Jin directed.

"Are you a doctor?" he asked.

"She's a PhD," I informed him.

Romero stuck out his tongue, and Mu Jin took his wrist and felt his pulse. "No spicy foods, no sugar, and more water," Mu Jin recommended.

"I love spicy foods and spicy women," Romero said, looking over to me.

It was the way he said it, so very sexy. Shit! Was I getting hot for Romero? I felt my normal labia twitch. I was a sucker for artists, especially sketch artists. Those charcoal-stained hands. Whew!

Mu Jin walked to the back of the sofa where Romero was sitting and massaged his neck and head.

"Close eyes," Mu Jin demanded.

Romero seemed to enjoy the massage and was moaning like he was slow-fucking.

I almost needed a cold shower. Then Mu Jin beckoned me to take over. Romero probably didn't realize I was now massaging him. I extended my hands to his neck and shoulders. He was solid. Yum.

"I'll make you a special tea, Romero. *Un te especial*," Mu Jin said.

"*Muchas gracias,* señora, *muy amable*," Romero said, being polite and grateful.

Mu Jin then exited for the main house to get the special tea. Romero asked if I could massage his feet. It hit me that I had no proof he was Dalia's husband. Then it could be some creepy stranger, or worse. I stopped massaging when Romero's phone vibrated, while my labia did also. He looked at his phone and read a text. He jumped up from the sofa, waved, and headed for the door.

As Romero exited, he shouted, "I'll be back."

By the time Mu Jin returned with a tea tin, Romero was gone.

"Where he go?" Mu Jin asked.

"Left in a hurry after a text message," I replied.

"I make you the special tea, OK?" Mu Jin suggested.

"I have to memorize lines, or I'll get fired," I said.

"I help you," Mu Jin offered.

Reluctantly, I handed Mu Jin pages of the *Henna's Revenge* script so she could read Basil's part. I should have been rehearsing with Olmo, but I had canceled.

I needed to learn the lines from the scene with Henna berating Basil for his poor bedroom performance. I hoped Mu Jin wouldn't mind the frank sex talk.

"*BAHSIL, you are clueless about how a woman's body works.*" Mu Jin cleared her throat and very emphatically delivered the lines.

Basil: "*Where do you want me to touch you?*"

Henna: "*Cracking my toes and my fingers is not sexy.*

Basil: *"It's chiropractor sex, Henna."*

Henna: *"There won't be any sex with that limp thing."*

Mu Jin laughed uncontrollably at this line and had to sit down.

I put my pages down and asked her to do the lines again as I wanted to be off book. Mu Jin wanted to know about the film. I found myself talking more about Olmo than the film. I showed her an old photo of Olmo from *Love and Secrets*. She was excited.

"I know that guy and show. He so nice!" Mu Jin said.

She sat down beside me and took my hand. She looked at my palm. "You like him, no, you love him," she announced.

"No way. I hardly know the dude, and he's too old."

"*Lao niu chi nen cao*. Old cow eats young grass. He good for you, Poppy. Need his yang," Mu Jin said.

"I haven't seen his yang yet," I noted.

The front gate buzzed, and I pulled up the camera on my phone. WTF? Guys flashing badges. Cops? I showed Mu Jin, who looked rattled.

"No cops. I no here, in China," Mu Jin shouted and ran to the main house. OK, check; Mu Jin had a problem with the police.

In case one of the cops was hot and single, I went to the bathroom to touch up my makeup. After I was presentable, I went to the front gate to meet them.

As I approached the gate, Mu Jin was in a coat and a scarf around her head, holding a mop and bucket.

As I let in the two cops, Mu Jin passed me on her way out and said loudly, "Floors clean, Missy Poppy. Come back next week, finish windows."

She hurried past the gate and onto the road. Where the hell

was she going?

As the two men in suits came through the gate, they flashed their badges and identified themselves as FBI agents.

This got scary fast. Was I being arrested? Were they looking for Mu Jin? Maybe she was undocumented. Why scamper away disguised as a housecleaner? Did one of Dalia's mourners drop a dime and report that there was an illegal burial of ashes on the property?

The FBI agents held up a photo, which looked a little like Romero. They asked if a Romero Robles or Cardoso Ortega had been here. I explained one of the previous tenants had died, and there had been many condolence calls with groups of people.

They were curious about who lived in the house and who owned it. I showed them my lease, and it stated that Lily Ju was the landlord. They seemed satisfied but wanted to contact Lily anyway. They also looked at me suspiciously, but maybe I was being my usual paranoid self. One agent handed me a card in case Romero showed up.

The FBI agents left, and shortly after, I noticed a light in the main house. Mu Jin was back. I texted her to ask if she was OK, and she came over to the guesthouse.

She arrived with bean buns and prepared the special tea. "Those FBI were looking for Romero," I said.

"Could be dirty business, we stay out," Mu Jin said as she poured the tea.

"I didn't tell them anything. So maybe they stay away," I said.

"That Dalia, nice girl, but mixed-up bad people," Mu Jin lamented.

"Was she in trouble?" I asked.

"Maybe long time ago. Ask Lily," Mu Jin suggested.

The tea wasn't helping my now-throbbing headache. While Mu Jin wasn't looking, I downed a double dose of OTC headache stuff and fell asleep on the sofa. Mu Jin must have let herself out.

I woke up in the middle of the night, and there was a book on the coffee table, *Sketches by Cardoso.* Mu Jin must have placed the book there before she left.

I leafed through the sketches. A few newspaper clippings fell out of the book. They were reviews from fifteen years ago with headlines like "Genius," "Miami's New Sensation," and "Cardoso Shines." The back cover had a photo of what appeared to be a very youthful version of Romero but with a full beard. I googled Cardoso Ortega, and a magazine article appeared, entitled: "From Celebrated Artist to Narco, the Fall of Cardoso." Holy shit.

I was going to need more meds with a vodka chaser. It was time to start documenting all the names in this saga related to the dead girl in my yard.

I started with Post-it notes and pasted them on the back side of the closet door: *Dalia Flores, Iris Ortega, Romero Robles, Cardoso Ortega, Acer Flores, Mu Jin Ju, Lily Ju, FBI, Dalia VIPs.*

Who next?

I turned to the clothing in the closet to get ready for my date with Olmo and asked myself—dead girl's dress or my own?

#narcoartist #cops #massage #sexysketch #unshaven #cleanwindows

CHAPTER SEVEN

IRIS 2.0

Leaving Miami in 2000 for New York felt like a new beginning—away from my mother Azalea and her toy boy, Moss. I was excited to set up house with my fiancé, Cardoso, who was getting a name in the Miami art world. He wanted more acclaim.

At first, I was overwhelmed with New York City—the size, the pace and the claustrophobic buildings. I didn't mix well with *gringos* yet, as I had spent my entire life in a Miami Cuban "wealthy" ghetto. Most of the Latinos I met in New York were Puerto Ricans and Dominicans. Even though we could speak the same language, there were cultural differences. These people were mainly poor and uneducated. I was a spoiled, Cuban snob with an attitude.

I was used to nice houses, boats, beaches, designer clothes and palm trees. I missed the pastel colors of the south Florida houses. New York City was all brown and gray. I knew there was a reason I was there, determined to tough it out and wait for an epiphany.

Cardoso threw himself into art class, the local scene and made tons of friends. They would hang out smoking weed, drinking, and trashing well-known artists, alive and dead. I was so fucking jealous of Cardoso. He found his passion and friends to share it with. Cardoso was also prolific and seemed to be on a roll creatively with everything he touched.

I confided in Papi O. by phone about my lack of passion for anything. "*Paciencia, m'ija,*" he told me. He was sure I would find my passion eventually and told me to have patience.

I took business administration classes at a community college. It was Papi O's idea.

The students were boring and just wanted a piece of paper to say they graduated from something. We were a class of misfits, and some didn't even speak English. Even the teachers were blah, no excitement. But then how much passion can you put in graphs, tables, and financial statements? Who cares? I hated accounting. There was a scruffy, bearded guy, wearing Birkenstocks even in winter, who taught software programming.

The marketing class showed promise, and advertising was more up my alley.

When I wasn't at school, I either moped around our apartment in our East Village neighborhood or wandered the streets. This went on for over a year. Then one day I stumbled onto a health food store called *House of Ash*. It had a "Part-Time Help Wanted" notice in the window. The manager, a heavily pierced, gay guy named Ash, seemed nice. He looked in his late twenties and was dressed in designer jeans, a t-shirt and an apron. Ash took me to the back of the store and introduced me to Amapola. She was a seventy-year-old, Cuban *mulata* with long, untamed salt-and-pepper hair down to her waist. She wore a muumuu and ran a mini *botánica* that sold medicinal herbs. Amapola also offered exotic potions and spells to overcome evil curses and bad luck. At first glance, I knew she was a *santera*, a priestess in the *Santería* religion, a crazy mix of African Yoruba and Roman Catholic.

When I was young, my mom would take me to a *botánica* in Miami near Calle 8.

Azalea would consult a *santera* on "lady" health issues. The plants, lotions, and potions in the *botánica* fascinated me. Miraculously, the evil-smelling herbs helped my mom with her heavy periods.

Ash was thrilled I was interested in the part-time job, especially when he heard I spoke Spanish and was Cuban like Amapola. They often had Spanish-speaking customers, and I would come in handy. "The Latin touch," Ash called it.

Amapola scoffed and shrugged. She muttered in Spanish, "She's young. They'll eat her alive." Then she stared at me and ran her fingers through my curly black hair.

"*Algo mal?*" I asked if there was something wrong.

"*Tienes raíces africanas, que suerte no se nota mucho.*" Amapola noted that I had African roots and was lucky you couldn't really tell. I was about to say I was proud of my black ancestors. But she was of a different generation and probably wouldn't resonate.

Even though Ash spoke no Spanish, her tone was obvious.

"Don't mind her moods." Ash dismissed the old woman's attitude.

Ash trained me in his business, the supplements, and the health foods. For a few days, he watched me interact with customers and sometimes left me alone to run the store. I felt comfortable, and I started to feel at home. New York didn't seem so awful anymore. I became at ease with many different types of people. The East Village was gentrifying rapidly, and it felt like a microcosm of the world walked into the House of Ash. I was feeling less Miami Cuban and more international. As the customers described their ailments or issues, I became empathetic. Sometimes, I would advise on supplements from the front, and other times, if they were New Age types, I would steer them to the back.

Eventually, Amapola was comfortable teaching me about her inventory of lotions, salves, tonics, potions, and herbs. She often referred to her age and how she could drop dead anytime. She was concerned about leaving her customers in the lurch. So, I officially became her apprentice. I wouldn't dream of telling my husband, Cardoso. He was a true nonbeliever, and I didn't want trouble.

I noticed Amapola had tarot cards, and a crystal ball on a small, card table behind a curtain. Ash remarked, "She's psychic and probably psycho, too, so watch out. Kidding. Not."

Ash was convinced Amapola was so powerful that she saved his business from bankruptcy. He was convinced the spell she put on the nearby health food store, now closed, kept him in business.

"How did she do it?" I asked Ash.

In a whisper, he replied, "It involved a doll, needles, and a lemon in the freezer." Amapola didn't even go near the competitor's shop to cast the spell.

She consulted a large, tattered book called *Mi Oráculo*, or my oracle. She said a supposedly famous Havana *santera* gave her the book. It consisted of handwritten notes and typed yellowing pages, sorted alphabetically.

At home, Cardoso made fun of my new job and called it the hippie store. I didn't dare tell him about Amapola as he hated the idea of *Santería* and would probably insist that I quit. One day, he surprised me at the shop. As he walked in the door, I asked Amapola, in Spanish, to get behind the curtain. Ash was not around.

"*Si, siento las malas vibraciones,*" Amapola said, claiming Cardoso had bad vibes. He came in and approached me for a kiss. Cardoso perused the supplements.

"Which one makes me hard for hours, babe?" he asked.

Thankfully, he didn't notice the *botánica* potions. He probably would have dragged me out of there. Once Cardoso left, Amapola emerged, looking bewitched.

She beckoned me to come to her and sit at the card table. She had laid out the tarot cards. "He's very talented. Look at this card," she said in Spanish, holding out a card with a sun.

"Is he going to be successful?" I asked.

"Oh yes, very. But he's going to throw it all away like garbage," she warned. Then she held out a card with a man hanging upside down. At first, I was shaken by this statement, then decided to forget about it. I tried to get up to return to the register. But she followed me with more warnings about the future.

"Not now, *Señora* Amapola," I insisted. But she ignored me as she shuffled the cards and asked me to cut them in two piles. She laid out a circle of cards.

"You have a calling to help people. You're a *curandera*," she announced.

"A spiritual healer?" I asked, and she nodded.

She predicted I wouldn't find my groove for some years, but I would be successful with lots of clients. Then I would hit a setback. She closed her eyes, took a deep breath, and said, "A woman named Amapola will save you. But it's not me, a younger woman." She then held my hands. "You must reward this Amapola or face terrible consequences."

At that point, I heard the bell ring as a customer entered the shop. As I stood up, the old *santera* said, "Don't forget. Amapola will save you. Reward her."

I became familiar with all of the products in the front of the house and the back. At some point, by osmosis, I learned how to blend the potions and knew the recipes for spells and lifting bad luck, as well as creating romance. Some clients only came to me, especially when Amapola was in a bad mood.

When I returned back home in the evenings, Cardoso was in full swing partying with artists and their groupies, drinking and smoking. They played music ranging from Miles Davis and Erik Satie to Granados.

One evening, the group were oohing and aahing over one of Cardoso's sketches. It was of me, naked, extending my hands above my head. He had some squiggles under my arms like some unshaven peasant. I begged Cardoso to remove those squiggles, but he refused. He continued producing art that was described as provocative and in true Caribbean style. I had no *"puta idea"* or fucking idea what "true Caribbean style" meant. His work looked tropical; palm trees, ocean, topless girls, sea-shells, beach trash and birds of unknown species.

I quit college and worked full time at House of Ash. I loved it. While I helped customers purchase supplements, Amapola would throw out tidbits about my past, present, and future. Luckily, she spoke in Spanish, so most people didn't understand. Once in a while, she stood in front of me to warn me about some future event. She would suddenly start chanting and swaying. Some customers would ask, "Is she OK?" or offer to call 911. Ash assured them this was normal and not to worry. I covered up her dementia by saying Amapola had the "gift," and her spirit guides gave no warning when they spoke to her. Several customers, *idiotas*, would come in the shop just to see Amapola act crazy and not buy anything.

She also supposedly channeled spirits like my dead sex-worker grandmother. The message was too generic about Fidel Castro's sex habits. Amapola claimed she would know when Fidel was dead. He would appear to her as he crossed over. But then she doubted he would die before her. "*Es como un gato, tiene nueve vidas.*" A cat with nine lives for sure. I asked her to channel my late father, and she said she couldn't pick up the signal. He didn't feel dead to her.

I listened carefully as Amapola consulted and advised clients on their ailments and problems. The customer would leave with a paper bag containing herbs, potions, and a handwritten note with detailed instructions.

One day, she asked me if I was pregnant. I wasn't due for my period for another two weeks but, *Santa María por Dios*, she was right. I was pregnant, according to a lab test.

Cardoso seemed thrilled at first about the baby and then lost interest. He seemed distracted and was working hard to please his teacher and mentor. When I told Amapola that I was really pregnant, she handed me one of her potions. Ash also gave me a basket of herbs and vitamins. I didn't take any of them. Just as I got used to the idea of being a mother, I started bleeding and lost the baby.

Amapola was not empathetic and coldly commented, "*Mejor así.*" Better this way. Ash was very caring and told me to take a few days off. I declined, as I loved working in the shop. Cardoso bought me a dozen roses and a bottle of wine. We never spoke about it. I admit I was kind of relieved.

We had been in New York four years when Cardoso announced he was offered an exhibition in Miami. We would be returning to Florida and I was conflicted about the move. Working with Ash was pleasant, and we had a nice synergy. But Amapola was becoming a nasty, Cuban bitch, not only to me, but also to the customers. It started to feel like she was getting a touch of dementia. What a disaster to have a *santera* with dementia. Who knew what mistakes could happen? And they did. Customers complained that her love potions and spells seemed to create an opposite effect. Instead of creating romance, hatred erupted. A spell meant to hurt one man's competitor created wealth and positive publicity instead.

I had it out with her in Spanish one day.

"These people are desperate. You're not doing them any good. In fact, you're hurting them. Something's wrong, *por favor,* let me help you," I implored.

Amapola became angry and threatened to put a bad spell on me. As she gathered some twigs and one of her mini rag dolls, she stopped and announced, "I don't need this as you're going to fuck up your life on your own, sweetheart!" She then threw the twigs and rag doll in the trash. If I wasn't leaving New York anyway, I would have quit right there.

After three years working at the shop, I believed I had enough knowledge to open my own health food store and *botánica*. I felt bad leaving Ash but was furious with Amapola.

On my last day working at House of Ash, I looked for the sacred *Mi Oráculo* book.

While Amapola wasn't looking, I stuffed the tattered book into my knapsack. I figured if Amapola realized it was missing, she would call me, and I would send it back. But I never heard from her. A week later, as we were driving south to Miami, Ash called to say Amapola had a stroke and died on the shop floor.

When I opened the oracle book, a folded paper dropped out, which read, "*Buena suerte,* Iris," and in small letters at the bottom, "*la necesitas.*" Basically, "Good luck, Iris, you'll need it."

Santa María Purísima, she knew I was going to take her fucking book. This didn't spook me at all. I was in possession of a magical book, and it made me feel powerful.

We returned to Miami in 2004 and planned our wedding. That was when I finally found out about the cash my father had left Papi O. for my upkeep since I was fourteen. It was for my education and a grand wedding. He was cagey about how much was left but wrote us a check for a fifty grand. Cardoso and I saved it for a future condo purchase. We wanted to live on Key Biscayne, with a water view from all sides. Papi O did offer a cash wedding gift of twenty-five grand.

A small wedding was the right choice as my mother-in-law, Mami Ortega, dropped dead at the rehearsal dinner between the main course and the dessert. Such a shame as she always had a sweet tooth.

Cardoso and I always thought obese Papi O would die before her but she probably had enough of him. A death of a family member within hours of my wedding triggered my *santera* instincts. A voice said to make up a potion to remove any negative energy, but I totally forgot. So, we were married the next morning with a handful of family at our side followed by a funeral a few days later. I often wonder if I had made that potion if we would have been spared the horrors to come.

Miami seemed busier than I remembered, with new high rises and more traffic. Since the 1990s, there had been an influx of South Americans fleeing inflation and political turmoil. From the new Latino restaurants, I sensed that Colombians, Venezuelans, and Brazilians had taken over Miami. Even a Little Haiti had developed. The Cuban community was shrinking, and it seemed we were now a minority. *Que pena.*

Cardoso and I soon shed our Cuban-centric perspective and easily fit in with the Miami melting pot and a now thriving city.

We moved in with my mom and Moss. My mom, Azalea, looked fragile and the once slim Indian had gained a lot of weight, with a thicker accent than I remembered.

They had shifted from Sai Baba full devotees to Baba lite. All the framed photos of the guru were gone.

"Scandal has touched Baba," Moss said gravely.

"I don't believe those stories, but Moss thinks they may be true. I'm heartbroken," lamented Azalea.

Moss showed us a British documentary about alleged child sex abuse by Sai Baba.

Cardoso couldn't stop giggling with an "I told ya so" attitude.

After watching the film, I became alarmed when Moss helped my mother struggle to stand up from the low sofa. I followed them to the bedroom and sat on the foot of the bed.

"What the hell is going on, Mami?" I asked.

My mom explained that she had a rare autoimmune disease that was eating away at her organs. She insisted, "It's under control." I was devastated but tried not to show it. I left the room as Moss helped her into her nightgown; she looked very frail.

When I told Cardoso, his first reaction was that we should move out. I was furious. He felt negative vibes all through the house, and they would interfere with his creativity.

It was about this time that I started falling out of love with Cardoso. His art and passion had changed him for the worse. The lust and excitement I felt as a teenager were gone. His words were cruel, and he seemed a stranger to me.

"How can you make me abandon my own mother at this time?" I pleaded.

Cordoso continued, "She has Moss to take care of her and he loves her or are you blind?"

"I admit he's devoted, but I should be here."

"But, my love, you have a business to run," he announced with a flare, then pulled out photos of a shop with the sign "Casa Iris."

"My dad bought the entire building for you," Cardoso noted while showing me a deed.

It read, "owner, Iris Ortega." The building address was in Little Havana.

"You can thank me as I had to force him to give me an accounting of all the money your *papi* gave him. Did you know your dad managed to send money even after he was dead?"

At the time, that piece of information went over my head, as I was so shocked about the shop. I hugged Cardoso.

"I can't believe it," I said, wiping tears from my eyes.

"You can do your *santería botánica* stuff. You think I'm *estúpido*? I knew what you were up to. Both Ash and that *vieja santera* said you were very talented and should have your own business."

I studied the photos of my new shop and the deed to the building again.

"I even visited Amapola once on your day off. I wanted a spell to make me become a famous artist," Cardoso added.

"Was there a doll, needles, and a lemon involved?" I asked.

"Just a lemon in the freezer and *mucho* money in her pocket. That bitch soaked me," Cardoso responded.

I couldn't stop looking at the photos of Casa Iris.

But then my thoughts reverted back to my suffering mother. I grabbed the oracle book in search of a healing potion for my poor *mami*.

There was a note in Amapola's writing on the page for autoimmune diseases.

"If your *mami* gets sick, make her this recipe." It was a list of herbs, and if necessary, a spell. Hopefully, I wasn't too late.

CHAPTER EIGHT

A DATE WITH OLMO

I agreed to go out with Olmo because I was curious. If anything, it would get me away from Dalia's fan club visits. It was Mu Jin's comment, "Old cow eat young grass," and suggesting I needed his "yang," that convinced me. Was Olmo a Mr. Right?

As I pulled up in an Uber, I saw Olmo in front of the restaurant in a wrinkled suit. He held a single rose and looked older than I remembered. Oh God!

I almost told the driver to keep driving, but I chickened out and coyly climbed out of the car. I needed a courage cocktail right then and there. When he spotted me, he drew closer with a big smile on his face.

"For the lovely Poppy," Olmo said as he handed me the rose and escorted me into the fancy restaurant.

It was a chic, French-fusion restaurant called Fleur-de-Lis, with bougainvillea climbing up a rustic, wooden gate. As we entered the patio, there were small café tables with floral-patterned tablecloths, wineglasses, and vases with no flowers. It was probably some new millennial fad or a Marie Kondo thing.

A young, pretty hostess, with the nametag, "Blossom," greeted us. She was annoyingly bubbly, with long, platinum hair pulled up in a chignon. Her flawless skin, perky red lips, violet eyes, and bushy brown eyebrows were *Vogue*-like. My God, I even told her she had great tits. Then the headwaiter, a handsome, African American man named Forest, showed us to our table. Olmo beat Forest to pulling out my chair.

"Hope you don't mind, but I'm old-school. I open doors for ladies and stand when a lady leaves the table," Olmo said.

"I can get used to it. There are so few gentlemen left in the world," I said.

We sat across from each other. Olmo kept smiling while I fiddled nervously with my napkin.

"Please tell me you're smiling naturally and not medicated," I commented.

"Oh no, never touched the stuff. I've never even smoked cigarettes, and coffee has never touched my lips," Olmo noted.

I was impressed with his willpower, yet assumed he was lying. He just kept smiling at me. His teeth were very white. I complimented him: "You have very nice incisors."

"Thank you," he said, dipping his chin and acting a little embarrassed.

"Did you know that opossums have eighteen incisors and armadillos have none? I learned that while shooting the outdoor television docuseries *The Wilds of Texas*," I said with confidence.

"That sounds like fun," Olmo said.

"They made me up like an '80s Vanna White on the Texas

prairies, pointing out odd animals. It paid well," I said.

There was silence, but Olmo kept smiling. Thank GOD Forest returned and handed us menus. Holy shit, twenty bucks for a lettuce wedge. I was afraid to look at the cost of the entrees. Forest asked if we had any dietary restrictions. Olmo looked at me.

"Nothing major." I paused, then added, "No super spicy, salty, or sweet flavors. No GMOs. I hate fighting with shellfish to get little pieces on a tiny fork. The food has to be dead when it lands on the table—nothing jumping, crawling, or swimming in a bowl. Oh, and no dark food; pastel shades if possible."

Olmo blanched, then flashed his white teeth again, but said nothing. If my long list of food wishes was a deal breaker, Olmo didn't show it. But the waiter, Forest, was quick to react.

"In that case, I recommend the fixed menu with several choices," Forest offered.

I glanced at the price of the four-course meal and tried not to gasp at the $140 per person. Was Olmo loaded?

"Looks like we can work around dark-colored food," Olmo said, perusing the menu, then added, "Maybe someday, you'll explain the pastel food thing."

"It started with being fed very bad, dark food," I said.

"You fascinate me, Poppy. You're so strange, but in a good way," Olmo remarked.

That was a backhanded compliment. I cleared my throat as the waiter handed Olmo a wine list.

"You said coffee has not touched your lips, but has wine?" I asked.

"Too much, I'm afraid, and that was long ago. Red or white?"

Olmo asked.

"The menu pairings selections cost a bundle," I noted.

Olmo patted my hand, then motioned to the waiter and ordered the pairings. "Non-issue, hon, and I can't take it with me," he said as he pointed toward the ceiling. Calling me "hon" was cute and retro. I could handle it.

"Did you get the message about rehearsals?" I asked.

"Yes, Fern, the director, wants to have a table read of *Henna's Revenge*," Olmo replied.

"Fern? I thought the director at the audition was a guy."

"Fern's one of those fluid souls. I called her a she, and SHE didn't look happy. She'll probably ask us to use the 'them' pronoun." Olmo stopped and looked worried. "Oh, I hope . . . didn't mean to offend."

Wow, that was something I would say. I waved my hand.

"Oh, don't worry. I'm a girl who likes boys, in the past, present, and the future," I said.

"Fern lost her grant from some LGBTQEFG outfit and only has some Kickstarter funds," Olmo reported.

"Why would *Henna's Revenge* qualify for LGBT funding?" I asked.

"The character Henna is a lesbian who preys on older, wealthy men." Olmo replied.

"I'm surprised at the violent LGBTQ theme coming from THEM," I noted. We both laughed.

"You and I better get woke about these pronouns or we'll never work again in this town. In that spirit, I suggested making Basil a cross-dresser," Olmo said.

I had to admit Olmo made me laugh, and he seemed charming. So, were there Olmo red flags besides maybe being born before TV was invented?

"Let's talk about you, Poppy," Olmo said, looking into my eyes. "Let's not," I responded and added, "You first, Olmo."

Olmo was saved from answering as Forest served the wine and said, "Dry, but fruity sauvignon blanc."

We were served our first course, some gray blob on a piece of lettuce. "The color is a little dark. Is it OK with you, Poppy?" Olmo asked.

"It's kind of gray, so it seems fine. But what is it?" I asked, staring at the hunk of solidified matter.

The waiter announced in a thick accent, "*Terrine de foie gras classique.*"

"In other words, goose liverwurst," Olmo chimed in.

We ate the gray slice in about two bites, and I said to myself it was probably about twenty bucks' worth. Strangely, Olmo also remarked, "That's what twenty dollars of liverwurst looks like. Enjoy."

He sipped his wine and rearranged himself, putting his hands on the table. "You win. I'll go first. I'm an open book. I was an unwelcome surprise to my theatrical parents."

Olmo was a Midwesterner and was raised by his maternal grandparents, as his parents were part of a traveling theater troupe. He spent summers with his actor parents and worked on the shows. They dressed up Olmo as a girl to play Baby June in the musical *Gypsy*. He eventually grew out of the white, frilly, dress and bloomers costume, but that wasn't until he was thirteen, when his voice broke.

"That was thousands of dollars of shrink to process," he said, then added, "At least my parent-induced gender confusion got me out of Vietnam."

We then clinked glasses, followed by me raising my hand in a Poppy pause. "Question. Did you like playing Baby June?" I asked.

"It was the cost of being with my parents, whom I adored," Olmo replied.

Olmo quietly sang a medley of songs from the show, starting with *"Let Me Entertain You"* through *"Everything's Coming Up,"* in a falsetto voice. I applauded, as did the diners at the next table.

"Today, they would arrest my parents and terminate their parental rights. But I have to thank them for giving me my love of acting and the theater," Olmo noted.

Olmo flashed forward to college and his junior year in Mexico. That was where he met his late wife, Violeta, an actress. When Olmo mentioned she acted in the *telenovela, Amor y Vivir,* I spat out my pastel food.

"Mom's fave Spanish afternoon show!" I shouted out. After I explained, Olmo wanted to meet my mom, Daisy, and reminisce about Violeta. I was anxious for the details about Violeta's death, but Olmo had to pee and left the table abruptly. Prostate problems?

I took his absence as a chance to do some cyberstalking. I found an Olmo Branch at a recent, high school reunion in Kansas, where he graduated in 1968. That made him sixty-nine or seventy, older than my dad, Palmer. Yikes! The article on *Love and Secrets* mentioned him leaving the show after his wife, Violeta, died. I couldn't finish cyberstalking before Olmo returned to the table and sat down.

The waiter filled our glasses, this time with an oaky chardonnay.

We toasted as Olmo remarked, "I'm having such a great time, Poppy. You're so refreshing, honest, and real. I meet so many fake women."

"I can be fake and dishonest when I want to. Remember, I'm an actress!" I said haughtily.

"And a good one. But I would love to read lines with you ahead of the shoot and have another fun dinner or whatever," Olmo suggested.

Wait: did the "whatever" mean sex? His comment struck a nerve. "Rehearse, yes, but let's wait on dinner or whatever," I replied.

"Yes, you're right. Tell me if I'm coming on too strong. But I'm so attracted to you," Olmo said.

"You may not be so attracted after you've heard my story," I informed him for his own protection.

"Hit me," Olmo said, leaning over the table and smiling.

"The family Shaw story is a little unconventional. I'm from Encino, I'm afraid."

"Nothing wrong with the valley. I live in Sherman Oaks," Olmo said.

We were served carrot soup and another glass of wine.

"Pale orange? Is that OK with Poppy?" Olmo asked. I gave him a thumbs-up.

"Parents alive? Brothers? Sisters?" Olmo asked while clinking my glass.

"One brother, Cedar, who makes infomercials. Parents, Daisy

and Palmer, still at each other's throats after fifty years."

"Aha. Know that movie," Olmo offered.

"I guess they're OK, but I stay away," I said.

"I'm sure they love you and are proud. It takes courage and bravery to start acting at forty," Olmo noted.

"I started way too late. But my acting coach, Rowan, is very supportive," I said.

"You study with Rowan? She's tough, ageless, and may be a vampire," Olmo said.

We both laughed. I liked this guy. I was going to put our ages on the table. "I'm forty-six."

"Really? I thought you were in your mid-thirties. That's why I waited so long to ask you out," Olmo said.

Bless him. But I wondered if it was bullshit. I leaned over and squinted.

"And I thought you were older than my dad, Palmer. That's why I hesitated."

"I'm sixty-nine," Olmo informed me.

"That IS older than my daddy," I said as I gulped down the rest of my wine. "Deal killer?" Olmo asked.

"Not for friendship," I said, holding up my empty glass for a toast.

Olmo grabbed the wine bottle and filled both our glasses.

"I'll drink to that," Olmo said, clinking my glass and winking.

As I set down my glass of wine, there was a text from the Dalia WhatsApp group.

"Poppy, I'm at the gate."

Didn't these people have any boundaries? Now, I had to

explain the Dalia business to Olmo. Didn't want to go there.

"Someone's at my gate. Sorry, need to make a quick call," I said. I stood up, and Olmo did as well, then sat down. What a guy!

As I walked away, a waiter was coming towards our table with dark food. Hell no!

I headed to the restaurant entrance, sat down at a table with a flowerless vase, and called the weird Sage. She asked me for the code to get in the gate so she could visit the Dalia tree.

WTF? No way was I going to give her the code. No way. Didn't like being the gate, tree, and dead girl keeper. I was so done.

I wasn't going to drop everything and run home, so I told her to come back in the morning. Sage texted back, "*I need to be near her tree like NOW. I've got painful ingrown toenails, a vaginal itch, and an open sore near my nipple.*" I wanted to text back, "Too fucking bad," but just ignored her maladies.

I returned to the table. Olmo stood up, buttoned his rumpled suit coat, and pulled out the chair for me. Big points. I glanced at him, hopefully not blushing, as a follow-up text from Sage appeared, asking if I had extra of Dalia's concoction for constipation because she hadn't taken a dump for two weeks. As I was about to turn the phone off, I heard another ping. It was a text from Acer with a photo of him, shirtless, holding a champagne glass overlooking a Manhattan skyline. *"Wish you were here!"* I didn't respond and turned off my phone.

I looked down at the covered plate at my place setting, I thought, *Please, no dark.*

The waiter returned quickly and lifted the silver cloche to reveal a lovely dish of roasted salmon.

"Pastel pink salmon?" Olmo asked. I gave him a wink.

"The salmon. Yes, lovely," I said, relieved, and added, "Sorry, but there's a girl trying to visit this tree at my place. Long story."

"Look forward to the story along with the pastel foods one," Olmo said.

Olmo and I continued to talk, eat, and drink. We discussed all his theater and TV roles, and how he beat out a well-known actor in the 1990s for the role of Mace Garland on the soap, *Love and Secrets.* The Mace character was abruptly killed off in season fifteen.

"I was lucky booking TV work, but I was never challenged. There is just so much you can do with vapid dialogue," Olmo lamented and launched into typical soap dialogue that seemed to have subtext. He made a sarcastic, serious expression and spoke in a Southern accent.

"I'm probably old enough to be your pappy. And there's Chuck, your high school sweetheart. You love him, don't you?"

I laughed and played along, also doing a Southern accent.

"Chuck? The captain of the football team? Ole Miss? Best-selling author? He means nothing to me now," I said while dramatically wiping my forehead. Then I leaned over the table and whispered, "Especially after Chuck bonked my sister and my mother, though not at the same time, and I think he even did my dad."

We laughed in unison.

Now on our fourth glass of wine, I was really getting light-headed and involuntarily spilled my medical history. Olmo stopped me at the X-rays of my ass and the leaky bowels. He suggested we call it a night and offered to drive me home. I was embarrassed and stayed quiet for the entire ride. I figured that should put him off and leave it as a professional relationship.

But Olmo didn't seem to be put off. He stopped the car in front of the gate, swept me into his arms, and kissed me, no tongue, thank God. It was so fast, I had no time to react. Did I really kiss a man older than my daddy?

"Am I too old for you? It's OK, I can take it," Olmo said.

For some reason, I was mysteriously drawn to leaning over and kissing him again. It was nice.

"Nope. It's fine. All good," I replied as he kissed my hands one by one. It was a kind, noncommittal act. I didn't want to face a film shoot with a guy who hated my guts for rejecting him. Or was I attracted to him? In any case, I was drunk.

As Olmo opened the car door and helped me out, my phone dinged with a text. Olmo and I had a quick hug at the gate, and then he got back in the car and sped off.

I stopped on the stone walkway and read the text from Acer. This time, it was a photo of him in a Speedo. Then came a dick pic. Was this normal behavior for a newly widowed husband? Acer then informed me that it wasn't his dick and sent another pic of him standing with a dude, exposing his massive pecs and bulging arms.

Seriously?

#maydecember #yang #goodnightkiss #deadvioleta
#pastelfood #dickpic #babyjune

CHAPTER NINE

———

HENNA'S REVENGE

The morning after my date with Olmo, Sage texted me that she was on her way over. It was seven fucking a.m. She wanted me to look for a Dalia healing potion, but she couldn't remember the name. The only way to shut Sage up and keep her away was if a Dalia potion didn't heal her multiple maladies. I ripped off the label of a new, cheap hand lotion bottle. I wrote on a Post-it note, "Earth Balance by Dalia," and taped it around the container. Then I left the bottle near the tree as if Dalia had materialized it.

I buzzed Sage in through the gate and watched as she skipped her way along the stone walkway. She was wearing a black sweatshirt over a pink tutu, striped hose, and boots. Was she still in junior high?

I didn't bother to meet her outside and watched from the window. Sage approached the tree, knelt, and picked up the bottle. She hugged it to her chest, then ran off and left. Hopefully, that was the last time I would have to deal with Sage.

There was an email message from Fern the director of *Henna's*

Revenge. Due to funding issues, it was now a fifteen-minute short film instead of a hundred-page feature. Phew! I was so behind in memorizing lines. She wrote to tell me to expect a new script in a week.

I texted Olmo to thank him for the dinner and asked him if he received Fern's message.

"Loved our dinner last night. Run lines new script next week at my place?"

"Sounds good," I replied.

I was super curious to see where he lived and also to get more info on the dead Violeta business. I'm so nosy.

During the next week, I dealt with more Dalia mourner visits. One overseas fan, Jasmin, said she was unable to visit the tree but wanted weekly photos of the mourners.

So, I had them pose around the tree, took pics, and posted them. This Dalia-fueled hysteria is fueled by her healing powers even after death. Unfortunately, Sage posted that all her ailments were cured with the "Earth Balance by Dalia" lotion. Sage told everyone to ask me about getting a bottle. OMG. I quickly replied, *"Sold out,"* and was tempted to add, *"Sorry, suckers."*

Olmo kept me updated on the *Henna's Revenge* shoot. Fern had lined up the crew and locations even though the script needed work. Olmo tried to persuade her to change the date and work on a rewrite that he offered to do. Fern refused.

The final script was sent, and Olmo invited me to his Sherman Oaks home to rehearse.

I was anxious to see his digs and poke around for more Olmo history.

He lived in a modest, three-bedroom bungalow with a screened-in porch and leafy grounds. The living room had high-end furniture, and it was nicely decorated in steel-blue tones.

"Before this, we lived on three acres in Brentwood," Olmo mentioned.

I knew there must be a story about downsizing and moving zip codes. I perused the photos displayed around his home. Most were of a young Olmo on TV and film sets, with major late-twentieth-century stars. The most prominent photo was Olmo and Violeta's wedding party and a band of mariachis. Violeta was a stunning woman. She wore a traditional, Mexican, red-and-white-embroidered, wedding dress. Olmo was in a tux and wore a red carnation as a boutonniere. Power couple.

I did more cyberstalking, and there was talk of Violeta in rehab after the *telenovela* ended and they had moved to LA after a short stay in Miami.

"Violeta was a looker. Must have been hard starting over again," I said.

"Hard is an understatement. She fell apart. Her thick accent only led to walk-on roles as a hotel housekeeper, a housemaid, or a taco vendor."

"While you were a major, heartthrob, soap star," I mentioned.

"She was a fiery, jealous type and even slapped the president of my fan club," Olmo reported.

"Was she sick?" I asked.

Olmo hesitated and sat down.

"Depressed mostly, and on a shitload of meds. Found her OD'd," Olmo said.

I sat next to Olmo and gave him a platonic hug. He obviously really loved her. Sweet guy. Too bad he was sixty-nine.

The new script was terrible. It was so bad that we would laugh and get silly, even without drinking. As I flipped through the pages, I realized there were exterior shots at the beach. I was mortified, as they called for me to be in a swimsuit. We were shooting in Malibu the next day.

None of Dalia's swimsuits fit, as she had clearly had a much larger chest. I asked if I could wear a cover-up, which would help my lack of self-esteem. Dalia had a gauze cover-up that was perfect.

Filming started at eight a.m. It was bitchin' cold. My nipples were stiff, and my ass was frozen. Surfers were wearing wet suits, and beach walkers were bundled like they were on Mt. Everest. Fern's crew were gender-fluid folks, except for one macho guy with extensive tats, heavily pierced and chugging Red Bull. But for all I knew, he could have had a vagina. They were all wearing heavy windbreakers while Olmo and I wore skimpy beachwear.

Olmo had on a flimsy, white shirt, open, and age-appropriate boxer trunks. He seemed in good shape with no beer belly. To my horror, I imagined there might be a pair of saggy balls and gray pubes in those trunks. I had to get that visual out of my mind.

My grandpa, Shaw, wore an old, wool, bathing suit that, when wet, dislodged and exposed his junk. My mother saw me gasp and put her hand over my eyes, but I was traumatized anyway at age ten.

Olmo gave me the once-over when I emerged on set. In the first scene, Olmo, aka BAHSIL, would pin me against a large rock.

The script indicated he would rip off my top and diddle with my nipples. But I told Olmo to tell Fern, NO WAY. She changed it to fondling a boob over clothes.

Olmo agreed to keep it PG and joked that maybe in the future, he could reenact the scene for real. I forced a smile and thought about saggy balls. However, I had to admit I got a little "chach" twitch when Olmo caressed my boob.

The next scene was centered on Basil and Henna sitting on a beach towel. The dialogue was so stilted, except for when Henna ogled a young woman in the distance. Basil agreed with Henna and said, "I could do her." Then Henna suggested a threesome and wanted Basil to ask the strange woman. He protested.

"I only want you!" Basil announced.

"You can have me and her if you want," Henna responded.

We had done ten takes, and we were completely frozen. In between shots, Olmo wrapped a padded coat around me to keep me warm.

After take eleven, Olmo whispered loudly, "I fear this is going to be a shit show." Fern must have overheard and shouted out, "It's all your dime, buddy."

OMG, Olmo was financing this nightmare film. He was paying my salary.

During a break, I texted Holly, *"Did you know the soap senior is financing the Henna short?"*

Holly texted back, *"I figured, but who the f . . . cares? It's paid work, and he's into you."*

Olmo was into me so much, he was spending thousands for this gender-fluid crew to shoot a crap film, just to be near me? I hoped Olmo didn't think he was buying a piece of ass. He already knew it had been rearranged at least once.

The next day, we were shooting the interior scenes in a rented house in Studio City. It was tastefully decorated and had a lot of windows. The lighting crew went to work to create a "day for night" effect.

I noticed an elderly woman in a rocking chair, over in the corner, knitting. I didn't remember anything about this character in the script. Apparently, Fern had arranged a discount on the location if we agreed to granny-sit. The sound guy, with headphones and a mic in hand, went around the room and stopped in front of the rocking woman.

"I can hear creaking. Can you make her stop?" the sound guy requested.

Fern looked annoyed and approached the woman, who appeared catatonic and was just knitting away. "Ma'am, can you stop rocking?" But the woman did not respond and continued knitting. Fern then taped the rocker to the floor to stop the noise. The woman didn't seem to notice and just carried on knitting. The sound guy did a thumbs-up, and we began shooting.

The living room scene was a confrontation between Basil and Henna, a newly married couple. Olmo was unhappy with the scene and started a heated discussion with Fern behind a fancy, Asian screen. I could see the silhouettes of their bodies and their wild gesticulations. They started whispering but ended up disagreeing loudly.

"This scene makes no sense. A threesome with a beach stranger, then Henna bludgeons him to death?" Olmo asked.

"You'll see, it'll make sense. It's a metaphor. Chill, bud. All good. Trust me," Fern replied.

The crew were flashing looks at each other as the argument escalated. The sound guy was shaking his head and then headed to the craft table. I noticed him blatantly packing up snacks in a knapsack. The makeup lady whispered to me that the sound guy was homeless and lived out of his car.

Fern and Olmo continued arguing.

"Fern, I'm sick of these so-called metaphors. Just make the DAMN movie that makes sense. I didn't sign off on these rewrites," Olmo said as he waved the script, then threw it on the floor. Fern and Olmo emerged from behind the screen and continued arguing.

"I know my business. What do you know, soap shit? Small-town theater? Take it or leave it, Olmo Branch," Fern shouted.

"I've paid my dues on all screens, big and small. I have been directed by the best. You, on the other hand, miss, mister, or whatever, may be talented, but you have no track record. I had confidence you could pull this off, show off Poppy's and my talents, make a decent short for a festival run. We have a bunch of silly scenes with bad dialogue," Olmo said boldly.

"We can shut it down now, Olmo. It's your call. I'll return all your money after I pay these guys," Fern suggested.

Olmo looked at me, and then seemed to calm down. "Let's continue. Hopefully, we can fix it in post," Olmo said.

I approached him, then put my hand on his arm and led him over to see Granny's progress on the blanket. She was halfway done. I made sure Fern was out of earshot and whispered.

"Olmo, let's improv the rest of the film," I proposed. Olmo looked at me and put his hand on my cheek.

"Poppy, you're so sweet and smart," Olmo said as tears formed in his eyes.

"Let's be bold," I said.

Olmo nodded; then oddly, Granny looked up and winked at me.

On the sly, I rifled through a closet of the homeowners. I grabbed a pink robe and handed it to Olmo. Fern smirked when Olmo appeared in a woman's robe, but she shouted, "Action."

She cut and restarted a few times until Olmo instructed her, "Shut up and just film, no cuts. It's my dime, remember?"

Fern's lover was a rational professional. She had a word with Fern, and we just rolled until the end with no cuts. Thank God!

In the next scene, Olmo improvised on the origins of Basil's cross-dressing.

"I was sitting on the bed, watching my mother lift her white, silk slip over her head and throw it on the bed. I crawled over, lifted the slip to my cheek, and it felt luscious."

"Did your mother notice you were a twisted little boy?" Henna asked.

"She loved when I tried on her hats, her shoes and jewelry. She found it amusing."

"Look, I could give a rat's ass about the cross-dressing as long as you can do something about your limp dick," Henna said, pouring herself a drink.

Olmo and I paused here. Surprisingly, Fern called out, "It's a keeper, let's move on." That bitch didn't want to admit that our improv lines were SO much better than her script. Olmo looked pleased and kissed me on the forehead.

"I'm forever grateful. I'll never put you through this again. Promise," Olmo said quietly.

Why did he assume there would be a next time?

The following day, we filmed the final scene. We returned to the house, and Granny was still in her rocker, taped to the floor. She had finished almost the entire blanket. Had she not moved from that chair for twenty-four hours?

The dialogue was going to get raunchier. I suggested we blindfold Granny and give her some earbuds.

"They say Granny's deaf and can't see worth shit," the sound guy said.

I was not in the next shot and stood to the side. Basil, still in the pink, chenille robe, was ad-libbing a phone call with his lawyer about divorcing Henna. I noticed Granny removing the tape from her rocker. Then she stood up unaided, holding the finished, red, knit blanket. I caught Fern's eye and motioned towards Granny. Fern gestured to the cameraperson to swing around and film Granny, with quilt in hand, walking slowly towards Basil. I was frozen in anticipation.

As Granny approached Basil, she announced, "That's the robe I gave my dear husband. That Henna's a cunt. Divorce the bitch." And then she threw her knitted red blanket on top of Basil. Fern looked delighted and told the assistant to get Granny to sign a release. She asked, "Is she SAG?"

I learned that other film crews rented this Studio City location and granny-sat on purpose. In a two-day shoot, she made a blanket. On a four-day shoot, Granny made a blanket and a couple of scarves for the crew. If they were there more than a week, Granny got a speaking role if she was up for it. We were lucky that during a two-day shoot, we got a blanket and a bonus killer line on camera. The woman was reported to be ninety-nine years old, and for sure, hers was the only good performance in the film.

As we left the set, Olmo put his arms around me and squeezed tight.

"I should have found a better script for us. When Fern lost her funding, I jumped in and thought we could do a rewrite. I'm sorry, Poppy," Olmo lamented.

"Forgiven," I said and pulled away.

"Owe you another dinner," Olmo said. I did a high five with him and left without another word.

Even though *Henna's Revenge* was not going on my resume, at least I had two consecutive days without dealing with Dalia-land. However, just after we wrapped, I received a text from Romero: *"Can I come over tomorrow? I'd like to sketch you."*

Should I call the FBI? Maybe not until Romero sketched me.

#beachfreeze #grannywatch #saggyballs #tatsgalore
#genderbending #drawme

CHAPTER TEN

ROMERO RETURNS

Did Dalia's ex-husband, Romero, have a nude sketch in mind, with a full or partial hoo-ha? Same position as the Iris nude sketch? I had shaved my underarms recently and would protest if he added the hair squiggles.

Was this going to be a booty call, or was he serious about drawing me? I already had cold feet, as I hated my bony body. That drug addict I dated said I looked like a teen boy naked, but it gave him a hard-on. I should have thrown him out before he got to my jewelry box and made off with a couple of cheap, gold chains and (tee-hee) some worthless costume earrings. Jerk.

I contemplated calling the FBI, but Mu Jin was at home, and it would risk a freak-out and forced repeat of the cleaning woman ruse. Couldn't imagine why they would arrest such a sweet, harmless woman.

Romero did look more bad boy than tortured artist. If the feds were interested in Romero or his alter ego, Cardoso Ortega, then there was a backstory. I so wanted to confront Romero with the articles, the book, and the Florida license of Iris Ortega. Was there a connection between Cardoso and Iris? Oddly, I didn't feel afraid, only a ravenous hunger for the truth.

If I had to pose seminude for him, I'd do it to get to the truth.

An hour before Romero arrived, Holly texted me to say she was nearby, having met with another client in Topanga.

"Can I drop off a script? Can't believe you still live with that dead woman," and added a screwed-up-face emoji.

"A male artist is coming over to sketch me."

"Do tell," she texted, adding question marks.

I sent a lips-sealed-face emoji.

Holly must have been around the corner, as the gate buzzer sounded a few minutes later. She breezed in, wearing a floppy hat, a peasant blouse, a brightly colored peasant skirt and men's sandals.

"This is my Topanga Canyon, boho outfit to blend in with the natives."

"Or the Dalia mourners," I said sarcastically.

Holly looked out the window.

"Is she still out there?" Holly asked.

"As far as I know. The fans keep coming," I replied. Holly handed me a TV pilot script called *Willow's Run.*

"This is the sitcom about a white couple who are golf club owners trying to keep their club white," Holly said as I leafed through the pages. "They want you to read for the part of Ivy, the husband's mistress and bookkeeper."

"And the wife is doing the young caddy?" I noted.

"The script is shit, but they attached bankable talent," Holly added.

I noticed Mu Jin waving burning incense around the tree again.

"Would have to be streaming or cable. I see some sex stuff, like this scene on the second page," I indicated to Holly. "Look, I put my hand down the guy's pants, during a lunch meeting at the club."

"If she doesn't pull out his dick or stick her face in his lap, it can be network," Holly noted.

She then wandered over and looked at the Iris sketch. "The guy who did that sketch is coming over," I said.

"Is he hot?" Holly asked.

"Yeah, I guess. Here's a photo." I showed Holly the coffee-table book. I purposely hid the articles about Cardoso Ortega turned narco.

"I'll leave you to entertain your sexy artist. How do you know him?" Holly asked.

"He says he was married to Dalia, the dead girl in my yard," I responded.

"Wow, you're so into this girl, now hookin' up with her ex? Playin' with fire," Holly said.

"Not planning on fucking him. At least not today," I mentioned.

"Hope you know what you're doin' and messin' with. Your track record is sketch, girl," Holly warned.

Before leaving, Holly told me to text her if things went south with the artist. I didn't dare mention that the FBI was interested in him. It felt dangerous. I kind of liked the feeling.

After Holly left, I changed into one of Dalia's Chinese silk robes. When I looked in the mirror, I saw a slut looking back at me. I then changed into jeans and a T-shirt. What was I thinking?

Holly left me to study *Willow's Run*. I hadn't even reached page two when there was a buzz from the gate. I looked through the camera, and it appeared Romero had arrived in an Uber. I buzzed him in, and he came straight through to the guesthouse and didn't even stop in the yard.

He was dressed in tight jeans, a designer shirt, and a blazer. He looked great but appeared not to have a sketchpad or drawing implements with him. Maybe this was going to be a booty call. He kissed me on both cheeks.

"Where's that Chinese doctor?" Romero demanded.

"Not here today," I answered. I had to lie, as I didn't want Mu Jin around.

"Too bad. She helped me with my headache. Also, I had questions about who owns this property," Romero noted.

"Funny, I had some questions for you too," I said coyly.

I sashayed over to the bookshelf and held up the book *Sketches* by Cardoso Ortega. Romero grabbed it out of my hand.

"Dalia kept my book. Did you see what I wrote?" Romero asked. He flipped to the second page and pointed to a scrawl at the bottom: *"Te amo"*

"Now, were you married to Dalia or Iris?" I asked, but Romero ignored me.

"The feds were here," Romero said while pacing.

I gulped and shook my head. Romero came over to me and held my chin up with his hand. I was terrified but got the twat twitch. Being addicted to bad boys was my old MO. However, my cooch told the truth.

"There were some men looking for you, but the photo didn't really look like you," I said and backed away.

Romero approached and pinned me up against the windowsill. It was like the *telenovela* I watched growing up with women being wooed by Latin hunks.

"I need to have what's left of her. A memory of our love. Let me dig up the ashes and scatter them in Biscayne Bay," Romero pleaded as he leaned into my face with hot and heavy breath.

"Miami?" I asked as I backed away from him.

"Yes, it was the beautiful view from our condo before everything went to shit in 2010. Her ashes should be scattered near there," he insisted.

"The ashes are not mine to give away. You should ask Lily, the property owner, or probably Dalia's current husband, Acer."

"Acer? I have no use for that *cabrón*," Romero said angrily, then released me.

"You know Acer?" I asked.

"That bitch gave him everything! Everything that was mine." Romero paced and shouted.

First, he tried to sell me on his eternal love, then he wanted her ashes, and then he called Dalia a bitch. Wassup?

Romero ran out to the garden, grabbed a small shovel, knelt, and started digging. I watched him from the doorway as he removed his blazer and threw it on the ground.

Then I saw it: a holster with a gun! What was up with the piece? I'd been worried about a booty call when I should have been worried about being murdered over a dead girl's ashes.

I found the FBI guy's card while Romero was busy digging. I hid in the bathroom and dialed the number. There was no answer, so I left a message.

"I think the man you're looking for is here, and he's digging in the garden. By the way, this is Poppy in Topanga. Come now," I said in a whisper and forgot to mention the gun. Stupid me.

I gingerly returned to the window and watched Romero feverishly digging with the small shovel. He was sweating buckets.

My phone buzzed, and it was the FBI calling me back, THANK GOD.

"Got your message. We're just the messengers. There's a deputy coming from out of town to deal with this matter. He'll be there soon. You'll be fine, take care."

The agent ended the call. He gave me no fucking chance to tell him about the gun. HEYSUS, please help me.

Romero was busy digging like a dog looking for a luscious bone. But that small shovel was obviously not helping him get deep enough to find the urn.

There was a buzz from the gate. The FBI dudes already? Not. It was that twerp, Sage, in the gate camera, holding a flowered plant. Christ!

Should I tell Romero that a VIP mourner was here? Would he shoot me? I slipped past him and headed to the gate to confront Sage. I wanted to discourage her from visiting the tree and witnessing Romero exhuming the ashes and taking them away.

Then again, maybe I should let Romero take the urn. If there was no Dalia underground, then no one needed to visit. There was an upside to Romero running off with Dalia's ashes. I could publicize the ashes had been stolen by her ex-husband and scattered in Biscayne Bay. Then all the fans could go to Miami and worship her.

I tried to dissuade Sage from visiting at this time and told her Dalia's husband was worshipping at the tree. I said he would prefer not to be disturbed.

"I would be very respectful and just drop my bush near the tree, then leave. Please let me in, Poppy," pleaded Sage.

I hesitated at first, but then if Romero planned on shooting me, would he shoot both of us? Not to be crass, but that would be one less Dalia mourner on the planet.

So, I let Sage in with her bougainvillea bush. She was dressed in the same sweatshirt, tutu and boots outfit. She put the bush down before we reached the yard and took out a folder to show me.

"These are my plans for the Dalia six-month death anniversary party," Sage said as she walked me through the pages in the folder.

"A what?" I exclaimed. Sage ignored my horror.

"Here's the guest list, which I pulled from WhatsApp, FB, and the growing Insta account."

"Who's posting on Insta? Not me! The tree is in my fucking yard!" I exclaimed.

"I started it. Some people hate FB," Sage said and added, "That drum group was a little expensive for the birthday party. I thought a more spiritual vibe, so I invited a Buddhist group. They are a super cheap alternative."

"Who's paying for this?" I asked.

"There's a GoFundMe account," Sage responded.

I was SO over this. I decided to take my chances and join Romero at the tree.

When approached, Romero had his jacket back on and was stomping on the ground where he had been digging. He didn't have the urn or anything else in his hands. I assumed he either didn't find it or changed his mind about retrieving it.

I introduced Sage as a Dalia fan.

"I decided to leave her there. *Puta bruja,*" Romero said. Sage didn't seem to know what *puta bruja* meant, and I didn't plan on translating, "witch whore."

"I'll never get over her death. If it wasn't for her cures and pep talks, I would have vomited myself to death several times," Sage admitted.

"Beautiful bush," Romero said, pointing to the plant that Sage brought.

"What was it like to be married to such a superhuman like Dalia?" Sage asked.

"She was my first love until—" Romero began to respond but was interrupted by Sage. "We're planning a six-month death anniversary party. I hope you'll come," Sage said.

Romero ignored her.

"My Uber is arriving soon," Romero announced.

"Will you come to the death anniversary party?" Sage asked. Romero walked up to Sage and confronted her.

"Not in the mood for a party. That dead woman and I didn't part on the best of terms. That woman had a very dark side," Romero said as he circled the tree, then headed down the path to the gate.

Sage burst into tears. I tried to console and distract her by helping her choose the best placement of the bush. Sage plopped down on the grass in a funk.

"How could he say that? She was an angel. She IS an angel," Sage lamented.

"Look, Sage. We don't know what really happened. Divorce is tough. She probably said some nasty things, and maybe he deserved it. He looks like a womanizer," I said, patting Sage on the back.

Suddenly, we witnessed Romero returning to the yard. He shouted as he approached the Dalia tree.

"You want to know how I really feel?" Romero exclaimed.

We watched Romero unzip his jeans, then take out his dick and pee on Dalia's burial site.

I gasped while Sage turned angry. She looked as if she was about to lunge at Romero, so I restrained her. I was worried that interrupting his golden shower would provoke him to blow us both away. Romero finished pissing, zipped up his pants, then crossed himself and walked to the gate. What a cliché move, pissing on a grave.

I spent the next half hour consoling Sage, who was sobbing. Then the gate buzzed, and I wondered if it was Romero, back for more antics. I could see from the camera it was a man in a suit, standing and waiting impatiently. He looked like FBI, but not the same one as the last time. This guy was African American and looked important. Mu Jin probably also saw the man in the camera and called me.

"Don't let man in," Mu Jin said and sounded worried.

"Don't worry, just stay in the house," I said, trying to calm her down.

Sage was frantically putting fresh dirt over Romero's pee puddles. She was contaminating a crime scene.

The gate buzzed again. "Who are you?" I asked.

"Deputy US Marshal Layton Blom. Please let me in," the man said.

That sounded official and dead serious. What was a marshal? Normally, I would google the difference between FBI and US marshals, but there was no time. I jotted down the name Deputy Blom on a Post-it and added him to the growing pile of characters.

"Just a minute, only got a towel on," I lied to buy some time.

I quickly set up my laptop on the dining table and motioned to Sage to have a seat. The video was a later one where Dalia looked very haggard and apologized at the beginning that her voice was raspy. Sage was mesmerized and even imitated Dalia's ending schtick of the hand on the heart and the phrase, *"siempre con mucho mucho amor."* Give me a break.

I then hurried out to the yard, buzzed the man in, and took a deep breath. I headed towards the gate to meet the deputy, who looked middle-aged, annoyed and concerned.

"I called you guys almost two hours ago," I informed him, to appear proactive.

"Just flew in from D.C. Glad to meet you, Poppy Shaw," the deputy said.

He knew my name. Oh shit.

"What about those other agents?" I asked.

"They are local FBI who were sent by me. I've been handling Cardoso and Iris Ortega for the past ten years," Deputy Blom stated.

I considered asking WTF handling meant.

#bootysketch #pistolpacker #beautybush #deathparty #goldenshowers

CHAPTER ELEVEN

CASA IRIS

I was happy to be back in Miami but still hated Cardoso, even though he and his *papi* bought me a business in 2006. It was my dream come true, my own *botánica*, Casa Iris, a storefront in a two-story building in Miami's Little Havana. It had always been a lively area with people at outdoor bars, sipping a *cafecito*, a *café con leche* or a *cortado.* The Cubans could go head-to-head with the Italians any day with coffee variations. You could hear Cuban music on every corner, plus there were old men arguing and smoking cigars, people dancing and men whistling at passing women. They say it was a replica of the old Havana.

My father-in-law, Papi O., had an office on the second floor. The access was a stairway from the back storage room. I watched Papi breathing heavily as he struggled to get to his four hundred pounds up the stairs and each time he shouted, "*ascensor, carajo.*" Basically, "fuck, I need an elevator." I feared he would collapse in a heap and suggested he create an office downstairs, but he needed privacy.

Papi O asked me to keep half of the storeroom for his inventory. I knew of his warehouse by the airport, but Casa Iris was for their local deliveries. He told me I didn't have to worry about anything, just run my business. The Casa Iris account had plenty of start-up cash.

"*No te precupes pa nada, m'ija.* Papi O. has you covered," he said. No worries, as his accountants took care of balancing the books and downloaded the register receipts. I just bought my inventory, sold products and services, and took the money.

Maybe Papi O. didn't think I was capable of handling the books? "Does your *papi* think I'm *estúpida y incapaz?*" I asked Cardoso.

"He wants you to concentrate on sales," Cardoso replied.

"One day, I'll insist on taking over running my accounts," I countered.

"Sure, sure," Cardoso said dismissively.

These Cuban guys were pieces of work and from another century. They were still trying to keep women out of the loop and in the kitchen, barefoot and pregnant.

The Casa Iris building had a history. First, it was a bar hangout for mobsters called Rosie's, from the 1940s through the '60s. There was even a photo of Sinatra on the wall. The first floor was a florist's for the past forty years. I could still smell the fragrant flowers; it was in the walls and the perfect segue to my *botánica*.

There was a large fridge in the storeroom and a back door to an alleyway with parking spots.

I planned on arranging my shop almost exactly like House of Ash in the East Village. But I created a completely separate room for the lotions, potions, and *santería* products. I wanted a more private arrangement than a cheesy, beaded curtain and a card table like that crazy witch, Amapola, had set up.

This was twenty-first-century *santería*. I had laptop terminals set up so a customer could search any malady, problem, or desire. The customer would be provided a list of products, DIY spells, or a personal spell by an accredited *santera* or *santero*. There was an extra charge if they wanted me to perform the ritual.

My roster of local, freelance Cuban and Dominican *santeras* and *santeros* generated significant business. And for an upcharge, there were the Haitian voodoo masters in Miami's Little Haiti neighborhood. Those Haitian dudes were fierce, with piercing eyes and wild hair. While my Cuban clients thought the Haitian spells were powerful, they needed translators, which was also an extra charge.

Eventually, I found a Haitian voodoo master who spoke Spanish. I had to warn my clients not to make any racist comments.

Cardoso offered to decorate the Casa Iris walls. He brought an art student, his assistant, Pixie, to help. She was seventeen and a spindly, petite blonde. Cardoso said she was a trust fund baby. Her real name was Linden Maple. Her family had oil fields and could afford Givenchy. So why did she dress like a cheap *puta* and shop at the Salvation Army?

Pixie arrived one day with her biker boyfriend, another artist. Together with Cardoso, they painted plants, flowers, and trees on the walls. The main mural, behind the register, was a splash of violet iris flowers. I insisted we place Cardoso's nude sketch of me in a prominent place. We hung it near the entrance to the *botánica* section. At this point, my underarm stubble on the sketch didn't bother me.

Cardoso and his team's murals were breathtaking. The shop's decor earned a spread in the *Miami Herald* Sunday magazine with photos: "*Casa Iris, a Botánica and Work of Art.*" The article brought a lot of attention and business to the shop.

Papi O. complained there were too many people around, as if he were afraid of theft of this inventory. In reality, he was trying to keep a low profile and avoid scrutiny of his dubious dealings.

The Casa Iris gala opening was a twofold celebration as my *mami*, Azalea, was getting better thanks to Amapola's potion remedy. I was regretful we parted on harsh words. But that old witch was a believer in destiny, "*el destino,*" but with a little help from spells and potions.

My business had a steady stream of customers for the health food products and medicinal plants. But I also had a lot of interest in my magical lotions, potions, and spells. Since I wanted to avoid any negative juju, I always had one of the freelance *santeros* on speed dial to deal with the spells.

I specialized in love spells. I preferred to stay away from the other kind that brought doom and gloom to enemies, neighbors, coworkers, bosses, ex-spouses and in-laws. Between Casa Iris and Cardoso's art dealing, we made some real money.

We moved to an oceanfront condo in Miami with a view of Key Biscayne. We had a great group of friends from the international art world. Cardoso was the toast of the first Art Basel Miami. I was less jealous of his success as I now had my own kingdom—Casa Iris.

One of Papi O.'s Mexican connections introduced me to the statuette of *Santa Muerte*, literally the "death saint." It was a scary-looking, cloaked, skeleton figure, carrying a staph. Mexican gangs used them as protection against rival gangs and the law.

I ordered a couple of cartons of these creepy-looking saints. The word got out, and not only the gangs bought them, but I also noticed gay boys buying the statuettes, especially the ones that looked female. It wasn't just a gang thing. It appeared that *Santa Muerte* was a one-stop-shop protective saint. The death saint and magic spells for gangs kept me going during the 2008 and 2009 great recession when the health food and other potion business was slow.

One day, I noticed one of Papi O.'s stock boys filling the bases of the saints with small packets of white powder. It was for a fifty-year birthday celebration for a local politician, and they were party favors.

I knew that sometimes Papi O.'s business crossed into narco territory, but he was also exporting computer hardware. Maybe when he called his company CHMS Inc., it meant coke, heroin, meth, and software? He claimed it was the initials of his business partners.

I stayed away from his business and let his people do all the accounting for Casa Iris. I didn't even look at the statements in the beginning. But when they asked me to sign off on the first year's accounts, I was shocked. They were claiming $10 million income.

When I dug deep into the statements and reports, I saw transactions that had little to do with Casa Iris business. There were invoices to vendors and contractors I didn't know, and for materials I didn't recognize. The business showed a large loss, and I calculated we broke even. I was afraid but ignored the red flags. *Estúpida!*

Papi Ortega was very interested in my spells. He seemed to be aging quickly, and I suggested potion for rejuvenation. Now that Mami Ortega was dead, we often saw young women on his arm at parties and restaurants. Cardoso said, "Just let the old man enjoy life, and let his *pito* do the walking. He earned it."

I consulted the *oráculo* book and found the spell Amapola used for "*impotente*," limp dick. I recreated it for Papi Ortega, and he seemed happy with the results.

He assured me all his physical strength was back. "*Todo!*" all of it! He swept his hand from head to toe, circling his protruding belly and around his groin. That was a little TMI for a daughter-in-law.

"Iris, you've been a daughter to me since you were fourteen," Papi O. said.

I gave him a big hug and responded in Spanish, "I love you, Papi O. You've been the only dad I've ever known."

"I promised your *papi*, Eneldo, who said, 'Look after my Iris, or I come after you,'" Papi O. reported.

"How can he come after you from the grave?" I asked, but Papi O. didn't respond and just took the vial I handed him.

"You surprised me, Iris. You're very good at this *santería* and health food business. Was that Violeta Branch, from *Amor y Vivir* in the shop yesterday?" Papi O asked.

"Yes, I'm treating her and the husband. They almost divorced and my love potion is working. So business is good." I replied with pride.

"*Excelente, querida*. But you still need help running the shop's finances." He added.

I thought that was a strange comment. I was *perfectamente* capable of running my finances and complained to my husband.

"He loves running everyone's life and he does it well, *mi amor.*" Cardoso noted.

Cardoso's book of sketches garnered amazing reviews, and he was becoming a local superstar. He was also discovering new talent. Papi O. rented him a gallery in Coconut Grove, which sold his art and other Latino artwork. Papi O insisted on handling Cardoso's finances also.

Cardoso hired Pixie as an assistant. I suspected she was living in the gallery. Some days, I noticed her underwear drying and a toothbrush in the gallery restroom. After a while, there was no sign of the biker boyfriend.

We were happily making money and had busy schedules. We really didn't talk much anymore like we used to, and there was minimal sex.

I had been in business four years when the shit hit the fan, big time. It started with my *mami*, Azalea. Having overcome her autoimmune disease thanks to the potion formula Amapola left; she developed congestive heart failure.

She seemed to give up and didn't want any treatment. Moss was heartbroken and broke down one night after she was asleep. He confessed that Azalea had married him for a green card.

"I know this is a shock, but I love your mother deeply, even though she's old enough to be my own mother," Moss said tearfully.

This Indian guy was my stepfather and only a few years older than me.

I was numb, going through the motions of the funeral. I made up my own potion to help me grieve and get through the ordeal. Cardoso was busy with his next exhibition.

Another fun family fact was that my supposedly dead father, Eneldo, sent flowers to my mother's funeral. Papi O. dismissed it as a sick Cuban prank or one of his associates sending on his behalf.

During the wake, a Chinese woman and her daughter approached me and said they knew my father. She introduced herself as Mu Jin and her daughter as Lily. I was distracted and just gave them my Casa Iris business card. But the young woman, Lily, whispered, "We should talk," and handed me her card with a glam shot. Lily was an actress, looked twenty something and reminded me of someone.

I showed Lily's card to Cardoso and then Papi O.

"*Parece tu familia mulata con sabor chino.*" Cardoso said noting that Lily looked like my mixed-race Cuban family with Chinese flavor.

"I saw her at the funeral," Papi O. noted, adding, "Her mother, that *chinita,* said she needed to talk to me. She knew your papi, Eneldo."

After the funeral, I left Lily a voice mail: *"Come on by the shop. Invite you for a café cubano."* She didn't return my call.

One morning, as I was busy in the shop, an expensive-looking, Anglo lawyer asked for Papi O. I escorted him to the back stairs.

After the lawyer left, Papi O. asked me to come up to the office. He gave me a tour of his desk, the combination to the safe, and files. I didn't dare ask him what was going on, hoping he would volunteer any information. He never did, and a few days later, Papi O. disappeared.

Cardoso said not to worry as he was probably shacked up with one of his *putas.*

I rifled through Papi O.'s desk and found a business card from a criminal defense attorney named Yarrow. Shit. Our usual lawyer, Tomillo, had died in a mysterious accident, and our accountant's phone was disconnected.

I left a voice mail for Mr. Yarrow. After a week, Cardoso was now worried and called everyone we knew, asking if they had seen his *papi.* Even his latest girlfriend was missing.

There were no clues in Papi O.'s bachelor condo. We filed a report with the police, but no one followed up.

Cardoso absorbed himself in work and spent most of his time at the gallery studio. He had bought a sofa bed for his office and claimed he liked to work on and off during the night. We hadn't had sex in months.

Papi O. had been missing for several weeks, and there was no news. To add to the stress, I had a very bad mammogram report. Just as I was making an appointment for a biopsy, an imposing, middle-aged, well-dressed black man walked into Casa Iris.

Deputy US Marshall Layton Blom flashed his badge and handed me his business card. He suggested I close the shop so we could talk. I was suitably spooked. I knew deep down someone had caught up with Papi O. He was either dead or in jail. I braced myself.

I noticed unmarked vans parked in front and what looked like a SWAT team spilling onto the streets. I thought there was a raid or a shooting nearby.

"How can I help you?" I asked as I placed the "Closed" sign on the shop door and bolted it. He also indicated I should close the grate over the windows.

"Can we sit and talk somewhere?" he asked.

I led him to the back storage room, where there were boxes of software, saints, lotions, and potions. I felt that the deputy was giving me the once-over as I bent down to unfold the chairs so we could sit.

"Your father-in-law, Lirio Ortega, has turned DEA witness and is in protective custody," said Deputy Blom, adding, "The DEA is about to burst through this door to seize all your inventory, devices, and documents."

There was a knock on the storeroom door, and Blom opened it to a SWAT team who stormed in, pointing guns. He flashed his badge to the squad leader, and they put their weapons down. The squad leader asked me where Mr. Ortega's office was, and I pointed to the stairs. The other team members started packing up the storeroom inventory of Papi O.'s hardware and the entire Casa Iris inventory, including my *Santa Muerte* dolls. I grabbed one before it was packed and flashed it at Deputy Blom. Somehow, I thought the death saint would help me. Blom held the ugly skeletal saint in his hand and dropped it in a box, like it was hot.

"I'm sure one day, you'll explain this thing to me," Blom said.

"It looks horrible but it's protection. Keep it," I advised him.

I watched in tears as they carried the boxes out of the store.

"This is for your protection. You and your husband are in danger," Blom announced.

"From whom?" I asked, choking up as they haphazardly threw my lotions, potions, crystals, and books in boxes. I was watching my world crumble.

"Your father-in-law was using Casa Iris and your husband's gallery to launder money for a major Colombian cartel. Mr. Ortega will testify against them. But our informants say the cartel is out for blood. You are targets," he warned.

I waved a *Santa Muerte* doll at Blom.

"So let them," I said, trying to hold it together.

"You don't want to fuck with these fellas. We've taken your husband, Cardoso, to a safe house hotel near Miami, and you need to join him," Blom said.

"We are innocent, Deputy Blom. We knew nothing. My father-in-law handled everything," I cried.

"Your names are all over the money transfers, and you will have to convince the feds you were not part of it. Or were you?" Blom asked.

I confronted Blom directly in the eyes and waved my hands.

"Of course, we weren't. What proof do you have? Aren't there laws to protect us?" I asked, then stood up and realized the world was crashing.

"The DEA recommends the witness protection program. The US Marshals Service is here to help you. First, a temporary safe house, then new identities and relocation in the WITSEC program," Blom informed me.

"Witness protection? Where are you sending us?" I asked.

"TBD, Mrs. Ortega. Also, forgot: we added your stepfather, Moss, to the list, but he's insisting on returning to India. My assistant deputies just saw him off at Miami airport," Blom said.

"Moss is only a civil servant bookkeeper. What does Moss have to do with anything?" I asked.

"He had dealings with Ortega and previously your father, Eneldo Espinoza," Blom responded.

I was so shocked and numb from the avalanche of events that I didn't question the connection between Moss, Papi O., and my father.

Blom said the marshals would put the house Moss shared with Azalea up for sale and send the proceeds to him in India. They would put our stuff in storage, and our luxury place would be sold.

"What's going to happen to this building, my business?" I asked, holding back tears.

"If it was purchased with cartel-related funds, don't count on it," Blom advised me.

I didn't even want to think about Cardoso's gallery and the million dollars' worth of artwork. Was that also lost? I was sick to my stomach, and then I remembered about the mammogram and biopsy. I thought a medical issue would get me a pass.

"Deputy Blom, I need to have a biopsy," I stated and broke down. Blom looked alarmed.

"We'll arrange it, Mrs. Ortega, don't worry," he responded.

"Call me Iris," I said weakly. He nodded.

While Blom was on his mobile, the SWAT team were still in

the storeroom. I grabbed a couple of Casa Iris shopping bags. I stuffed all the cash in the register, my nude sketch, and my oracle book into the bags. I also grabbed some potions, needles, and the yarn dolls used for spells. I felt a little empowered with at least some of my *santera* paraphernalia.

I looked at the marvelous Casa Iris flowered murals for the last time. Some lucky bastard would take over MY kingdom. Deputy Blom signaled we had to go. I exited with him and a few SWAT team members with guns drawn. They led me into a black van with smoked windows. I held my shopping bags tight, as they were filled with the only items I saved from my Casa Iris.

I was only thirty, and my life was now pure *mierda*. Shit.

CHAPTER TWELVE

DEPUTY BLOM

I was dumbstruck after Deputy Blom's statement that he was "Iris and Cardoso Ortega's handler." We were standing in front of the Dalia memorial tree. As I was about to ask for more detail, we heard whacko, Sage, having a meltdown. She was inside the guesthouse, soaking up the Dalia videos. Even from the yard, we heard Sage screaming, "You can't be dead!"

I pointed towards the guesthouse to explain the outburst.

"That's Sage. She's an unbalanced Dalia devotee and often comes to worship at the shrine," I said to Blom.

Blom approached the tree and the area Romero had pissed on. "Is Dalia supposedly buried there?" Blom asked. I nodded.

"Let me get the crazed fan out of here so we can talk," I proposed, again taking the offense.

"I've been following the Facebook posts but wasn't sure if this was just a memorial tree or a real burial site. In some states, it's against the law to scatter human remains on a property," Blom informed me.

"Wasn't me. Not my idea," I said, raising my hands as I headed back into the guesthouse.

I tried to calm Sage down and told her visiting hours were over. I persuaded her to take a Xanax, saying Dalia would approve. Then I ordered Sage an Uber.

From the window, I could see Deputy Blom taking photos of the tree and the guesthouse. I escorted Sage to the gate and made sure she got into the Uber. Good riddance. What a pain in the ass.

When I returned to the yard, the deputy was inside the guesthouse, poking around. He was opening cabinets and drawers, like he was deciding if he wanted to rent or buy. He stopped perusing, then removed his jacket, revealing a gun in a holster.

"Damn it, I was this close," Blom said, gesturing with his thumb and forefinger.

"Close to what? Blowing your or my brains out?" I muttered.

Blom stopped and stared at the nude sketch.

"Brings back a decade ago memories, not good, by the way," Blom said.

"Romero said he drew that, but I'm confused," I noted.

"The dude's violating the agreement and selling art under the name Cardoso Ortega. He, Romero, has been ignoring my texts warning the cartel may find him," the deputy said.

OK, a lot to unpack here, I thought.

I told Blom that Romero had a gun, acted very angry, said not-so-nice things about Dalia, and then, as a finale, "Performed a golden shower on the poor woman's grave."

Blom winced. "Sounds like a typical dramatic Cardoso or Romero move."

"What did you mean by 'handling' Iris and Cardoso?" I asked the deputy.

Again, the deputy didn't answer my question and continued his monologue.

"I was so close to retirement, and on my last day, the boss, the new, young upstart, calls me in, that little shit," Blom said as he made himself comfortable on the sofa. Maybe this guy needs to retire, as he wasn't making any fucking sense.

"Deputy Blom, I'm not following you. Are you OK? Need a drink or some meds? All legal," I said, crossing my heart and kissing my own hand.

"Poppy Shaw. Your name is so familiar," Blom remarked.

"Maybe you've seen me on the big or little screen," I mentioned casually.

"I don't watch nothin'. My work has been a twenty-four seven for over thirty years. I was about to retire when I was dragged kicking and screaming back into the Ortega nightmare," Blom noted.

"I found a license in the closet for an Iris Ortega. Looks a lot like Dalia," I noted.

"IT IS DALIA!" Blom said, jumping up from the sofa. "I'll take a drink, vodka straight up. I'm on duty, but what can they do, fire me?"

"I feel like I'm under investigation. What does any of this have to do with me?" I asked. Then I made a mental note for the next Post-it, "Dalia is Iris."

Blom circled me like I was a prey animal. I backed away and served him a vodka straight up.

"Poppy Shaw. Poppy Shaw. Did you know Dalia's last name?" Blom asked.

"Dalia Flores. It's on her website and YouTube channel," I replied.

Blom made a buzzer sound like an old game show.

"Wrong. Her name was Dalia Shaw before she married that loser, Acer," Blom informed me.

"You know Acer?" I asked and totally spaced on the "Shaw" angle.

Blom didn't answer at first, then gestured for a vodka refill. He had some balls. This US fucking marshal, drinking vodka in my home on the taxpayer's dime, acting vague and weird. Since he had a gun and I didn't, I had no choice but to go along.

After I poured the deputy a refill, I walked over the bookshelf, then handed him the Cardoso Ortega sketchbook. He leafed through it and shook his head. Correct. "So, Dalia was married to Acer before she died, but she was also married to Romero, but who was Cardoso?" I asked. Then I silently chanted, "I am not confused," several times.

"Dalia and Romero were Iris and Cardoso Ortega in previous lives. The Ortegas were part of a Miami drug cartel that testified in a narco money-laundering case. Then they entered WITSEC, the witness protection program under my care, ten years ago," Blom said.

"Witness protection? Isn't that for murderers?" I asked, and now, I was not sipping but gulping down vodka.

"They were kinda indirectly involved with murders," Blom informed me.

"Kinda indirectly?" I blurted out.

"But both of them violated their protection agreements, and I'm not sure Acer is part of the shenanigans," Blom replied.

"What shenanigans?" I asked.

"I could tell you this complicated story, but I first want to know HOW you're involved, Miss Shaw," Blom said, being very intimidating.

"Who? Little ole me?" I said in a corny theatrical voice, then realized my sarcasm could make him super suspicious.

"Yeah, you. Who are you, and why are you living here? Also, who are those two living in the big house?" Blom demanded.

"I'm just Poppy Shaw. Those two in the big house are Lily Ju, which means 'two flowers' in Chinese, and Mu Jin Ju, which also means 'two flowers,' or three? Another vodka?" I asked.

Blom drank up, slammed the glass down, and gestured no more.

"This is no game, young lady," Blom said. I was so flattered he used the word "young."

"Bless you, Deputy; no one has called me young in ages. Maybe you can text my agent, Holly, and tell her you think I'm young. I'm SO flattered," I said flippantly.

"I came here and thought you were connected with this gang, but somehow, I think you're not the type," Blom commented. I was kinda insulted.

"Why? Do I appear too ditzy, too stupid to be involved in a crime?" I asked indignantly.

"Not at all. Your background doesn't put you in their orbit," Blom informed me and added, "but I'm still not convinced you and those Chinese ladies are not involved. Who owns this property?"

I shrugged and launched into my story.

"Look, Deputy. I was a boring office manager turned struggling actress. I met Lily in acting class while we were being sheep during an alien invasion. Over margaritas, she offered me the guesthouse for cheap. Then I saw them bury an urn under that tree. Lily believes she told me part of the deal was being Dalia's mourner manager, but not true. I was hijacked into the position and forced to deal, as you saw, with unhinged and deranged fans. They visit her burial site in droves, have parties, and have ruined my life." I got emotional and needed more vodka.

"What was the relationship between Lily and Dalia?" Blom asked.

"I guess they were close, like BFFs. Lily promoted her website and YouTube channel," I said.

"I knew about that and didn't like it. Dalia was too visible, but because of the cancer, I let it go," Blom said.

"Cancer treatment, tough. She had a lot of wigs, still in the closet. I guess her hair was falling out from the chemo," I mentioned.

"Can I see the wigs and any other items Dalia left behind?" Blom requested.

I panicked. Stupid me. I shouldn't have said anything. He might take all of Dalia's shit as evidence of whatever crime she supposedly committed. I could lose all my magical clothes and never book an acting job again.

I gingerly led the deputy to the walk-in closet and quickly moved boxes and clothes together. I tried to comingle my stuff with hers. Blom saw the Post-it notes on the back end of the closet. I quickly ripped down all the notes and put them on a shelf. I pointed to the wig boxes. He took out a wig and petted it.

"And the rest of the clothes?" he asked.

"Some are hers," I said, thinking I'd point out the items that I didn't like or that didn't fit me. Blom first focused on the wigs and took a long, dark brown one out of a box.

"I can see her wearing this," Blom said as he held the wig. Whew, creepy.

I pointed to the handbags and scarves. No way was I going to give up any shoes or the bulk of Dalia's clothes. They were my key to success.

"I'm taking this stuff as evidence. I need some bags," Blom informed me.

I pulled a few large shopping bags from a shelf, and he nodded.

I threw in a few sweaters, and some were even mine. Ha! I packed a few handbags and some scarves not in my color palette. Ha! Blom threw the wig into the bag. Gosh, what was he going to do with that?

Blom took the bags outside and placed them near the tree, then took crime scene tape and plastic gloves out of his pocket. With gloved hands, he picked up a shovel that was on the side of the main house. He dug up the tree, then poked around and found the urn, which he placed in a bag. Then he put crime scene tape around the tree, grabbed the bags, and headed to the pathway.

"I'll be in touch. Don't go far, Poppy," Blom advised me as he left.

Mu Jin was apparently watching from the main house and

came rushing out to the yard.

"Who that man?" Mu Jin asked.

"He's a US marshal. He said Dalia is Iris and the Romero guy is Cardoso, the artist. They were involved in Miami drug gangs," I answered.

"Where he take Dalia?" Mu Jin asked.

"I didn't ask and not sure I want to know," I replied.

"That girl big trouble. Just like her father," Mu Jin remarked.

"Father? You knew him?" I asked Mu Jin as she examined the crime scene tape.

"Never mind," Mu Jin said.

I took photos of the crime scene tape and the empty hole where Dalia's urn had been. *Bye-bye, Dalia, now you're government evidence for who knows what crime.* I texted the photos of the crime scene tape around the tree and the hole to Lily. I told her a US marshal had removed Dalia. I added text to the photos.

"No more Dalia, so no more need to mourner manage?" I asked. Lily contacted me immediately on FaceTime.

"Please don't post those photos. I need you to pretend she's still in the ground," Lily pleaded.

Mu Jin grabbed my phone to speak to Lily.

"Lily. Make sure all those papers sign and legal. Don't want trouble," Mu Jin said.

"Yes, Ma. Don't worry. But have to keep the Dalia fans coming. I promised," Lily said. I grabbed the phone back from Mu Jin.

"There was a US marshal here. He says Dalia was in witness protection," I informed her.

"We knew Dalia had some issues, but it was all behind her.

We still need to preserve her memory. She was a wonderful person," Lily cried.

"Maybe, Lily, you have to close the Dalia dead club. Don't take any more money," Mu Jin shouted into the phone.

"Money? You're taking money from the mourners?" I asked.

"I have to pay Ginger to keep up the website and the channel," Lily said.

I then realized Lily was soaking the Dalia fan club.

"Close it all down. She dead, Lily. Enough!" Mu Jin insisted. Lily was getting tearful.

"Poppy, please allow people to come. At least for the death anniversary party," Lily pleaded.

"I'll allow for the party, but then it's over. I'm going to move out," I announced.

"No! Please. I'll drop the rent again," Lily offered.

"Unless you drop it to zero, I'm outta here," I said.

Those words came out involuntarily. Yes, I should move and take the magical Dalia clothes with me. Surely, they'd work off-site.

"OK, rent free for the next six months," Lily said. I was shocked; so was Mu Jin.

"No way," Mu Jin said.

Then Lily and Mu Jin argued in Chinese so I couldn't understand, followed by Lily getting my attention.

"Poppy, how about you don't pay next month, and we'll talk after the party?" Lily said.

I gave her a lukewarm "OK." But I was not happy.

We ended the call, and Mu Jin left the guesthouse. I could see her shaking her head as she passed the crime scene tape around the tree in the yard.

I entered the closet to dress for my date. Olmo texted me.

"Are you OK, hon?"

"Friggin' amazing, hon!" I texted back, lying.

"Ready for our date? Can you wear that Hermès scarf?"

Olmo asked, which was creepy. It was the same one he had bought for his dead wife, Violeta. Ew. I texted a thumbs-up emoji. Then I panicked. Did I hand that scarf to Deputy Blom? Shit!

As I searched for an equivalent designer scarf, I realized I was shit-faced. Olmo was going to think I was a sloppy, afternoon drunk.

Now I needed an evening outfit for my date. As I rummaged in the closet, I suddenly heard Dalia's voice: "When you're sad, visit your clothes."

I totally freaked out and ran out to the living room and noticed my phone was suddenly playing a random YouTube Dalia video. The urn was gone, but she was still around.

#sageshow #triplevodka #freerent? #witsec #hermes #voices #deputy #deadwife

Chapter Thirteen

MR. RIGHT OR MR. WRONG?

I sat down on the guesthouse closet floor, chanting, "*Nam-myoho-renge-kyo,*" and concentrated on an outfit for my date with Olmo. After a minute of chanting, I looked up at Dalia's wardrobe and was drawn to a light purple, pastel skirt, a matching floral top, and purple espadrilles. I had almost handed that ensemble to Deputy Blom as evidence; so happy I didn't.

Olmo texted, *"Arriving early."* I did NOT want to explain the crime scene tape in my yard, so I waited for him outside the gate. He pulled up in a rental car, as he was shopping for a new one.

I had to admit he looked good. He wore a charcoal-gray jacket, a light blue, linen shirt, with a few buttons undone, and linen pants.

But goddamn, I knew his saggy nutsack was floating around in those trousers. I had a love of and fear of balls. It was related to Grandpa Shaw's old wool swimsuit that, when wet, exposed his junk. When I was ten years old, his nutsack got stuck in the slats of an Adirondack chair. I was the only one around. Grandpa pleaded, "Help save my balls, Poppy." I pushed his balls gently through the slats until they were free. It was our secret.

Maybe because Olmo was older, I flashed back to Grandpa Shaw's balls.

"Oh, Poppy, you look sensational," Olmo said and pecked me on both cheeks.

"This old thing?" I said and wondered what Olmo would think if he knew I was wearing a dead woman's clothes.

"You are wearing pastels, how appropriate," Olmo pointed out.

I had a silent Poppy pause as a feeling of *déjà vu* came over me. There was suddenly something so familiar about Olmo, as if I knew him in another dimension, time, or space.

"Back to FDL, for another nice evening of French cuisine?" Olmo suggested.

"FDL? Ah, you mean Fleur-de-Lis. Great!" I said.

"From now on, it's gonna be our place," Olmo affirmed. As we drove, he grabbed my hand and kissed it.

We arrived at Fleur-de-Lis. It was as gorgeous as ever. The bougainvillea was overflowing, and this time, there were flowers in the vases on the outdoor café tables. At the restaurant, we were greeted by Blossom and Forest.

"Are you ready for a superb meal of pale food, *á la* Française?" Olmo asked as he seated me, then scooted tightly into the table.

He put his hand on my right shoulder, leaned in, and kissed me on my left cheek. He returned to his seat across from me and asked, "Do you mind if I take control?"

That was SO sexy. I was really hot for this guy, all sixty-nine years of him. "Control of what?" I asked coyly.

"I've prearranged the meal. And whatever else may happen tonight," Olmo said nonchalantly.

Olmo didn't order the wine pairings this time. He probably remembered from the last time when I was hammered after three glasses and told stories about my colon.

He ordered a single bottle of champagne.

"We're celebrating," Olmo said and added, "I looked at the *Henna's Revenge* raw footage. You and Granny are terrific."

"So, you can salvage something?" I asked.

"At least ten minutes. I'm renaming the film *Pink Chenille*," Olmo noted. The waiter came promptly with our first course.

"Ah. Hearts of palm, artichoke, onion, clementine, in lemon vinaigrette. It is perfectly pale," Olmo informed me.

I was so touched and looked into Olmo's eyes.

"No one else has taken my fear of dark food as seriously as you have. Thank you," I said, smiling. We clinked flutes.

"I think you owe me the whole dark food story," Olmo suggested.

"Thanksgiving, when I was twelve. My mom's sister served me dark and slimy spinach. I wanted mashed taters and white meat, but she threw a dark thigh on my plate with dark, mushroom gravy. I gagged," I said.

Olmo refilled my glass with more champagne. We clinked glasses again.

"So far, I hear a picky girl at a normal Thanksgiving dinner."

I did a Poppy pause. Olmo laughed. I continued.

"And there's more. My mom said her sister's turkey was too dry. That was when the big fight began."

"A good ole family Thanksgiving brawl. Been there," Olmo said, finishing his salad.

"First, it was why my mom's trust fund was bigger, which morphed into boyfriend stealing, followed by calling each other alcoholics. True times two," I said while sipping my champagne.

"So, both sisters lushes, interesting," Olmo remarked.

"It got physical, with dark food flying across the table," I said.

"Did anyone get hurt?" Olmo asked.

"Stained clothing, crying, and collapsing in each other's arms. Then my aunt served me sour blueberries, and from then on, no more dark food for me," I said.

"It sounds trauma related. Ever speak to someone?" Olmo suggested.

"Never told my therapist as I spent so much money on my other phobias. The pastel food thing was low priority," I responded.

We sat in silence again, and Olmo smiled at me. The waiter came with the main course.

"Frog legs for you, Monsieur. And for you, Mademoiselle, a terrine of light green vegetables and cod," the waiter announced as he set down our dishes.

"Frog legs. The skin has anti-aging properties," I noted.

"Are you suggesting I peel off the skin and put it on my face?" Olmo asked.

"If you don't finish them, wouldn't mind taking home a leftover leg or two," I suggested and touched my face.

"Joking? I guess not, because you're Poppy," Olmo said, laughing.

"Sorry, I hope I didn't ruin your appetite. Enjoy those legs," I said.

"Goddamn! You're so honest, raw, and funny. What am I going to do with you?" Olmo said, reaching for my hand across the table and kissing it. He grabbed the champagne bottle and filled both flutes.

His mood shifted, and I knew he was going to say something serious. "Poppy, what do you want in life?" he boldly asked.

"That's a loaded question. Honestly, I don't fucking know. And you?" I asked.

"I know. I want to die in love," Olmo responded.

That line made me cry on the spot. It was so beautiful. I was speechless. My cries turned into snivels and the hiccups. The people at the next table looked concerned.

"I'm sorry, it's just . . ." I started to speak and couldn't get the words out.

"It's OK. I didn't mean to upset you," Olmo said, trying to console me.

The headwaiter, Forest, came over with a box of tissues and placed it in front of me. "Breaking up is hard to do," Forest said, assuming the worst.

"No, he just said he wants to die in love. Oh no, are you dying, Olmo?" I asked, still sniveling.

Olmo was now embarrassed and asked for the check.

"No, hon, not dying yet. Let's get you home," Olmo said as he helped me up from my chair, put his arm around me, and led me out of the restaurant. We stood facing each other while waiting for the valet to bring the car around.

"Was I a spectacle? I'm sorry," I said.

"You were so cute, breaking down. And it was real," Olmo noted.

I had recovered and spontaneously gave him a kiss on the mouth. He then grabbed me tight and kissed me deeply, this time with tongue. As he pressed against me, I felt his member growing. *Good job, Poppy, haven't lost your dick-raising skills.*

In the car, Olmo was quiet. When we were at a red light, he put his hand on my leg and massaged it. If the red light had been longer, I felt like he would have gone in for a twat squeeze.

"I want to know the exact time, date, and location of your birth," I announced.

"Why?" Olmo asked.

"For astrological purposes," I replied.

"I'll have to check the exact time. But promise me you'll tell me what you find out. Good or bad," Olmo said.

"I'm sure it's good," I said as I reached over and patted his thigh.

We arrived at my gate and parked. Olmo and I did some heavy high-school-style petting, in the car and in front of the surveillance camera.

As we made out, Olmo had an apparent hard-on, which I touched quickly. I had more than a twat twitch: a full-on sensation running throughout my whole body. I said my goodbyes and thank yous for dinner and headed through the gate to the guesthouse. We planned a date for the coming weekend.

As I was falling asleep that night, I was thinking I wasn't prepared to go further with Olmo until I had validation. I needed more science beyond Mu Jin's palm read and talk of needing Olmo's "yang."

The next morning, I called Fig, the astrologer to the stars. He was a French astrologer, better known as Fig the Frog. I only met him once and he wore a purple cloak decorated with the planets along with a turban and dark shades.

I arranged a reading to take place the next day, as he had a cancellation. Usually, it took two months to book a session with Fig the Frog. He was now doing readings from a half-way house in West Hollywood. It wasn't clear why he was there.

He compared mine and Olmo's astrological charts and was so impressed that he removed his dark shades. The he leaned over and whispered.

"I call these planetary conjunctions between you and this Olmo, as *l'amour toujour, oo la la, mon dieu, le grand* sex, baby. It's good."

Fig went into a light trance to concentrate.

"Karmic. You have been together in previous lives: slaves building the Pyramids, soldiers in the Crusades, assistants to Torquemada, tortured Elizabethan poets, heretics, Eskimos, Turkish assassins, African tribal leaders, drowned Portuguese sailors, and Russian prison cellmates," Fig said in his heavy French accent.

I was exhausted just listening. Couldn't even imagine living all those lives alongside Olmo. Luckily, Fig was recording the session, as I couldn't keep up with all the reincarnations and history lessons. Fig also read my future. He noted "a TV role of a lifetime" was coming my way.

I was certain it was the part of Ivy in *Willow's Run*. As soon as I left Fig, I called Rowan to book some coaching time. I didn't want to take any chances and blow the *Willow's Run* audition. If

Fig was correct, it was my breakthrough role.

Rowan answered the phone but not sounding like herself. She was recovering from a minor stroke. This was upsetting. I realized I had been taking her for granted and probably believed she was immortal and a vampire. I never imagined life without Rowan's direction and support. The actress turned teacher was my anchor.

Fortunately, she was up for phone coaching once she had the script. I was certain Rowan would walk me through the Ivy role and prep me for the audition.

"I'm having trouble, Rowan, getting the right tone in my voice," I lamented.

"Ivy is a manipulator, smart and sexy. Think of a cat purring before you speak a line," Rowan instructed.

I purred out loud and then read a line of dialogue.

"Do it next time purring silently, then deliver the line. Otherwise, you won't get a callback, sweetie," Rowan said, laughing.

"You're terrific, Rowan. Can't do it without you," I said.

"Yes, you can, my dear. Just channel that drive and curiosity for the character," she instructed.

After we reviewed all my lines, I mentioned I had been out with Olmo Branch.

"I'm so jealous. He's a lovely man, well-mannered and sensitive. That Violeta was a lucky gal, and she blew it," Rowan reported.

"Because she died?" I asked.

"Tragic. I'm sure he'll tell you all the details someday. Poor guy, it was complicated and messy," Rowan replied. I wondered what Rowan meant by "messy."

"There's a big age difference," I noted.

"My problem was the opposite. After he was widowed, I came on to him, but he said I was too old at fifteen years his senior. I thought Olmo was my Mr. Right. Perhaps he's yours, Poppy," Rowan suggested.

That comment gave me the chills. As I was basking in romantic feelings, my phone dinged with a text from Romero, the artist.

"I still want to draw you. Rain check? Don't believe Blom. I made mistakes, she did too. Sorry she died, payback for all those spells."

Well, that explained it. I'd been under a dead woman's spell. Now what?

#saggyballs #slats #pastels #figthefrog #spells #reincarnation #sexting

CHAPTER FOURTEEN

HAPPY HOMESTEAD

Plucked from my Casa Iris, my pride and joy of the last four years. I was numb as we sped away from Little Havana and my place of business. Was my old life really cancelled? Would we end up in jail?

I sat, catatonic, in the back seat of the black van flanked by two young deputy marshals. We careened down the streets of Miami and headed to a safe house outside the city. Deputy Blom was in his own car following us, along with another unmarked car, to protect us. They didn't want to chance the Colombians narcos following us.

After a half hour, one of the deputies indicated we were almost there. I could hear planes, and one of the deputies told me we were near an Air Force base.

"Homestead?" I asked.

"You got it," the deputy answered.

Homestead was south of Miami and became famous for being flattened by Hurricane Andrew in 1992.

Once the van stopped, I spilled out of the vehicle in front of the Happy Homestead Inn. It looked like it had not been repaired since Hurricane Andrew. Even in the dark, it looked like a welfare motel. The parking spaces were lined up in front of the first-floor rooms and other spaces opposite. There were a few parked cars in the spaces in front of rooms. There was a fenced-in pool with a few cheap chairs and tables. I could see a couple of overflowing dumpsters off to the side.

The planes continued to fly overhead. As we drove in, I caught sight of an empty lot alongside the motel that looked like a dump. It was so different than our luxurious Miami Beach condo, where we could see the cruise ships on the way to and from the Caribbean.

The Air Force base provided the constant noise of planes landing and taking off. The deputy marshals showed me up to the room where my husband, Cardoso, was staying. The paint on the doors was peeling, and we entered a dark corridor with old, brown carpet. As I walked into the room, I spotted my own luggage that the marshals had packed and brought from our condo.

Cardoso was on his mobile, whispering. Deputy Blom took the phone from Cardoso's hands and shook his head. Cardoso was furious.

"*Cabrón*, what are you doing? You take away everything and now my phone."

"US marshal rules. Once you have a new identity, you'll get a new phone," Blom said. Then Cardoso exploded.

"New identity!? I'm Cardoso Ortega, famous artist, toast of the Miami art world! Now you're erasing Cardoso and Iris Ortega just like that?" Cardoso shouted, waving his arms wildly.

"It's that or be gunned down by the *Colombianos*," Blom responded, trying to show off a Spanish accent.

I was too sad and exhausted to speak.

"And my gallery? My artwork?" Cardoso asked.

"Need to have your attorney make a deal," Blom suggested.

"And where is my father?" Cardoso asked while pacing.

"Your father and his girlfriend are in another location in state," Blom said.

"Girlfriend?" Cardoso asked.

"We sweep up all the immediate family and close contacts, including lovers, who could be in danger," Blom responded.

"If you or I had lovers, they would also be under protection," I said to Cardoso.

"Your father is with a woman named Tica," Blom said, reading from his notes.

"Tica? That's not a girlfriend! She's an old, gold-digging, Peruvian *puta*," Cardoso shot back.

"She was living in the hood, so she'll probably be better off in witness protection," I added, mustering some strength to speak.

"Let the cartel ice her. She's been bleeding my *papi* for jewelry and cash," Cardoso said.

I regained more strength and realized what had happened.

"I should have taken over my own books and run a decent business. *Coño*!" I said.

"You have eyes. Why didn't you look? It was probably obvious what he was doing and you, *estúpida*, NADA! NOTHING!" Cardoso shouted at me.

Blom glared and approached as if he might have to separate us.

"Stop. *Basta*! Enough, too much negativity. *Fuera*," I pleaded and gestured for Cardoso to move away from me. He went into the bathroom and slammed the door.

Blom excused himself from the room and said he was arranging dinner.

Cardoso emerged from the bathroom and approached to hug me, but my heart was not in it. I felt defeated.

"We'll get through this together, *mi amor*," he said, kissing my hand.

"I don't think so. We could be charged, go to jail. Our names are on everything your father did," I warned.

I unpacked my Casa Iris shopping bags. I stored the cash and the oracle book under a pillow. A business card with a headshot fell out; it was Lily's. She really had my *papi's* eyes but with an Asian flavor. I tucked the card away in my makeup bag. I placed my nude sketch under the bed; then I sat down with my head in my hands and cried. Cardoso left the room.

I curled up in a fetal position on the bed. It was like trying to sleep on a fucking runway.

The next morning, Cardoso was not in the bed next to me. I heard his loud voice outside the hotel. I peeked from the balcony. Cardoso was downstairs talking to Blom by the pool. I couldn't hear what they were saying, but Cardoso was making a lot of hand and arm gestures while pacing around the pool. I ran down in my pajamas and sandals to find out why Cardoso was carrying on. A black van drove up, similar to the one that brought me to the Happy Homestead.

Two men in suits opened the car doors. A female was led

out of the van. Cardoso ran over to the new arrival. I recognized Cardoso's gallery assistant, Pixie.

"Why is she here?" I asked and turned to Blom.

"Sorry, I thought you knew," he whispered.

Then I realized why Pixie was here. My *pendejo* husband was screwing the *puta*, Pixie.

Now she was in protective custody with us at this shithole.

"*En serio*, seriously?" I asked, loudly enough so everyone could hear me. Blom pleaded with me to keep it down.

"It was nothing, *mi amor*. I didn't know she was coming." Cardoso tried to convince me.

"Find him or me another room. I'm not staying with him, and I want a divorce," I announced.

I was furious and looked it. I tried pushing Cardoso into the dirty pool. The deputies held me back. Then I was propelled by a demonic spirit and ran over to Pixie. I grabbed a handful of her hair but ended up with a barrette. I stuffed the barrette into my pajama bottom pocket. Pixie screamed while the deputies peeled me off her. I spat at Pixie's feet and threw an aluminum chair at Cardoso.

As I stormed back into the shithole motel, I could hear Pixie shouting. "I'm no drug dealer. Can someone tell me why I'm here, for God's sake?"

I heard Blom trying to calm her down. "Let's talk quietly over there."

I turned around and watched them escort Pixie to another part of the motel. I closed myself in my room and consulted the oracle book. It made me feel empowered. I prepared to put a spell on Pixie for husband stealing. I took that *puta*, Pixie's, barrette, attached it to one of the yarn dolls, and hung it upside down in the bathroom. I didn't specify the calamity, only that she should suffer.

Deputy Blom knocked at my door and indicated they were moving Cardoso to another room. I let Cardoso into the room to pack his belongings. He entered the bathroom and must have seen the yarn doll in the bathroom. I heard him shout, "Witch" and "Shit." Obviously, he meant me.

"Bruja de mierda!"

Cardoso came charging out of the bathroom, grabbed my *oráculo* book and headed outside. He screamed, "That *bruja* put a spell on Pixie."

Blom looked worried, and together we ran after Cardoso, down the stairs and outside to the pool area.

Cardoso first set the book on fire, then threw it into the dirty pool. I could feel Amapola rising from the grave to curse Cardoso. Blom continued to look worried. Cardoso told him about the spell I put on Pixie and suggested he go up to my bathroom and see it for himself. Blom shook his head.

Then Pixie saw the fire from her balcony and ran down. She became so hysterical, the deputies had to call in a doctor to sedate her.

I grabbed a few charred bits of the oracle book, some Post-its and pages that were loose. I threatened Cardoso with a spell.

"I can do it even without the book. You'll see. I'll shrink your penis to the size of a pea," I suggested.

Blom sat down in one of the plastic chairs with his head in his hands. It appeared that he had never dealt with angry Cubans before.

"Witnesses twenty-one and twenty-two, please don't make this a living hell," Blom pleaded and then took charge. He ordered Cardoso and Pixie back into the motel.

Blom set up two, cheap, aluminum, poolside chairs and motioned to me to sit near him.

He looked around frequently to ensure safety. In an effort to calm me down, Blom talked about marriage and its challenges. He shared his wife's concerns about their long separations and his dangerous cases. Frequently, Blom was out of state and had to leave her alone in their northern Virginia home.

"When she complains, I say, you'll be sick of me when I retire and I'm home twenty-four seven," Blom noted.

"Sounds like you love each other very much," I noted and was a little jealous of Mrs. Blom.

After Blom left, I went to bed feeling the deep loss of my oracle book. It had been my anchor, my source of power and my income. I would have to start inventing potions and spells from scratch.

The next day, Miss Linden Maple, aka Pixie, was gone. Her rich family made a deal with the DOJ, and they sprung her. A limo pulled up, and Pixie pranced through the parking lot. She was hustled away by some bodyguards. Cardoso was furious.

Cardoso and I didn't speak for days. But we had to be together to speak to our attorney, that gringo lawyer, Mr. Yarrow, whom Papi hired. Both Cardoso and Blom came to my room. I think Blom wanted to make sure there would be no violence between Cardoso and me.

The attorney, Yarrow, arrived. It was the same guy who had visited Casa Iris a few weeks ago. Cardoso paced, but I stayed silent, controlling my anger and rage about the whole business. Blom left the room.

"Nice to meet you formally, Mr. and Mrs. Ortega. I have letters from your father," Yarrow said as he opened his briefcase. He handed us each an envelope. Cardoso ceremoniously threw his letter in the trash, then shouted.

"Where is my *papi*? If the cartel doesn't get to him, I will," Cardoso vowed.

"Why bother, Cardoso? The damage is done. Right, Mr. Yarrow?" I asked.

"Your wife is correct, Mr. Ortega. It's a done deal. He's made a deal to testify," Yarrow responded, taking out a large file folder.

"Before you begin, I want a divorce from this," I said, pointing to Cardoso.

"Fine with me, Iris. You're a vindictive, dangerous bitch," Cardoso said.

"You made me that way, *HIJO DE PUTA*," I responded as Cardoso raised his fist and turned his anger toward Yarrow.

"And where is my fucking artwork?" Cardoso asked Yarrow.

"In storage, being inventoried and appraised," Yarrow answered. Cardoso sat and looked at Yarrow dead on.

"I want it all back!" Cardoso demanded in a menacing tone.

"Can you get us, or at least ME, moved to a nicer place?" I begged.

An incoming aircraft drowned out Yarrow's voice. All I heard was "next steps." Those next steps included testifying in a grand jury, then maybe a trial. If Papi O. named enough names and that led to arrests, we might be able to go into witness protection earlier. We were now known as Witnesses 21 and 22, in the *United States v. CHMS Inc.* case of money laundering, drug trafficking, and extortion.

"I will ask for a list of assets that the government seized. I warn you, most of it, including your business, Mrs. Ortega, and your gallery, Mr. Ortega, was also purchased with laundered drug money," Yarrow informed us. My heart sank again.

After the meeting with Yarrow, I sat on my little balcony. There was a knock at the door. It was Blom with bags of takeout from Pollo Loco and the items I requested from Walgreens, including a toothbrush. Blom sat with me, and we ate our Pollo Loco takeout together.

"How did it go with Yarrow?" Blom asked.

"How do you think? Have you ever had your entire life ended just like that?" I responded, snapping my fingers.

"You're right. For the past twenty-plus years, I've shepherded families and the mobsters, drug dealers, and other criminals into the WITSEC program. I pride myself on protecting and just observing," Blom said.

"Probably because if you ever felt the way we do, it would kill you," I offered.

"I have to keep a distance. I couldn't protect effectively if I became emotionally involved. It happens to some agents. It's called the Partington syndrome, named for Agent John Partington," Blom said while picking up a chicken part.

"Is that when you get too chummy?" I asked.

"Agent Partington, one of the founders of WITSEC, got real close with a Mafia family.

It also happened to one of my partners. He actually wanted to marry a narco's mistress whom he was assigned to protect," Blom said.

"So how do you avoid getting too involved?" I asked, leaning over and staring into Blom's eyes.

"I think about all the criminal things you have done or could do if we let you loose," Blom said.

"But I didn't DO anything," I offered.

"Maybe, but you were an unwitting accomplice to some serious crimes," Blom said.

"Not a good answer," I said, letting my robe open to reveal my legs. Blom seemed to stare and then changed the subject.

"Here's some interesting bedtime reading. A copy of the DEA and DOJ's case against your father in-law," Blom said, handing me a fat file.

He was right. It was interesting reading, with details of every transaction including names, dates, and account numbers. The documents also contained descriptions of how and where the money flowed. It was fascinating, and I had plenty of time. So, I studied it for the next weeks like a course—Money Laundering 101. I made notes on what Papi O. could have done not to get caught. In my next meetings with Yarrow, I asked him many questions and many hypotheticals. It was all part of my education on money laundering.

There had been no word about the trial for weeks. Then the press started to report on rumors. One Sunday, Blom brought the

Miami Herald, which had previously written up a beautiful article on Casa Iris and wonderful reviews of Cardoso's art. There was an article, with Cardoso's photo, entitled, "From Artist to Alleged Narco, the Wonder Boy Disappears." I could already imagine the meltdown he would have when he saw the article.

Cardoso was now staying two floors below me. I could see his balcony, where I noticed he had set up an easel. He was fucking painting! I couldn't believe Blom arranged that. Cardoso had on headphones through which he was probably listening to old, Cuban boleros.

In between plane landings, I screamed insults at Cardoso from my balcony. Even the *Santa Muerte* dolls I hid in his room didn't seem to have an effect.

Blom was around daily. At dinnertime once, he mentioned his wife would be jealous of me. She wanted him to take another position in the department so that he could be home every night for dinner.

"What would she be making you for dinner tonight, Deputy?" I asked.

"Maybe stuffed pork chops, garlic mashed taters, and pie for dessert," he responded.

I felt Blom was softening up towards me, and I gave it a push with one of my love potions. Maybe Blom was getting the Partington syndrome that he described? Was I getting a *kinda* Stockholm syndrome, falling in love with my gatekeeper?

Besides having my business and identity taken from me, I was still facing a breast biopsy. I convinced the marshals that I should have the biopsy at Miami's Jackson Hospital under a fake name. I trusted my Cuban oncologist, Dr. Clavo. I insisted on staying under his care even if it meant possibly being hunted and killed by the narcos. Even though I was headed to a hospital, it was good to get out of the Happy Homestead Inn and away from the plane noise. I was well-disguised in sweats, a baseball cap, and large shades. As we headed up Interstate 95, north near downtown Miami, I cried softly, remembering what we left behind. I was admitted to the hospital under my mother's name, Azalea Espinoza. Blom arranged for a posse to protect me.

We exited at West 12th Avenue and entered the hospital from an alleyway. "VIP entrance," the assistant deputy informed me.

But I didn't feel like a VIP. I was a shadow of my former self; a woman betrayed by a husband as well as a father-in-law and facing an uncertain future.

CHAPTER FIFTEEN

———

ACER FEVER

One morning when I popped out for a run, a red Jag mysteriously appeared parked outside the gate. I assumed it was Dalia's missing Jag that her husband wanted to sell. The keys were in an envelope in the mailbox, along with a registration in the name of "Acer Flores." I sent a photo of the Jag to Acer, the grieving widower, NOT.

Me: "Is this what you were waiting for?"

Acer: "Si! Si! Be there day after tomorrow. Can't wait to meet."

He accompanied the text with a photo of himself, shirtless and skimpy shorts showing off his junk.

Me: Don't think they'll let you on a plane.

Acer responded with a photo of himself in a tux next to Dalia wearing a gorgeous black lace evening gown. I ran over to the closet to look for that gown. Strange I hadn't spotted such a marvelous frock earlier, but it was hiding in a zippered garment bag. Score!

Since I was in the closet surrounded by her clothes, naturally, there were Dalia vibes. There was a text from Rosita, one of the VIP mourners. Dalia fans were ruining another precious day. It was so weird, like I had a roommate who was never around but I managed her social schedule.

Rosita and several other devotees wanted to picnic around the tree and asked if I wanted to join them. Hell no. I had a lunch date planned with Olmo. I replied to Rosita's text, asking to please put off the worship picnic to the following week. Good riddance, at least for now.

Next, there was a voice mail from Olmo, in which he told me to call him urgently. Did not sound good.

"I had a call from Rowan," Olmo said, in a dark and gloomy voice.

"Isn't she great? I had a breakthrough with the TV role," I said.

"You told Rowan I was too old for you and there was no future. And I should reconsider dating her even though she just had a stroke," Olmo reported.

"Not true! She said she was jealous. Hey, what's going on? Who's sabotaging whom? Is this a way to break up or test me? It's nonsense, bullshit. I like you, Olmo, a lot," I said.

"Poppy, I thought about it, and our age difference is too much. Go find a younger man. You deserve that. I'm releasing you," Olmo said.

"Releasing me? We've been out on two dates," I said.

"Poppy, I'll always want you. Don't forget," Olmo said and ended the call.

Goddamn son of a bitch. I worshipped that witch Rowan,

just like the fans worshipped Dalia. Now I'd been cockblocked by an old woman. I depended on her, and now she had ruined what might have been a real romance. Fig was wrong also. What happened to those past lives and the *ooh la la*, poof, gone. Over before it began. Damn that man. What older dude dumps a younger woman? Fuck Olmo!

I had to turn my energy to something else. Luckily, Acer sent me countdown texts and photos of his impending arrival. He began two days before our meeting and texted in six-hour intervals.

I was getting nervous and wondering how old Acer was. I assumed Acer and Dalia were the same age. But I could be wrong.

In the meantime, a special Dalia outfit was in order to greet her husband. Should I wear that black lace evening gown that was in the photo Acer sent me? Or was that going WAY too far? Maybe it would freak him out.

He texted from LAX after landing from New York and wrote, *"One hour more."* Acer arrived at Bilberry Lane in an Uber. I saw him in the gate camera, and he looked HOT.

He was a slick, Latino businessman, wearing an expensive suit, a white shirt opened to show his six-pack, and shades. He looked early thirties.

I buzzed him in and met him on the walkway.

"Encantada, Poppy, such a pleasure," he said and kissed my hand.

We entered the yard. Acer looked at the tree and said, "You know, I did love her." Should I tell him the US marshal dug her up?

As we entered the guesthouse, he mentioned it smelled of

Dalia, like she had just swept across the room. All I could smell was the mulch Heysus had laid in the yard earlier that morning.

"How long had you been married?" I asked.

"We were together five years, then lived apart for a while. I own a very successful restaurant, Que Rico, in New York. Dalia had her business and many followers," Acer responded casually.

"So many people visit the tree," I noted.

"She was everything to everybody. Or she became whatever you wanted her to be," Acer said wistfully.

Acer gave me a once-over and noted, "You look good in her blouse."

"This is actually mine," I said. Then I wondered, was it hers? I handed Acer the envelope with the Jag keys and registration.

"Thanks. Let's have dinner tomorrow night at the Marigold Hotel. It was Dalia's favorite," Acer proposed.

I agreed. Before leaving, Acer spent time at the tree and crossed himself. Then I walked with him to the gate. He held my shoulders and kissed me on both cheeks. I had a minor cooch twitch, a sign that she needed attention and some TLC. Acer jumped into the red Jag and sped away.

First business was to google his restaurant. I found "Que Rico, proprietor Acer Flores" on Yelp. It was in Union City, not New York City. It was in New Jersey and looked like a bakery. The reviews looked fake and were all five stars.

He must have other income streams. How could a baker afford a bodyguard, jet-setting, those clothes and fine dining? More fucking Dalia-related mystery.

I became a little obsessed over Acer before our date. I reread all his flirty texts, which got me fantasizing about his lean, Latin body, so deliciously handsome and suave.

I downloaded the snapshot of Acer and Dalia that he had sent in a text. Seeing the two of them together made me uncomfortable, so I cut Dalia out of the picture.

I put Acer's face on my pillow, slipped out of my clothes, and lay down on my bed. I think I wore out the batteries of my trusty 'Bam Bam,' imagining him on top of me.

Shame on me for projecting some hot romance with Dalia's husband, but I felt entitled. It was a consolation prize—hot sex for all the mourner management. And honestly, the Olmo thing was done, and it had been ages since my last sexcapade.

I wrestled with the question of which Dalia garment I should wear for my date with Acer. I decided to wear something of my own, and a pair of her shoes. A bright orange pair of Manolo sandals.

I manipulated the final touches and was blotting my lips as I heard the beep-beep of a Jeep Grand Cherokee at the gate. I hopped into the back seat and realized I hadn't checked the license plate.

"OK, Miss Poppy, Mr. Acer wanting you to be happy," the driver said.

"Wait. This is not an Uber. How do you know Acer?" I asked.

I noticed the driver was a middle-aged, East Indian man, with a thick accent.

"It's a long story, Miss Poppy. Mr. Acer not wanting to trouble you and the expense take an Uber, so sending me. Safer this way," he explained.

"Safer," I responded like a ho damsel, not in distress. I quickly canceled my Uber successfully as it was more than ten minutes away.

"He was wanting to pick you up himself, but had to see a man about a man in Sherman Oaks, something doing about a Jag, and figured you called an Uber, so here I am. Cool?"

"Cool. Excuse me. Please tell me, what is your name?" I asked.

"Bakul Indukamal Moshayan, but just call me Moss."

"Moss it is," I said.

"My name means 'sweet-smelling flower in the water.' Reminding me that I am now smelling Miss Dalia. It's her perfume," Moss commented.

I was frozen. He knew Dalia? Didn't remember putting on perfume.

The car suddenly stopped halfway down the driveway. Moss turned his head, looking solemn. *God, now what?*

"Forgetting to ask big favor, Miss Poppy. May I go and worship at the Dalia tree?"

Well, fuck me.

Moss spent twelve minutes chanting Indian devotional hymns to the damn olive tree. Should I tell him, "Nobody home, no urn, no Dalia, MIA"?

"You know, a poppy is a pretty flower but bad trip," Moss commented, then chuckled.

"What?" I blurted out. I was regretting not taking an Uber.

"Safe with me, Miss Poppy," Moss said.

Moss drove me to the front of the Marigold Hotel. Moss hopped out and ran around to open the door for me. He extended his hand and helped me out of the car.

"Never hesitate to call. I'm Acer's main man, Indian homey. I protect him, and I do same for you," Moss said confidently.

"Thank you?" I said with a slight intonation and an unfurrowed brow. I had my monthly Botox treatment done a week ago. Nothing on my forehead moved for weeks after. The emotion needed to come from my eyes.

"What do you mean, exactly?" I asked, squinting.

"Big world out there, Poppy. Best have eyes in back of head. I am eyes for you," Moss said while cupping my face. This was too weird.

Was Acer that big of a hotshot to need a bodyguard?

Acer arrived to greet me. He and Moss shared a private joke, probably at my expense. Acer then put his hand on the small of my back and led me from the parking lot toward the main entrance. Moss stopped us.

"Forget bad flowers, stupid comment. You are so noble to be the caregiver of Dalia's legacy. By helping others, you will rise to the next level," Moss said, then headed back to the car's driver's side and hopped in.

"Love that one, man. Another great Sai Baba saying," Acer said as he slid his arm around my waist, then whispered to me, "He's a follower of the guru, Sai Baba."

"Is that a secret?" I asked. Acer laughed and shook his head. Acer and I walked towards the hostess stand.

This was the first time I had a close look at Acer. He was so goddamn handsome. And that smile of his. I was definitely a teeth girl. He was dressed very appropriately for the setting, formal, yet beachy. He was wearing dark jeans, a white button-down shirt, just open enough, and a black linen blazer with the sleeves pushed up his forearms.

I paused for a second while he took off his sunglasses to reveal those dreamy eyes of his. I then panicked, wondering if he was checking me out the same way.

Did he find me as attractive as I found him? No time to be insecure. Spinning in my own head, we landed in front of Camellia, the hostess. She was beyond gorgeous. If Sophia Loren and Raquel Welch could make a baby, it would have been Camellia.

"Hello, Camellia. Great to see you again," Acer said smoothly and added, "How is Juniper?"

"She's fabulous, Mr. Flores. Thanks for asking."

"Meet Poppy. We have a 6:45 reservation on the top deck, overlooking the ocean."

There would be more Post-it notes tonight: Moss, Camellia, Juniper, and Sai Baba.

On the roof deck of the Marigold, we were seated with a magnificent view from north Malibu all the way south to Palos Verdes. You could see Catalina Island in the distance.

"This is so wonderful," I honestly exclaimed.

Camellia chimed in, "This is a small, local club for creatives in Malibu and the surrounding areas. There is the restaurant, the upper and lower bars, conference rooms, a gym, a spa, and a boutique hotel."

"Very exclusive. You need three other members to vouch for you. I had six," Acer boasted.

"May I start you with a cocktail? Your waiter will be with you shortly." Before Camellia left, she put her hand on Acer's shoulder and said, "By the way, I heard about Dalia. I am so sorry. She was such an inspiration. Juniper and I are just devastated. Going to get you candles." Camellia went to another table.

I asked Acer in a low voice across the table, "Who's Juniper?"

"Her twin sister with a terrible snoring problem that Dalia cured with a spell. That girl could wake up the *diablo* himself," Acer replied. Should I ask how he knew about Juniper's snoring?

Camellia placed lighted candles on our table and continued Dalia reminiscing. "The last time Dalia was here, she was so frail. She almost fell off the balcony from puking so hard, poor thing."

"Please tell Leaf I'm very grateful. Anytime you're in New York . . ." Acer said.

"I feel badly I didn't make it to the memorial. But I would love to visit the tree," Camellia said.

I choked on a piece of bread, then muttered, "Sure, anytime."

Acer ordered Cristal Brut, and I wondered how a baker could afford this.

"There is so much I want to know. Let's start with Moss. How do you two know each other?" I asked while fiddling with the napkin in my lap.

"Moss is an old family friend of Dalia's. Crazy story about an ashram in India," he said, placing his sunglasses on the table. "Panthers," Acer noted.

"Pique diamond panthers?" I pondered.

The glasses had crouching panthers on the sides of the frames, solid lenses, and a pique diamond bridge for the nose.

"Would you like them?" Acer inquired.

"Honestly, they are amazing. I would die for them."

"Well, I hope you don't, die that is. I want you to have them. Dalia gave them to me."

I took a Poppy pause. I realized I'd said I would die for a dead girl's gift to her husband.

"Please forgive me, Acer," I said.

"Poppy, you're raw, beautiful, and you're hilarious. Dalia is laughing her ass off," Acer said.

Leaf, our waiter, was using his finest talents putting on a good show for Acer, and possibly me. He did say he recognized me. It always feels good to be noticed.

Acer and I raised our flutes for a toast, and the night progressed well. Was I falling for this guy? Lust? *Fuck, I don't know.*

The shrimp appetizer was delicious and in my color scheme. It was amazing Acer ordered only pastel foods, like he already knew. Then another bottle of Cristal Brut appeared.

"How did you and Dalia meet?" I asked, piercing the halibut filet with my unused dinner fork.

"I met her at Jackson Hospital in Miami."

"Holy shit. I was in that hospital too!" I exclaimed.

"Really? I was there to get some lab work done for an ongoing health situation. I was awaiting my appointment, and she was getting her first chemo treatment," he responded with a mouthful of neutral-colored food.

"Did you get together then?" I asked as I took another sip of bubbly.

"Oh, I wanted to, but the timing wasn't right," Acer lamented, adding, "We kept in contact for a long time. I was opening my bistro, Que Rico, and she wanted to invest. We started dating, then we got married," he then said, swallowing a bite of pork tenderloin.

"What was your health issue?" I asked as I moved food around on my plate.

"Hypogonadism," he said, stabbing another piece of meat.

I gagged a little and asked, "Oh. Something to do with your balls?" Couldn't escape balls again.

"Yes, *cojones*. Not enough natural testosterone when I was younger," Acer reported.

"Does that mean too small or too big?" I asked coyly.

"Why not check for yourself?" he laughed and added, "Don't worry, they work."

"I had a tumor in my colon ... surgery, a diaper, excessive bleeding ... think of the shape of a V cut in your rectum. How's your food?" I lamely asked.

Acer was now coughing and drinking water to recover. Was that TMI on my part?

"Maybe you, me and Dalia were all in the Jackson hospital at the same time?" I pondered.

Leaf, the headwaiter, approached.

"Anything else, Mr. Flores?"

"Yes. Is the Bloom Room available?" Acer asked. Leaf nodded, and Acer pushed some cash into his hand.

"Of course, sir. Always ready for you and your guests," Leaf informed him.

We rose from the table, and Acer stared at my footwear. I

had forgotten I was wearing Dalia's sandals. He bent down and touched them.

"Her Manolos? I bought them for her," he noted.

OK, now, normally, my gaydar would be way up, but so was his wiener when he pulled me towards him and pressed against me.

"Join me in the Bloom Room?" Acer whispered in my ear.

"Sure, Baby," I mumbled.

A drunk Poppy and a young, Latin hunk, with a hard-on, only means BIG trouble.

#olmobye #badrowan #manolos #juniper #cristal #panthers #bloomroom

CHAPTER SIXTEEN

JACKSON

Who would have thought the government used shitty hotels as safe houses for witness protection? It was 2010 and not 1950, *coño*.

It was great to get the hell away from the un-Happy Homestead motel even though I was going into Jackson hospital. I would have a breast biopsy, then wait for the results in the hospital. The US marshals would not chance moving me if I needed more tests and I hoped it would drag out weeks. This way, I wouldn't need to see that asshole, Cardoso.

I was taken to a private hospital room and two young deputy marshals would be stationed outside my door 24-7. They carefully checked the room and the window angle and swept the landline for taps. Thankfully, they left it there as I had no cell phone.

They only person I needed to contact was Lily who showed up at my Mom's funeral with a Chinese mother. Lily looked like my Dad and I sensed a connection.

I waited until the deputies left the room; then I used the

bedside phone to call Lily. It went to voice mail. I wanted her to visit me in the hospital. I didn't care if Blom got pissed off. I could say it was an accident and Lily was visiting someone else. I was so curious if I was related to this Lily. I wasn't going to transform into another person in witness protection without finding out.

A young, sexy Dominican, Acer Flores, delivered my lunch tray each day.

"Azalea?" he asked. "*Bonito nombre,*" he said as he set up my tray. I agreed it was beautiful name and told him it was my mother's.

It was clear we had chemistry as our conversation in Spanish flowed easily. Acer barely spoke English.

He pointed to my Casa Iris shopping bags that I had brought, including the sketch. Acer pointed to the shopping bag and the tagline.

"*Botánica?*" Acer asked.

"*Si. Fue una excelente* botánica, now closed, *cerrada,*" I answered.

"*Mi abuela fue santera,*" Acer shared and described his Dominican grandmother's greatest accomplishments as a *santera.* He was sure the bad spells had turned against her as she died an excruciating death.

"*Un gusano la comìo viva, dentro afuera.*" Acer explained her horrific death by a worm eating her from inside out.

We tested each other on the meanings of Cuban and Dominican expressions. Miami was now a blend of Caribbean Spanish, so I advised him to pay attention, or else he could be saying "call me" and someone would interpret it as "fuck me."

Acer had just arrived from Santo Domingo. I guessed correctly that he was working with a "borrowed" Social Security number. His dream was to get a green card and open a restaurant. He showed me the artist's rendering of the logo for *Que Rico*, a restaurant serving Dominican fusion food. I wasn't sure which food he was "fusing," and neither was he. He just thought "fusion" sounded hip and cool.

After a few days of his daily visits, I started to get hot and bothered when Acer delivered my food tray. As I was naked under the hospital gown, I let it open to flash a little *concha*. He grinned, and the next day, he actually reached in and gave it a squeeze. At first, I felt like a dirty cougar, "*una vieja sucia*," as he was nineteen and I was thirty-three. I dreamed of revenge sex with Acer. The only man I had ever known sexually was Cardoso. It was my time to explore.

"I'm going to be on the graveyard shift tonight. Expect a surprise," Acer announced.

Around two a.m., Acer managed to grab a cardiac machine on wheels. Since he was dressed like hospital staff, he was able to get past the deputy marshals stationed outside my room. At that hour, the deputies were groggy and sleepy. They didn't question why I needed a medical procedure at two a.m.

Acer gingerly wheeled the equipment near my bed. He popped open a small drawer that revealed a bunch of condoms. Apparently, there was a communal arrangement by staff to sneak into patients' rooms for consensual sex. Acer removed his white coat and feverishly undressed while softly singing an old *son montuno*, "*Llevala pal rincon y apriétala.*" The song is about getting a woman into a corner to squeeze her. I was hoping for much more.

I lifted the white blanket and beckoned to a now-naked Acer. He flew into my bed, dramatically grabbed my hospital gown, and ripped it off. My first thought was how I was going to explain a torn gown to the nurses. I didn't need to worry, as Acer had already brought a fresh gown for me. What a thoughtful and clever guy.

It was marvelous and delicious to have this strong young man on top of me. For ten minutes, I forgot I might have cancer. Acer tossed one condom onto the floor and was about to put another one on. That was nineteen-year-old stamina. No need for a lotion or potion to get it up and in.

Just as we were about to go into round two, there was a knock at the door. "Everything OK in there?" asked one of the deputies, who was now alert. Acer took control.

"Test almost finished," Acer shouted in heavily accented English.

The second time, he entered me from the side. He was so forceful that I pulled up the bedside bars and hung on so we wouldn't fall on the floor. *Ave María Purísima*, I was too excited to even have an orgasm. After his climax, he kissed me deeply and jumped up.

He dressed quickly and wheeled the apparatus out of the room. As he exited, I heard him say, "Everything OK, Mrs. Azalea. We'll do another test tomorrow."

He made sure the deputies heard him and prepared for a reprise the following night.

The deputies peeked into my room after Acer left. I pretended to be asleep but was basking in afterglow.

My afterglow quickly faded a few hours later when the doctor came with very bad news: I had breast cancer. Since I was so young, the prognosis was grim, as the cancer could spread quickly.

I felt life drain out of me, and I could hardly think or speak. The doc recommended a double mastectomy, chemo, and radiation. My life turned upside down for the second time.

Later, a youngish social worker came into my room with an armful of cancer pamphlets. She shared a personal story to presumably help me face my prognosis and encouraged me to assemble a support team.

"I had a double mastectomy in this very hospital. I survived with my mom, my dad, my husband, and Jesus Christ at my side," the *loca* said.

"If Jesus is still in the building, please send him over. My parents are dead, and my cheating husband will be an ex soon after I get these chopped off," I said while pointing to my chest.

The social worker didn't give up. I planned on going in for the kill so that she would never come back to my room.

"That's so sad. Isn't there anyone you can count on, hon?" she asked in that sugary-sweet voice.

I reached into one of the Casa Iris bags, took out a *Santa Muerte* doll and waved it in her face.

"I'm counting on him to help me, *juebona*," I said loudly.

The skeleton doll in a cloak freaked her out. She ran out of the room, and I never saw her again.

I told Dr. Clavo not to send any more social workers. He knew I was going into witness protection and counted on them to provide counseling.

The doctor also suggested we have a meeting with Blom, the attorney, my husband, and me to discuss my treatment. Cardoso was such a narcissistic bastard; he was the last person I wanted to turn to.

I was numb with the devastating news. I realized there was no one close to share this burden with except Deputy Blom. He entered my hospital room as I was having a breakdown and sobbing into a pillow.

"I spoke with Dr. Clavo. It's rough. I'm sorry. I'll try to help," Blom said and pulled up a chair close to my bed.

"Send me back to my shop. I'm going to die anyway. Who cares if I get gunned down by the Colombians while selling vitamins?" I noted.

"First, you're not going to die, and second, it's not so simple," Blom informed me.

"There's so much I wanted to do. A family, a baby, a bigger business. Help people," I said while holding back more tears.

"You can still do it," Blom said, trying to cheer me up.

"That old witch was right. I was going to fuck up my life, and she didn't need to put a curse on me," I said.

"When I was a boy, we were dirt poor. There was no hope I could even make it through grade school. Couldn't read or write. They said I'd only be good at plowing fields, if I was lucky," Blom said.

"Were you labeled retarded?" I asked.

"Yeah. In reality, I was dyslexic," Blom replied and added, "I was saved by my sixth-grade teacher, who sent me to a specialist. After a few months, I was getting straight As. I was the high school football captain and valedictorian, and then I was accepted to college. There are fields that probably still need plowing." The deputy chuckled, but I was not amused.

"I don't see any comparison to having breast cancer, facing disfigurement and hair loss, and maybe dying in my thirties," I noted.

Blom stood up and looked out the window.

"Correct, no idea what it's like to be raised by a drug lord, married to a crazy artist from another family of drug lords, getting cancer, and being forced into witness protection. You win, babe," Blom said as he turned and looked at me.

We both laughed. I liked that he called me babe. It made my *concha* twitch.

That night, Acer appeared at one a.m. with a different medical apparatus on wheels. My face was puffy from crying. He caressed and consoled me when I told him about my cancer diagnosis.

"I'm dying, Acer. Fuck! *Coño, me voy a morir!*" I whispered as my eyes welled up. Acer tenderly took a Kleenex and wiped away my tears. I lowered my gown and held my breasts.

"*Los van a quitar.* They're cutting them both out," I cried.

Acer removed my hands and kissed each breast tenderly. Then he began sucking on my nipples. He then placed his fingers in my *concha* and twirled them so fast that I came within a minute. As I recovered, he took off his pants and underwear, revealing a massive hard-on. As he parted my legs, he whispered,

"*Reconstrucción, unas nuevas tetas estupendas.*" Acer suggested I would end up with a great pair of new knockers as he entered me bareback. Why care about a deadly STD or getting pregnant if I was going to die? Better to have a nice new pair of tits while lying in a coffin.

The next day, Blom visited, sitting on the edge of my bed. He looked concerned. "I would bring your husband here to the hospital, but it's too dangerous," Blom informed me.

"No need. He's the last person I want to see," I said.

"I've never had a witness in my care going through such a medical ordeal," Blom said, adding, "Gonna do my best."

I patted his arm and said, "Doin' OK so far, Deputy."

The attorney, Yarrow, arrived along with Dr. Clavo. They crowded around my bed. Even though I had only had a biopsy and could easily move around, they acted like I was fragile.

"I recommend a double mastectomy even though it's only in one breast. It's the aggressive type," Dr. Clavo noted.

"What about reconstruction, Doc?" I asked.

"I don't recommend it until at least six months to a year after surgery," the doctor said. "Where will I be?" I asked, turning to Blom.

"We can arrange for additional surgery at another hospital," Blom suggested. "Depends on her insurance," responded Dr. Clavo.

"I assume, Deputy Blom, it's all on the government's tab?" Yarrow asked. Blom nodded.

I perked up, threw my blanket off, and stuck out my chest. "Great. A new pair of tits paid for by Uncle Sam," I exclaimed.

"Given the circumstances, I can petition the DEA and DOJ to accept a deposition instead of appearing in court," Yarrow suggested.

"Then the narcos wouldn't see us in the courtroom? No need for protective custody, right?" I asked with hope.

"The depositions will be available to the defendants. They probably already know. You're still in danger, trust me," Blom chimed in.

Blom stayed behind.

"You don't have to go back to the Happy Homestead," he announced, and I wanted to kiss him.

Gracias a Dios! I would be taken to the Washington, D.C. area for WITSEC orientation and then relocated with my new identity. Cardoso and I were given several options for relocation. But since we were divorcing, we wouldn't know which location we picked or our new identities. *Excelente*. The further I could get from Cardoso, the better. I wanted him out of my orbit permanently.

Yarrow had already filed the divorce papers for Iris and Cardoso Ortega, so by the time we had our new identities, I would be a single woman. Hallelujah. Then I thought of being in a new place, not knowing anyone.

There was Lily and the close connection I felt with her. I called her again. This time, she picked up. I told her that my father-in-law was in big trouble and I was lying low. I gave her my hospital room number and told her to come looking official.

"Wear a white coat and a fake badge, with pens in the pocket, and bring a clipboard," I suggested.

"I love *Grey's Anatomy*; I know the look," Lily said.

I was thrilled when Lily walked into my room the next day. She looked so cute wearing the white coat and her hair in a bun. She had half specs perched on her nose.

Even though I had only met her once, I felt I had known her my entire life. She also suspected we were related. Her mother, Mu Jin, had been vague about her biological father, and Lily had little memory of him. She took her mother's last name, Ju.

"Lily Ju are two flowers together, lilies and chrysanthemums in Chinese. Also, a great stage name," Lily noted.

Lily said she had a photo she thought was her dad. It showed my *papi*, Eneldo, and me just before he disappeared. *Santa María de Dios y los Santos.*

Could Lily be my half-sister? I did the math, and it meant that Lily was born years after they said my *papi* had died.

"Lily, why did you and Mu Jin come to my mom's funeral?"

"My mom was told to find Lirio Ortega, as he had money for her from my dad," Lily explained.

How was Papi O. involved? Couldn't ask him now, obviously, but maybe someday Mu Jin would explain. In the meantime, I considered Lily my sister.

One of the deputies entered, and Lily pretended to write on the clipboard. She asked me questions.

"Smoke? Recreational drugs? Narcotics?" Lily asked as I shook my head to each question.

The deputy left after Lily started asking about sex.

"How many sex partners? All men? Last date of intercourse?" Lily continued, stifling giggles, as I was too.

"Last night," I whispered, and Lily's jaw dropped.

We stopped giggling when Acer arrived with my food tray. Lily perked up when she saw the cute Domincano and mouthed "hot" to me. I made a gesture indicating it was him I had bonked.

"No way," Lily whispered.

"Way," I whispered back.

"Excuse me, ladies," Acer said as he set up my tray with a naughty grin. He leaned over and said, "*Hasta la noche*," indicating he was coming later that night for more fun.

After Acer left, I told Lily about my cancer and upcoming mastectomy. Lily cried and hugged me.

"You will survive, and I'll help you," she said emphatically.

"I promise to contact you wherever I land," I assured her.

"You won't, and you'll forget about me," Lily said, pouting.

I got out of bed and walked to the closet. I took out a Casa Iris shopping bag containing Cardoso's framed sketch of me.

"To prove it, I'm giving you this for safekeeping, little sister," I said and handed her the sketch.

Lily looked at the sketch in awe. She put it back in the Casa Iris bag and hugged me tearfully.

After she walked out with the bag, I had an epiphany. If I got out of this hospital alive, I'd be "Dalia" and reboot my botanica shop as Casa Dalia.

The next day was a blur. They came in early to prep me for the surgery. Acer was able to come in for one last boob squeeze, which made me feel worse. It reminded me again that I was losing major pleasure points and some major woman parts.

On the day of my surgery, Acer pressed me for information about why I had guards outside. I was a little groggy from the pre-op drugs. He'd figured out I was in some sort of custody. *"No hay futuro, acabada"* I mumbled about not having a future.

"Me voy a New Jersey *con mi familia, la* Panadería Flores, *cerca del aeropuerto,"* Acer informed me.

"Got it. Flores family bakery near Newark airport," I repeated.

It made sense, as there were many Dominicans in the surrounding area.

Acer made me promise to find him after I straightened out my troubles. Just as I conked out, I whispered, *"Esperame, querido."*

He whispered back in Spanish, "Of course I'll wait for you, my love."

When I woke up from surgery with no breasts, I was in a different hospital in another state.

CHAPTER SEVENTEEN

BLOOM ROOM

Dinner was over but Acer signaled more to come when he rubbed against me with his hard-on. He whispered in my ear, "Bloom Room." I remembered saying I looked forward to seeing his *testículos*.

The Bloom Room was a suite in the Marigold hotel. I thought we took an elevator, but it might have been my champagne hallucination. Acer had a card key, and we entered the room, which was very dark. He seemed to know his way around and escorted me to a long sofa. Acer wasted no time and started undressing me, but he stopped short of my underwear. "I'll be right back," he said as he exited the dark room.

Was he leaving me there alone? He was already hard, so I didn't think he needed any enhancement like a penis pump or a Viagra boost. I sat frozen, until I heard the salsa music.

"I'm preparing something special for you," Acer said from the other room. He then appeared, still dressed, and started to dance to the salsa music.

At first, I thought he wanted me to dance with him, but he began to strip. I just stood and watched the show. He led me to a large comfy chair and gently pushed me into it.

He then jumped on the coffee table as if it were a stage. He took each clothing item off and threw the garments around the room. He looked very professional as he gyrated and was grinding his pelvis to and fro. He spaced out the removal of clothing, perfectly timed with the music. I sobered up a little at this point, and WTF?

Once he was down to his bikinis, he climbed all over me, like in a strip club. I wondered if I was supposed to get out a dollar bill and stuff it down his front. Suddenly, off came the bikinis. He was only wearing a dick sock.

"That's why I excused myself, to put this on. For you, baby. Don't you love it? Make you hot?" Acer said, pointing to the sock.

I felt fairly neutral about the dick sock. Would he take it off for sex? It looked like cotton. Yuck. Why do men think they have to try so hard? Yes, pun intended.

He then slid off my bikinis and my bra, leaving me naked in the chair. Then he leaped back up on the coffee table and danced alone. It crossed my mind that he might be an escort and expected me to pay him—baker, stripper, escort?

The salsa music stopped, and a Latin romantic ballad played. Acer, only wearing a dick sock, uncorked some champagne and poured out two glasses.

"Did you like my dance? It was my show finale at Dante's Inferno."

"*Muy impresionante,*" I complimented him as I stared at his half-erect dick in a sock.

"At the end, the other boys would form a pyramid. I was at the bottom, dry-humping a random woman from the audience," Acer reported.

"Would have loved to have seen it," I said, not clear on the visual.

Acer's phone buzzed, and he took the call in the bedroom. I heard him arguing in Spanish.

I quickly googled Dante's Inferno on my phone. It was in Newark, New Jersey. Not too far from his so-called bistro, *Que Rico*, which still looked like a bakery. When Acer returned, he was wearing a Marigold Hotel robe.

"Loved the dance. Did you strip when you were married to Dalia?" I asked.

"She made me stop when we opened *Que Rico*," Acer replied. "The bakery?" I inquired.

"Dominican fusion bistro," Acer said loudly and sounded annoyed.

Acer then lifted me out of the chair and walked me naked to the bedroom.

He lowered the lights and lit a candle on the nightstand. He lay down next to me, opened his robe and whispered a question.

"*Si me permites, te presento a mis testículos.*"

He asked if he could introduce me to his balls. Seriously?

I forgot about the cheesy strip dance. I was now living a real Spanish afternoon, on steroids.

Acer didn't waste any time, and I was more than ready to receive him, with a condom, of course. I was beginning to think he was younger than mid-thirties. He was hard again within minutes. I asked playfully, "How old are you, anyway?"

Acer drew the number twenty-seven on my tummy. Shit, I was old enough to be his mother! Cougar for the night.

He suggested we move to the Jacuzzi tub. Once the water was high enough, Acer started the jets. I felt adventurous and tried to blow him underwater. It didn't work out as well as I had fantasized. It was very difficult to stay underwater and keep his dick in my mouth while the force of the jets bounced me all around. Plus, I couldn't hold my breath very long. When I popped after the third attempt, I had gotten so much water up my nose, it just made me laugh. Once we caught our breath, he leaned in, kissed me, and told me I got an A for effort.

"Poppy, *pura loca*. Crazy. Never done that before," Acer remarked.

The next morning, I awoke in an empty bed. The morning sun came peering through the walls of glass. The view was spectacular. I could hear the waves crashing the shoreline at the same tempo as the throbs pounding my head from all the champagne.

I had to giggle at the sight of clothes and pillows strewn around the large, smartly decorated bedroom. The room's pale blue tones were soothing to my tired, bloodshot eyes. Not one regretful thought had yet crossed my mind. I decided to relish the comfort of the bed until a ping on my phone forced me out of heaven. It was a text from a Dalia fan.

Those goddamn mourners. It was eight a.m., and a Dalia devotee wanted to visit the tree. I would have loved to announce that I just fucked Dalia's husband, not once but a gazillion times.

Moments later, Acer appeared in the bedroom with two

coffee cups.

"How are you this morning?" he asked as he set the cups down on the bedside table.

"*Ha sido el mejor sexo de mi vida!*" I blurted out, surprising myself that I could still utter a complete, grammatically correct sentence in Spanish.

"The best sex you have ever had?" he asked with a chuckle and climbed into bed beside me.

"*Si, si,* señor," I replied.

"Is there anything more you would like to know about my balls?" he said, giggling as he leaned over for a kiss.

I took it, the kiss. I did not care if I had halitosis or not. He didn't seem to mind one way or another. He grabbed me forcefully, and we made love again. After my fifth orgasm, I enjoyed my cold cappuccino. Acer got up and handed me a hotel robe.

A beautiful, pastel breakfast arrived twenty minutes later. We ate outside on the balcony, wearing matching robes. At one point during the meal, I apologized for poking around his sex organs. I meant not the actual poking of his unit, but my interest.

"Poppy, you are curious, and I love it," he said, laughing.

I was relieved by his answer, settled back, and enjoyed our meal together. It was a lovely morning, with the sun shining and the waves crashing against the sand.

After breakfast, we had a last quickie, then showered and redressed in our evening clothes. He looked as good as ever. Absolutely handsome.

My phone pinged again. "No more mourners," I said as I pulled my phone out. It was a text from Holly.

"Call me back ASAP. New pages for the Willow's Run audition."

I panicked as I was already off book on the original scenes. Now what? No Rowan to coach me. I would need to memorize several new scenes in a day.

"Acer, I've got to go. Script changes for my audition," I said in a panic.

"Moss is downstairs, waiting to take you home," Acer mentioned.

"Moss? Waiting? He knows I spent the night with you?" I questioned.

"Yes, I hope it's not a problem. I am an honest man, no secrets. Moss knows everything. He runs my business, and we make lots of money. More sexy, no?" Acer said, moving closer to me.

"Money isn't everything," I replied, a wet blanket on his Latin ego.

"I really like you, Poppy. Get together next time I'm in town?" Acer asked. I nodded and gave him a quick kiss on the lips.

We headed out of the hotel. There was Moss, the big, burly, right-hand man of the dude with whom I spent the night doing circus acts.

Moss opened the back passenger door, and I jumped in. Acer's demeanor seemed changed, and our last hug felt platonic. My Bloom Room bloom was fading rapidly. As we drove off, I was not planning on conversing with Moss.

"Everything OK, Miss Poppy? Have a good time with the Dominican?" Moss asked.

"Lovely time. He's a good host," I responded and started feeling guilty about fucking Dalia's husband.

"So happy he had a nice evening with a nice woman," Moss announced.

That was a strange comment. I did owe a thank-you text to Acer.

"Gracias for a wonderful evening."

There was no response. It didn't bother me. It was pretty clear. Acer was not Mr. Right, more like Mr. Last Night. A one-shot deal.

We reached Bilberry Lane in record time. As we approached my place, Moss asked, "Miss Poppy, will you allow me more time with Dalia?"

I hesitated and really couldn't deal with him hanging around. Besides, I was hungover and tired. The Acer glow was now buried like Dalia in the yard.

"Could you come back another day?" I politely suggested. Moss hopped out of the car and walked around to open my door.

"No worries, another day. As Baba said, patience and perseverance lead to a meaningful life," Moss said as we shook hands and parted.

He waved, then drove off and honked as he exited the driveway.

I noticed Mu Jin watching me from the doorway of the main house. Busted.

"I see you go with another old man. Maybe he's better yang than the other guy," Mu Jin suggested. She spoke loudly enough for all the neighbors to hear.

Shit. She thought I spent the night with Moss. Should I bother clarifying?

"Not what you think, Mu Jin," I said as I headed down the stone pathway on the walk of shame. Mu Jin caught up to me on the pathway.

"So worried, almost called police when you not come home last night. Flowers delivered last night by the other old man," Mu Jin informed me.

As I approached my doorway, I noticed a bouquet. There were two dozen blooming red roses on my doorstep and a handwritten note.

"I'm so sorry. Please call me, Olmo."

Then my phone started blowing up with my name and headlines in the trades, "Scandal on Willow's Run set," and "Poppy Shaw Shaming" Oh shit!

#stripperbaker #dicksock #tubsex #ballsgalore #testiculos #walkofshame #roses #sorry

Chapter Eighteen

CASADALIA.COM

Blom was the first person I saw when I woke up after my surgery. I didn't realize that I was in a different hospital, until I noticed the icy windows. This was not Florida.

"Iris, you're in the Bethesda, Maryland, Army hospital now. We had to get you out of Jackson. The cartel was looking for you. My guys screwed up," Blom said.

"What? Where?" I asked, still groggy.

"Someone saved your ass, Iris," Blom said.

Blom took a hospital bracelet out of his jacket pocket and dangled it.

"You were wearing a different bracelet when we picked you up from Jackson," Blom said. He handed me the bracelet, then asked, "Name familiar?"

I looked at the bracelet, and it read, "Poppy Shaw."

"*Ni puta idea.* No fucking idea," I replied.

I shook my head and placed the bracelet on my side table.

"Someone switched bracelets. The medics actually loaded

this Poppy Shaw onto the chopper transport. Luckily, one of my assistant deputies noticed it wasn't you. They took this Poppy back to the recovery room, hoping the narco assassins hadn't found you."

"Did they find the guys who came to kill me?" I asked.

"The hit squad was never found. Probably exited the hospital. My guys scooped you up, and here you are. Hopefully, they didn't kill this Poppy Shaw, thinking it was you." Blom chuckled and added, "Bad joke."

I suddenly remembered what the old witch *santera* had said: "Someday an Amapola will save you." Poppy means "Amapola" in Spanish. She told me to take care of her, and it would undo any of my bad deeds.

"So, where the hell am I now, and why?"

"Maryland. Safe place and near the WITSEC orientation. Cardoso is already in a safe house nearby," Blom informed me.

"Don't let me anywhere near him," I said, glaring at Blom.

My recovery was tough in Bethesda hospital. There were no Acer nightly booty calls, and I felt ragged and demoralized from the radiation and chemo. *Ay Dios!* The cure was worse than the fucking disease.

Blom said I had to meet with the DOJ attorneys to discuss the depositions and the terms of my protective custody. In my gut, I felt it was futile. I could die of cancer, and no amount of money would help me. What the hell was there to live for? What and who were waiting for me in my new life? I would have to build from scratch and do something new. *Santa María de Dios,* how much could a person take?

I sometimes hoped the *Colombianos* had gunned down Papi O. and Cardoso. That would have helped me face the future with fewer emotional vendettas.

I avoided the meeting with the DOJ for days until Blom was getting pressured. "For you, Papi, I'll do it," I said. I began calling Blom "Papi" once I arrived in

Bethesda. He knew it was an endearment and didn't seem to mind.

I admit to fantasizing about the deputy taking me away for a wild weekend in a five-star hotel and only ordering room service. I was not usually attracted to black men like my mother.

But Deputy Layton Blom was an attractive and caring man. I didn't see color anymore.

One of the young deputies on guard outside my room was very chatty. He said it was possible to cut deals with the DOJ and also get paid for testimony. Also, he said to make sure they compensated you for your cleared seized assets, those not connected to money laundering.

I was so grateful for the advice, I would have offered the young deputy the opportunity to fiddle with my *concha*, but he confided that he was gay.

After I reviewed the breakdown and value of our assets, I was insistent on bonus cash. "I think I need an extra something for testifying, plus my share of our liquidated clean assets," I announced to the attorneys on a conference call. Cardoso, Blom, and our attorney, Yarrow, were in the meeting.

"Same here, and I want my art back, plus my share of the assets," Cardoso said. "The government will hold your art in storage, until you leave the witness protection program," a DOJ attorney informed him.

"You mean we can leave the program? I thought it was for life," I commented.

"It's all voluntary. But we don't suggest returning to your old life, until you're out of danger," Yarrow informed us.

"So, Cardoso Ortega can make a comeback!" Cardoso exclaimed. I hated when he referred to himself in the third person. *Egoista!*

Cardoso was delusional in thinking he could return to being an artist under his old name within a few years. The DOJ agents warned him about being visible in the art world.

Blom and Yarrow indicated it could take ten or more years for the Colombian narcos to die off or for us to fall off their radar.

"So, draw your ass off, and don't put your name on it," I suggested to Cardoso.

They advised Cardoso to get comfortable, lie low, and not show any new work even with his new name for a while. Someone could recognize his style. I then heard Cardoso cursing in the background and the words, "*Hijos de puta.*"

"OK, guys, I know this is hard. Let's move on to new identities and logistics," Blom chimed in.

"I already know my new name, Romero Robles," Cardoso said, rolling the *r*'s.

"Since you're divorcing, not a good idea to share each other's new names and locations," Yarrow warned.

I searched for a paper and pen on my side table and found Poppy Shaw's hospital bracelet. I wrote down, "Dalia Shaw."

Perfect new name.

Later on, when I told Blom my chosen name, he didn't seem to click with Poppy Shaw and the hospital switch. But I wanted to honor the woman who probably saved me from my second brush with death. My first being cancer and my second almost being assassinated by Papi O.'s enemies.

I also asked to be relocated to a place far away from Cardoso.

I wanted to go to New York, but Blom said it would have to be New Jersey. Since I had lived in Manhattan, it was advisable to steer clear so I wouldn't run into someone I knew.

"We're putting you in a place where you can blend in. There's a huge Latino population in New Jersey: Cubans, Dominicans, Puerto Ricans," Blom mentioned.

"Why do I need to be with Latinos? Because I have a slight accent? How would you feel if I said you should stay with black people?" I asked.

Blom had to agree and apologized.

"My bad. I forgot about what it's like to be stereotyped. Trust me, I should know. The program policy is relocation in places where one can blend in."

"Did you know I'm part black, Deputy Blom?" I asked.

"Yes, you are, kid. I've seen a photo of your father, Eneldo. You're my people." He replied laughing.

That night Cardoso called me in the hospital, drunk. He told me they were relocating him to a small, California, desert town. He would be a high school art teacher where they needed bilingual staff. He was not happy and unleashed a litany of curse words against his father, the Colombians, the government, and me.

"I bet you're going to go to New York, Chicago, or San Francisco. That Blom guy has the hots for you and probably arranged a prime location," Cardoso shouted on the phone.

"I guess you'll never find out where I am," I said.

"Don't worry, I'll find you, *coño,* and make your life miserable. Someday I'll piss on your grave!" Cardoso shouted, then ended the call.

Blom had arranged for my treatments and boob reconstruction in a top New York hospital. I showed Blom the pamphlet on my future reconstruction surgery that showed the types and sizes of boobs.

"Here's info for a nipple tattoo option." I held up another pamphlet. He pretended he wasn't uncomfortable, but his hands were trembling.

"It's OK, Papi. Won't embarrass you. I'll turn my head, and you can circle the pair you like," I suggested.

"I'm no expert," he said and handed back the pamphlet. There was a tick mark on round 38C's.

"Good choice, Papi. Natural. Not porno or stripper size."

I spoke to Blom about setting up a Casa Dalia. But he said I was barred from returning to my old business. I was so depressed about the future. Every time Blom asked me what kind of job I wanted, I just cried. Then the side effects of the chemo made me feel like *mierda,* with vomiting, hair loss, and weakness.

Blom tried really hard to cheer me up and brought my favorite takeout food. He found the equivalent to Pollo Loco near the hospital.

Some of the hospital staff thought Blom was my husband,

especially after he brought me flowers. When he arranged the 'round-the-clock' deputies outside my room, another rumor circulated. They thought I was the wife of a Mexican cartel leader in protective custody.

As I started to feel better, I made some plans. In addition to a new set of tits, my grand plan was Casa Dalia, a twenty-first-century *botánica*. The marshal relocation team and Blom said a brick-and-mortar store was out of the question, so I planned online only. CasaDalia.com. But all I said to Blom was to find me a job in a health food store. He seemed not himself that day.

"What's wrong, Papi? You look sad," I noted.

"Tired. Just up all night talkin' with the missus," he said. There was a pause. I gestured to indicate that I wanted to hear more. By that point, we could communicate without talking.

Blom sat at the edge of my bed.

"We've been trying to get pregnant for many years," he informed me, adding, "She's talking adoption now. But I'm not a fan."

"Are you the problem, or is it her?" I asked diplomatically.

"It's her. I tested top notch," he said shyly.

I took out my notepad and wrote a list.

"Before you go down the adoption road, she should take this potion," I said as I handed Blom the piece of paper.

He read aloud, "Alligator pepper, false unicorn, red clover? They sound like Disney characters. Where would I get these?"

"If you hadn't shut down Casa Iris, I could have prepared this potion in minutes. Find a botanica, and they'll mix it up for you," I suggested.

"I'll ask if she wants to try it. *Gracias,* Iris. I mean Dalia," Blom said tenderly.

I didn't see Blom much for the next few weeks. I was released to a safe house, with a lot of other people heading into witness protection. People came in and out. Once in a while, I hooked up with some embezzlers and money launderers. I tested my theories about ways to circumvent the authorities. There was one hot, Aussie guy named Ainsley, whose idea of dinner was only liquid. We giggled during witness protection orientation. I loved his accent.

"These blokes not letting me return to Australia to set up another Crocodile Dundee tourist trap. Has to be stateside," Ainsley said.

"I lived near the Everglades in Miami, lots of crocs there," I mentioned.

"Not a chance, mate. Closest they offered was working the jungle ride at Disney World in Orlando. Crikey," Ainsley reported.

The US marshals had hopes that Ainsley could be on a path to being a character roaming the park, a train conductor in period costume, or a voice-over for the Pirates of the Caribbean ride.

Ainsley and I got drunk, made out, and ended up in my room. I carefully steered him away from my falsies. I was afraid he would see the scars in place of my boobs.

He gave the falsies a quick squeeze and headed down south. It made me forget that I was still facing more treatment and then breast reconstruction. Ainsley was a slam-bam type and came fast and was exhausted. He was no Acer.

After my final chemo treatment at Bethesda, I felt empowered.

I was not yet ready to die of this disease. I would take my chances and rely on my potions to heal myself.

After a few months and after Papi O.'s trial was over, I was ready for relocation. Blom had arranged for an apartment in a town called Lyndhurst. I searched the address on Google Earth and it looked like a hood. Blom assured me the apartment building was new. Ha. He handed me a large packet with my new identity documents and my "backstory."

Someone at the US Marshals Service was a fiction writer wannabe. They wrote that Dalia Shaw was from a New Jersey mixed Latino and real American family with ties to the *Mayflower*. I could join the DAR, Daughters of the American Revolution. *Por Dios*. I heard that there were a lot of women of color now in the DAR.

They invented a Cuban connection on my mother's side, with Spanish heritage dating back to the Inquisition. Was I related to Torquemada? They also concocted a story about my fictitious father and his fatal factory accident. Everyone in my family was dead.

I had documentation that Dalia attended college and had worked in a pharmacy. They provided birth and death certificates along with a passport and driver's license. There was even an associate degree in health sciences in the name of Dalia Shaw.

I had to memorize my backstory. I couldn't graduate from witness protection orientation until I passed a test on my new identity.

Finally, I was ready to go to New Jersey as the now-single Dalia Shaw. The divorce had come through, and I was done with

Cardoso. They suggested I change my hair color and look. That was easy, as I was wearing wigs since I suffered hair loss from chemo.

I had a $2 million stash and another half million mistakenly deposited into my account for Cardoso's artwork. I said nothing. Fuck him. He owed me for destroying my *oráculo* book and screwing that *puta* Pixie.

Blom handed me the keys to my new apartment in New Jersey; a new car was parked outside the safe house in Maryland. Blom seemed to be taking a long time to show me all the bells and whistles on the brand-new, red Toyota Camry. We had a moment when he gave me the keys. He kept his hands in mine, leaned over, and whispered, "In another lifetime, it may have gone differently."

"What if I had been black?" I whispered back.

"May surprise you that my wife, Heather, is Waspy Wisconsin white," Blom informed me. That was a shock. I always pictured his wife as a petite, cuddly lady, maybe not a real *negrita* but *mulata*.

"There's still time, Papi. You know where to find me," I said provocatively.

I was pissed off. So, he did have feelings for me but didn't have the *cojones* to act on them. I was sure Heather Blom was nice, but could she match my Cuban papaya action?

The deputy approached me with a quick platonic hug and said, "This isn't the end. I'm still in charge of your case. Call me when you get settled in NJ."

I remembered what Acer Flores told me about his family in New Jersey. I looked up the Flores Bakery near Newark airport and surprisingly, it was only a few miles from my new apartment in

Lyndhurst. Was that a coincidence, or was the universe speaking? For a moment, I thought Acer was involved in my relocation, but that couldn't be possible.

He was an undocumented Dominican with no skills apart from his *rabo,* although being a dick master would probably serve him well in the New Jersey suburbs. I decided not to contact him until I got my new pair of *tetas.* Now that Deputy Blom didn't want any part of me, I was determined to move on.

I had a plan about my future: I would be a health coach and a healer. Not some *juebona cualquiera,* or a stupid crazy *santera* or a health store cashier. I wanted to help people, especially cancer patients. If I could do the occasional spell to help people fall in love or curse their enemy, and that was OK too.

I was also determined to use the money-laundering skills I studied using my two million plus. I wanted to prove I was no longer Iris Ortega, the innocent girl, *la niña inocente.*

Money mattered, and I wanted to prove I was a player in the big leagues. The opportunity would come as soon as I got my new pair of tits. Nothing could stop Dalia Shaw, a healer with street smarts.

Fuck cancer. I would start my empire with CasaDalia.com. God help me.

CHAPTER NINETEEN

#WILLOWSRUN

Those bastards ruined my life with hashtags and they're stuck in my brain. Now it's Poppy payback time.

#tvpilot #sitcom #goofypremise #golf #nailedaudition
#myclothes #Ivy #happyholly #bigcommision #toptalent
#divadirector #pickyproducer #chaos #toxicset
#toptalentexit #badcasting #teamconflict #writersroom
#nodiversity #badscript #badpress #crazycatering
#kaleonly #nopastelfood #poppytroublemaker #cyberbully
#fakenews #foodshaming #fired #newIvy #trophygirl
#deviousdirector #sadholly #nopay #hollypissed
#industryghosted #allmyfault #neverworkagain
#shitshow #notmyfault #badpress #twittershade
#poppymeltdown #Xanax #vodka #help #therapy #callOlmo

Aaah. I'm feeling so much better after venting and vomiting hashtags.

Chapter Twenty

ROSEMARY AND JULIET

Imagine losing a plum TV role for refusing to eat a bowl of kale?

My big break and it slipped through my fingers, followed by cyberbullying over my pastel food requirement. "#pickypoppy" became the latest trending hashtag.

Who would have thought such an innocent phobia would erupt in Hollywood's latest scandal and become the butt of late-night jokes? One comedian told a nasty joke, asking if sperm was pastel colored. A talk show host proposed my phobia was also related to people, implying I was a racist: "Sorry, I only talk to pastel-colored people."

Fucking Fig the Frog told me it was the "role of a lifetime." He should have been disbarred or whatever they do to quack astrologers. I guess he left out the part about getting fired and my name being dragged through the mud.

"She only eats pastels—refused to eat kale," one airhead actress wrote on her Insta, together with a meme of me making an ugly face over a bowl of kale.

I found out the director wanted his girlfriend for the Ivy part. This was even before the kale incident. They were looking for any excuse. I was branded "difficult," "toxic," and "not a team player."

My agent Holly fired me as she thought me uninsurable and un-bankable. She called me a liability.

"Unfit to be hired for a VERY long time, except for maybe cleaning the studio toilets or babysitting some producer's brat. Maybe in a year, you can resurface after a nose job and a name change or just pack it in," Holly lectured me by phone.

Maybe she was right, and I should pack it in. How many jilted first wives, cougars, menopausal BFF's, MYLF's and miserable empty-nester roles are there? Was I chasing an impossible dream? Was it true what that vampire Rowan said that I have raw talent? What the hell does that mean, raw? An uncooked vegetable, sushi?

I thought Holly was exaggerating. Soon after, she and a long list of people in the business ghosted me. The only meaningful texts I was getting were from the Dalia mourners. Were these now my only "friends?" Fuck, I hoped not.

After the trades reported on my firing, Olmo texted:

"Call me if you want to talk. I'm here for ya, kid."

I had been so caught up with the *Willow's Run* nonsense that I hadn't reached out to Olmo, since he delivered the roses on my doorstep. I didn't think I had ever thanked him. Shame on me. *Where were your manners, Poppy? Obviously evaporated like your CAREER!*

I texted Olmo back:

"Sorry, haven't been in touch. You obviously know what I've

been up to. Not good. Sorry I didn't thank you for the roses. They were lovely and lasted until I was fired off the show. Would like very much to chat."

Olmo called me right away and heard my damsel-in-distress voice. It didn't help that I started crying when he asked if I had eaten. He suggested that he come over with food.

He arrived with little boxes of pale Chinese food and a bottle of chilled, white wine.

Bravo. He also brought braised pork balls in dark brown sauce as a test. "Thought you may want to start experimenting?" Olmo proposed.

I was so happy it wasn't fucking kale that I kissed him. I would think about the pork balls.

As we ate the Chinese food, Olmo regretted ending things the way he did.

"I had several younger women dump me after date five and others looking for a meal ticket," Olmo said sadly.

"We never got to date five," I noted.

"Women my age have so much baggage," Olmo complained.

"And I don't have baggage?" I asked sarcastically.

"I can handle your baggage, I think," Olmo noted and squeezed my hand.

I told Olmo about Fig's prediction and the past life reading. I played him the recording of the session. Olmo seemed overwhelmed with the historical references.

"Forget about the Crusades, the Inquisition, and revolutions. I think we should try getting past date five. Since we have worked and rehearsed together, I count this as date six," I announced.

Olmo hugged and then kissed me deeply. "I think I already love you, Poppy Shaw."

My phone dinged with another WTF text from an acquaintance and more condolences on the bad publicity and getting fired, as well as some cheerful emojis. I showed Olmo.

"I have many stories of toxic productions with big-name stars ending with fights and even police presence," Olmo chuckled.

"Should I just pack it in, Olmo, and go back to being a BORING office manager?" I asked. Olmo waved his chopsticks.

"Absolutely NOT. You're a fucking great actress, Poppy." Olmo declared.

He tried to convince me that my story would blow over and no one would remember in a few days. I obviously looked like I was not convinced to carry on.

"Thirty years ago, the scandals lingered much longer. People now have short attention spans, and the news cycle is nanoseconds. You'll work again soon," Olmo predicted.

The publicity around the death of his wife, Violeta, lasted a long time. She was well-known for her role of Orquídea in *Amor y Vivir*. It had been dubbed in forty languages. Olmo said he didn't work for almost a year.

"I thought she overdosed. What did that have to do with you?" I asked.

"She wasn't alone in the bed," Olmo informed me.

So, this was what Rowan meant by complicated and messy. "Another man?" I asked.

"Another woman: our housemate, Rosemary. It was a murder-suicide. But I was arrested and under investigation," Olmo replied.

196

"This storyline sounds straight from *Amor y Vivir*," I offered. Olmo laughed, sipped his drink, took a deep breath, and exhaled.

"Rosemary was the president of Violeta's fan club," Olmo said.

"How big was Violeta's fan club?" I asked.

"It had dwindled after the show ended. The remainders were crazies," Olmo replied.

"I wonder if my mom was in the fan club. She would count as a crazy," I said.

"This Rosemary had never been married, had no kids, no job, and was estranged from her family. No paper trail, like she had appeared from under a rock."

"Red flag," I noted.

"Rosemary worshipped Violeta. Showered her with gifts and attention. Violeta was depressed after her show ended and my career took off. Rosemary stepped in as an enabler," Olmo said.

"No good," I commented, filling my glass again. I wondered if I should ask if there was a lesbian love affair.

"I was so damn caught up in my work, I paid no attention as this Svengali took control of my wife. Rosemary had her convinced she should divorce me."

"How did Rosemary wangle the move into your home?" I asked.

"We were living in a big house in Brentwood. I had to go on location for six weeks. Violeta begged me to let Rosemary stay and keep her company. The woman never left. What a dumb fuck I was. That woman was in love with my wife."

"Holy shit," I said.

"They once tried draining our joint bank account. Luckily, the bank manager called me," Olmo recalled.

"So, they didn't get any money?" I asked. Olmo shook his head.

"When I confronted Violeta, we had a big fight. Rosemary called the cops, telling them I was abusive. So there was a record."

"Was there anything physical between them?" I asked.

"I don't think so. Violeta was drugged twenty-four seven. Wouldn't rule it out. But Rosemary was not much to look at: stringy, greasy hair, overweight, and butt ugly, IMHO," Olmo said.

"Love comes in all packages," I noted.

"Rosemary was not a package you wanted to open, trust me. She smelled bad, rarely changed her clothes, and spoke in a horrid, shrill voice," Olmo noted.

"Nightmare. Why didn't you kick her ass out?" I asked.

"I was a pussy. Every time I broached the subject with Violeta, she would become hysterical, so I caved," Olmo replied.

Olmo had come home after an all-day shoot. He found the women in bed with gunshot wounds. Violeta's tranquilizer vials were empty.

"What really happened?" I asked.

"Violeta was drugged, then shot by Rosemary, who then took her own life. It took a while for it to blow over. I didn't work for almost a year," Olmo lamented.

"Rosemary had called the cops earlier to say I had threatened them. She also called the *L.A. Times* and *The Enquirer*. There were camera crews filming me in handcuffs being led out of my house, and the removal of the body bags."

"That's awful. Poppy pause," I said; I needed some more food.

I was so engrossed in Olmo's story that I didn't even notice I had eaten some pork balls. Olmo saw me take a few bites, high-fived me, and continued his sordid tale.

"I was interrogated and held in custody until the medical examiner ruled it a murder-suicide," Olmo said, refilling his glass and mine with wine.

"Holy shit. That's a *Lifetime* movie, and if there was any evidence of sexual misconduct, an episode of *Law and Order: SVU*," I remarked.

"All of the above. Unfortunately, the law enforcement were not as nice or glamorous as on TV. They were nasty and cruel until the high-priced lawyers showed up. In those days, the studio where I was shooting *Love and Secrets* came to the rescue. They quashed the publicity and bailed me out."

"Bet that doesn't happen anymore," I noted.

"That was as far as the studio was prepared to support me. Within weeks, my character, Mace Garland, was killed off in a ridiculous story line. It involved Mace choking on a chicken bone. Lazy writers," Olmo said.

I patted Olmo's back, as he appeared upset recalling the incident.

"It must have been rough dealing with several tragedies: her death, her relationship with Rosemary, and your own struggles," I commented.

"For years, I couldn't get the scene out of my head, of the two women lying there in bed, holding hands," Olmo remembered painfully.

"Rosemary and Juliet, I mean Violet," I corrected myself.

Olmo snapped his fingers. "That's a great name for a play, *Rosemary and Juliet*," Olmo remarked.

"Then write it," I suggested.

Olmo hugged me again. "I will," he said.

"OK, you win, Olmo Branch. Your scandal was way more serious than mine. At least I haven't been arrested, yet," I noted.

"Yet?" Olmo asked.

"If my scandal doesn't blow over, I may have to change my name. I thought about taking a dead girl's old identity," I announced.

Olmo looked puzzled, so I took him to the window and pointed to the olive tree.

"Underneath that tree was an urn with the ashes of Dalia. People come to worship. But the US marshals dug her up and took her away," I informed him.

I led Olmo to the back of my closet door.

"You're the first person I'm showing the Dalia backstory."

I pointed to the numerous Post-it notes on the back of the door.

"Iris Ortega, Cardoso Ortega, Romero Robles, Acer Flores, Dalia Shaw Flores, Moss, Deputy Blom," I called out.

I explained about the witness protection, Dalia's videos, and her two husbands. Olmo looked mystified and alarmed. He read the next set of Post-it notes and asked questions.

"Dalia VIP mourners: Sage, Rosita et al?"

"They get preference when visiting the tree."

"Camellia and Juniper?"

"Twin fans; Juniper had a snoring problem cured by Dalia."

"*Que Rico?*"

"Dominican bakery."

"Dante's Inferno?"

"A strip club in Newark, New Jersey."

"CasaDalia.com?"

"Dalia's website, selling lotions, potions, and magic spells." Olmo nodded his head and looked at me.

"Super impressed with your investigation, but you do realize that this is bizarre and scary shit?" Olmo commented.

"Uh-huh, welcome to my world," I said.

He looked over all the Post-it notes again, then the clothes in the closet. "Whose clothes are these?" Olmo asked.

"Um, mostly mine, some hers," I replied, not wanting to share my secret.

Since I hadn't heard from Blom, maybe it was case closed. But Olmo thought that it wasn't the last of the Dalia business.

"With all this investigation, did you consider she might not be dead?" Olmo pondered.

I shook my head.

"Too many people watched her dying in the videos. She looked real close," I replied.

We had enough of the crazy and disturbing stories and drank more wine. It led to afternoon and sleepover sex. I felt so safe in his arms, and he had absolutely no trouble in the erectile department. I didn't dare look at his balls and saved that exploration for another time. It was time I came to grips with the fixation. Grandpa Shaw's balls problem was too many decades ago. More therapy?

We did it again, and surprisingly, it only took twenty-nine minutes for the sixty-nine year-old to get it up again unassisted.

Fig was correct, *ooh la la*, and yes, a deep connection. Mu Jin was also correct; I enjoyed his yang, and felt we were a match, spiritually, physically, and emotionally. I thought Olmo felt the same, although he still had insecurities.

"Poppy, just give me advance warning if you're going to dump me." I just hugged him and asked, "Five, ten minutes OK?"

I was so confident that Olmo might be Mr. Right, I suggested he meet the family Shaw: Daisy, Palmer, Cedar, and his bridezilla, Saffron.

Olmo agreed without any hesitation. I hoped it wouldn't go sideways. What could go wrong, bringing home a guy older than my dad? Olmo, the husband of my mom's favorite telenovela actress, Violeta Branch, who was now the subject of Olmo's new play, *Rosemary and Juliet.*

#mediafrenzy #sorry #deadwife #porkballs #shakespeare #familyshaw

CHAPTER TWENTY-ONE

—

FAMILY SHAW

Just before Olmo picked me up to reluctantly visit my family, I had a burning question. There was no one to consult except Siri and Alexa.

ME: "Siri, I'm taking my new boyfriend to meet my parents. He's older than my dad. What is the best way to handle the situation? PS: They hate everyone."

Siri: "I am sorry for your dilemma. Perhaps you could choose more wisely. I found this on the Web."

Me: "Thanks for nothing."

I hoped Alexa would be more helpful.

ME: "Alexa. My boyfriend is older than my father."

Alexa: "Google is not older than your father."

ME: "Alexa, what's the best way to introduce my older boyfriend to my family?

Alexa: "I don't know that but recommend the book: Daddy Complex."

I went into my closet to get some guidance. It was always the best private source of communication with Dalia. I waited for the Dalia wizard, then heard a voice.

"Just go to the party. Be you and let Olmo be himself. Your family is nuts. Hold hands and be strong. He loves you."

Olmo showed up in a red, Jag, sports car with the top down. He jumped out and opened the passenger side door.

"Nice ride! Where did you get it?" I asked as I slid into the seat.

"Bought it from some Dominican who was in a hurry to fly back to New Jersey," Olmo replied. I froze. It was Dalia's jag! I said nothing and then remembered we were going to meet my family. I took a pause and a deep breath.

"Are you sure you want to do this, Olmo?" I asked.

"Of course, I want to meet your family. The people who made Poppy possible," he responded.

He saw my apprehension, took my hand, and kissed it. He tried to console me.

"If I can handle hostile, bad-tempered, crusty, old directors and toxic, judgmental, vengeful actresses, I can handle your parents."

"There's no category for Daisy and Palmer Shaw. Just in case, let's have a safe word if we need to get the hell out of there," I suggested.

"Sure, hon. Safe word is Polaris," Olmo proposed.

It was Daisy's birthday, which was always a major event. I feared the family Shaw would potentially be even more dysfunctional and bizarre than usual.

"I brought your mom a gift. Something that belonged to

Violeta," Olmo announced.

I was stunned, literally breathless. His gray hair was blown back from the wind, and for some reason, he looked younger to me. I gazed at him, and he noticed.

"I love you," he said.

"No, I love you for being so kind and thoughtful. A gift for Daisy? From Violeta? I mean, a gift from you, but something from her?" I awkwardly tried to explain myself. "Wait! You still have possessions of Violeta's?" I blurted. I felt so jealous, even a bit betrayed.

He looked at me, smiling. I melted. Then I forgave myself for being such a bitch.

"I want it to be a surprise, for the both of you. Do we need to stop for champagne?"

"Daisy likes sangria; I brought a bottle of brandy, some rhubarb, strawberries, and mint. A new recipe for Daisy's special day," I said with an extreme attitude adjustment.

Moments later, my phone rang. The connection was awful, a high-pitched ringing noise. I hung up. My phone rang again: same noise. And it rang again. I thought it best to let the call go to voice mail. I reached for Olmo's hand, and at that exact moment, the Waze lady said, "Your destination is on your left."

I froze in fear, as it was showtime.

We arrived at my parents' home. It was the same house I was raised in but looked recently remodeled. It had been over a year since I had seen my family, and I was walking back into the entanglement.

Daisy and Palmer were outside as we pulled into the

driveway. They were aging well, but both looked glassy-eyed. She was wearing a cover-up over a bathing suit and was still a size eight. Palmer had on Bermuda shorts and a golf shirt.

Daisy walked towards us while Palmer wandered into the garage without saying a word. WTF.

"Why don't you answer your phone? I needed you to pick up some ointment. Oh, is this him? Really, Poppy, do you have to bring home every guy you screw?" Daisy asked while giving Olmo a once-over.

I wanted to die. Olmo didn't flinch. He reached out to shake Daisy's hand.

"Hello, Daisy. A pleasure to meet you, I am Olmo. Poppy and I don't just screw. Happy Birthday, you look fabulous. I've been gray since my thirties, so don't let my hair color fool you," Olmo said, smiling his never-ending smile.

"*Cuántos años tiene el viejo*? Plus, you're late," Daisy said, assuming Olmo didn't understand Spanish.

"*Este viejo tiene sesenta y nueve, señora*," Olmo responded to her question in the third person indicating the "old man is sixty-nine."

"Happy Birthday," I said and double-cheek-pecked Daisy. A hug between us was unusual.

Olmo swooped Daisy up, twirled her around, and landed her on her feet. Both heads of hair were tousled, and both were slightly dizzy afterwards. Daisy adjusted her swimsuit straps and fanned herself as if she was having a hot flash.

"Never mind about the ointment," she whispered in my ear, taking Olmo's hand.

Palmer appeared from the garage, holding a garden hose, and seemed catatonic.

"Cedar and his wife, Saffron, are outside by the pool. Palmer, come along," she said and motioned for us to head around the back. Palmer did not react.

"I don't like this Saffron; she's a lush. But what does a mother do when a nitwit is married to her only son?" Daisy said to Olmo.

I wanted to kill her, slowly. I didn't remember Daisy ever appearing so evil.

Something changed her after her last face-lift. She had become a cunt. Maybe she always was one, and I never noticed.

Olmo leaned into me and whispered, "Polaris," as we made our way to the pool deck. "Too early," I whispered back.

From the empty glasses, pitchers, and beer bottles, it seemed the party had started WAY before we got there.

Palmer had followed us with the running hose. He finally acknowledged that I had arrived and dropped the garden hose that was still spewing water.

"Water shortage, Palmer. Gonna get fined again," Daisy shouted as she settled in a chaise lounge where she was now holding court.

My dad wrapped his arms around me, which was weird. Again, we were not an affectionate bunch.

Palmer reached out to Olmo. "I'm Palmer Shaw, welcome."

"Olmo Branch, thank you," Olmo replied and shook Dad's hand.

"Olmo, maybe you can help me find a good place to bury Fred," Palmer said.

"Fred?" Olmo asked.

"I built Fred a plastic palace and expansive Habitrail. It's more like a maze than a cage, with bridges and tunnels. We thought he had escaped, but he was just lying peacefully in one of the tunnels. Starved to death, I guess," Palmer explained.

"I hated that fucking rodent. Ding-dong, Fred is dead, and on my birthday," Daisy shouted.

"Hope you patented the hamster maze, Dad?" Cedar shouted.

He walked towards Palmer and Olmo with a shoebox and placed it on the ground.

I approached my brother, Cedar, and messed up his hair, like I did when I was a kid.

At thirty-four, he was getting a middle-aged beer belly.

"Long time, sis. Haven't seen you in any major roles or commercials. How's that acting working for you?" Cedar asked.

"Love you too, little brother. Meet Olmo," I said. Cedar did a fist bump with Olmo.

Olmo and Palmer discussed the best resting place for Fred. I was nervous about leaving them alone.

I waved to Saffron, who was in the pool. She blew me a kiss.

My sister-in-law, Saffron, had already dropped into her fake, Southern accent. She spoke like that when she was buzzed or manipulating someone. She was petite, thirty, and intolerable. Her career in advertising ended after she was caught using her company credit card for liposuction treatments.

"Oh, for Christ's sake, someone pour this birthday babe some sangria," Daisy ordered. I found a half pitcher and poured the rest into her glass.

"Alexa, play some Latin jazz," Cedar asked as he stripped naked and jumped into the pool.

I retrieved a fresh batch of sangria from the kitchen. When I returned to the pool deck, Olmo was seated on Daisy's lounge chair. The two were deep in conversation.

I brought out an array of Spanish tapas. I filled my glass and stabbed a grilled shrimp.

Cedar was nude in the water while Mom was seducing Olmo. Saffron was on her phone, sitting on the pool stairs. Palmer was digging a hole for Fred near the forsythia.

"Olive?" I asked Saffron, holding out a condiment dish.

She ended her call.

"I'm allergic. I thought you knew," she sassed in a Southern accent.

"No, Saffron, I didn't know. Must suck," I sarcastically remarked.

Saffron stood up and picked at other tapas on the table.

"Happy Birthday, Mom. Lovely spread," Saffron said.

Ew, she called Daisy Mom. I pulled over a chair next to Daisy and Olmo.

"Hi hon, how are you doing?" I said and pinched Olmo's thigh.

"Shame on you, Poppy. Not revealing you were dating Mace Garland from *Love and Secrets*. Every night, in real life, he slept with Violeta Branch from *Amor y Vivir*. I fantasized about sleeping with Violeta." Then she added, "Sorry, Palmer."

I had a flashback of Mom making out with one of the Spanish afternoon gals. I must have buried that memory.

"Saffron, get Cedar out of the pool. We are having a family meeting. Palmer?" she cried out.

A family meeting meant one of two things. First, a dead pet needed funeral planning, which was already happening with Fred. Second, someone admitted to an extra-familial affair. It looked like it had something to do with Olmo, as he was waving a small box with a bow. Oh shit.

"Alexa, turn off the music, right fucking now," Saffron slurred.

My brother emerged from the pool and stood near me. His naked, long dick was dripping chlorine. "Polaris," I whispered to Olmo.

"Everyone look, Olmo brought me a birthday present," Daisy announced.

"*Feliz cumpleaños?*" Olmo said, presenting her with the small box, which she opened.

"*La cruz*! The cross? Is it really the necklace she wore on the show?" Daisy asked excitedly.

"*Si, señora,*" Olmo confirmed as he stood and filled a plate with food.

Dad paid no attention to the special announcement or Olmo's present. Palmer was still digging a hole for Fred's final resting place.

Daisy announced it was getting chilly and the party was moving inside. As Olmo helped Daisy up from the chaise lounge, she grazed her hands across his ass.

Cedar walked past Daisy. He couldn't resist throwing shade on his mother. "Same old Daisy." We all headed to the kitchen.

"Poppy, you will never be free of her," he said.

"What the hell does that mean?" I asked.

"Our mom will fuck anything to get her way," Cedar replied.

"Dad says they only did it twice, to make me and you," I said.

Palmer was still digging a hole for Fred and must have had his hearing aid turned up.

"I have had sex more than two times with your mother," Palmer shouted.

"And many others. Mom and Dad were swingers before it became a thing," I said in a loud voice.

"Remember college?" Cedar reminded me, still naked.

I was half listening to Cedar while I had my eye on my mother. She had flipped off her shoes and was unbuttoning Olmo's shirt.

"Polaris," Olmo whimpered, but he didn't fight her off.

This was insane. My own mother was pawing my boyfriend, and he was letting her.

"Mom came to visit me at college. She dropped off lasagna and stayed to make breakfast," Cedar said. Daisy chimed in.

"It was mothers' weekend. Imagine, both CVS and Walgreens sold out of condoms. Not sure about the other moms. Honestly, I would rather cook the boys pancakes."

"That's not what the frat boys said. Daisy knew a little too much about street drugs and taught them how to make white trash sangria," Cedar informed me.

"The moms were doing the boys?" Olmo asked as he discreetly buttoned up his shirt. As he tried to get far away, Daisy kept hauling him back towards her. I was pissed.

"Daisy only offered food. My roommate paid me fifty bucks to have her return each weekend with lasagna," Cedar said.

The doorbell chimed. I opened the door to our neighbor, Cherry Bush, the hoarder. I couldn't believe she was still alive.

She looked even larger than I remembered. Palmer wandered in and sat down.

"Did I interrupt something?" Cherry asked, then handed me a cake.

Daisy still had her claws on Olmo but managed to shout, "Cherry, look, it's Mace Garland!"

Cherry collapsed in a chair that nearly broke under her weight.

"And you have him all to yourself? Share, Daisy," Cherry begged as she struggled to get up. She lunged at Olmo with open arms.

"Polaris," Olmo shouted as I peeled Daisy and Cherry away from him.

As we were leaving, I heard Palmer ask Daisy, "Wasn't Mace Garland the last guy she brought over?"

On the ride home, I asked Siri, "Where is Polaris?"

Siri: "Polaris, the brightest star in Ursa Minor and 434 light-years away from Earth."

That should be far enough away from the family Shaw.

#redjag #swingers #mylf #deadfred #openmarriage
#fuckalexa #fucksiri #polaris

CHAPTER TWENTY-TWO

QUE RICO

My most joyful memory of the past decade was having been fucked by Acer Flores, the undocumented hospital orderly at Jackson Memorial Hospital in Miami. It was now 2012 and I had been in New Jersey for two years treading water.

I was still processing my new life as Dalia Shaw, having lost my business and started over again. I was still angry at my now-ex-husband and my father-in-law. I was probably angry that no family was there for me to get through cancer and the double mastectomy.

My breast reconstruction surgery was a step forward. I was happy to gain back my woman parts and forgot about the pain and agony. *Dios mío.*

It was time to reconnect with the hot Dominican, Acer Flores, so I stalked his family bakery. The Flores Bakery, *panadería,* was in Union City, New Jersey, about twenty miles from my apartment in Lyndhurst.

It was easier to disguise myself in the winter as I could

wear a hat and a large overcoat. I also wore a wig as my hair had thinned out from chemo. Some days, I just watched Acer through the bakery window in his cute, white baker's outfit, arranging the breads and buns. One day, I actually went inside and bought empanadas. I noticed the woman at the register, who was probably his aunt.

"Acer, *no olvides* las empanadas."

Then his aunt walked to the kitchen entrance and told Acer to pack that order of empanadas before he left. Where was he going?

I waited in my car and noticed Acer leaving the bakery. He jumped into an old, banged-up car. I followed him all the way to downtown Newark. He parked near a male strip club called *Dante's Inferno*. I wondered if he was a waiter or a stripper.

I changed my top in the car to show off my new pair of 36D's. The last time Acer had fondled my *tetas* was in the hospital, and they were 36A's.

Dante's Inferno was pretty sleazy and full of drunken women of every age and walk of life. It was a sad place, smelling of disappointment, desperation, and frustration.

Acer was chatting with the other male strippers. It sounded like his English was much better, although he still had a heavy accent. The stripper boys had on beach robes and dark shades, ready for their first dance. I caught Acer's eye and gestured for him to come over. He didn't seem to recognize me. Then I looked him up and down and said, "Que Rico," and winked. I knew the name of his dream restaurant would get his attention.

He was speechless, then burst into tears when he recognized

me. One of his fellow dancers shouted, "Yo, Acer, stop ballin', pussy, and get yo ass over here."

Acer wiped away his tears on the sleeve of his beach robe and headed to the stage.

"*Hablamos, después,*" he said and hugged me.

I wondered what he wanted to talk about after the show.

Acer, with his muscular, tanned body, was the best dancer and seemed to get the most tips. The women threw themselves at the strippers. None of it excited me. I was horrified when a naked, young man, only wearing a dick sock, tried to pull me towards him on stage. Gross. *Que asco!*

Acer and I hooked up later that night and went to my apartment.

"I thought I had lost you, forever," he said as he fondled me in bed.

"I said I would find you when I got my new pair," I said, flashing my *teta*s and then reaching for his erect *pito*.

We spent an entire weekend together, although he had to return to bake bread at three a.m. Without even discussing it, Acer moved in little by little. He had been renting a room at his cousin's house, and my bed was welcoming for him. I had no objections to daily sexcapades with the virile, young Dominican. I didn't bother asking if he had a girlfriend. I assumed whomever he was involved with wasn't a route to a green card, which I knew he wanted since Miami.

In the meantime, I had launched my website, CasaDalia.com, that sold potions for healing. I included a personal mantra with each order. I recycled online mantras from other healers. This was not a big moneymaker, so I needed another vehicle to make serious cash.

Acer was still dreaming of opening his *Que Rico* restaurant, serving Dominican fusion food, although he still hadn't figured out what the "fusion" would be. It just sounded cool to him. I decided to use the $2 million I received from the government settlement to start the business. I would practice the money-laundering skills I had learned from the experts and the feds, using the *Que Rico* restaurant under Acer's name.

I called Deputy Blom for guidance on getting a green card for Acer through marriage.

In reality, I wanted to see if I could make Blom jealous. I had prepared a fake, heartfelt story about our lengthy love affair. When Blom found out Acer was thirteen years younger, he sounded skeptical. I later learned he was sixteen years younger. Acer was only seventeen when we met in Miami. Jailbait.

"On paper, Dalia, it looks like a green card scam. It may not pass the smell test. Are you sure about this?" Blom asked.

"I'm very sure. Listen here, Papi, this is probably my only chance. I'm damaged goods on all levels," I noted.

"Not true. You're still the same radiant and bewitching woman I scooped up from Casa Iris in Miami," Blom said.

"But I failed to bewitch you," I noted.

"Does this Acer Flores know about your past?" Blom asked.

"He only knows me as Dalia Shaw," I replied.

I was tempted to say Acer wasn't that bright, only hot and sturdy. This was a marriage of convenience with a lot of sex benefits. If I was going to die young, I might as well get banged nightly by a twenty-year-old and use him as a front to make money.

Blom said he would look into the green card. He wasn't thrilled about me getting married. It complicated my relocation and witness protection program. But Blom would give me a pass, given my circumstances.

"You deserve some happiness, even if you're in cougar territory and may get your heart broken by this boy," Blom warned. That was so sweet.

Days later, we had a private marriage ceremony with Acer's New Jersey family. I also invited my housekeeper and told her to say she was a cousin. Acer's family was suspicious that I had no immediate family present at the wedding. But they were grateful I was getting their nephew a green card and overlooked the age difference.

When I handed his aunt and uncle a fat check for the bakery, they kissed my hands and referred to me as *"la Santa Dalia."* If they only knew how far I was from sainthood. I married Acer so that the business was in his name only and he could not testify against me if I ever got caught.

Acer and I had a weekend honeymoon in Atlantic City, and we never left the room.

Acer was as virile and sexy as I remembered from our middle-of-the-night hospital booty calls.

The *Que Rico* restaurant opened as an extension of the Flores Bakery. The only fusion dish on the menu was Asian flavored sauces to dip the *tostones*. Otherwise, it was pure *comida del Caribe*: all dishes with rice, beans, and plantains.

The restaurant became popular, and the money was rolling into Acer's bank account.

His gratitude was abundant in and out of the bedroom. He enjoyed buying me clothes, shoes, and accessories. He had great taste for a bakery boy with little education.

Although Acer stopped stripping, lady fans from the club followed him to *Que Rico*. They would flirt with Acer and the hot, stripper boys he hired as waiters. They would stop flirting with the men when they saw me enter, looking judgmental. I got the reputation as the bitch wife.

I did the books and told Acer to handle the kitchen and front of house. We were turning a profit, but I was ambitious. I was ready to start money laundering.

Out of nowhere, I received a letter through the US marshal secret postal service from my now-ex-father-in-law, Papi Ortega.

He was still somewhere in protective custody with his Peruvian *puta*. The return address and his location were blacked out. Papi O.'s letters were always full of apologies and hoping he could make up for destroying my life. In this letter and a subsequent series of letters, Papi O. suggested restaurants and bars within a fifty-mile radius of my New Jersey apartment. I was surprised he knew where I was. I paid no attention to these restaurant suggestions until it hit me. Maybe this was a code of some kind, so I started visiting these bars and restaurants.

Each time I would locate the owner of the bar or restaurant, I mentioned my father-in-law sent me, without using his name. Some didn't react, but others would sit me down for an informal chat. It wasn't long before I was able to assemble a network of businesses that wanted me to launder money. I never asked why they needed my services. DADT. Don't ask, don't tell.

Just as I was underway with washing money through our Union City restaurant, the US marshals forwarded a letter from my stepfather, Moss. He was supposedly in India, but I couldn't tell where the letter came from. In his note, Moss recommended an Indian restaurant and told me to make sure I attended the upcoming *Diwali* festival.

The Indian restaurant, Lotus Room, was in midtown Manhattan. I did visit on the first day of *Diwali*. There was a very fat Moss sitting in the corner, surrounded by a pack of Indian bros. Moss was almost unrecognizable. He had obviously spent several years doing nothing but eating. He also had an air of importance. How did he find me? No one was supposed to know where I was or my new name.

"Uncle Moss!" I said to cover up the identity of my stepfather. He played along.

"Yes, my lovely niece, Dalia. Your uncle Moss is very disenchanted with India after so many failed business ventures," he informed me.

"So, you're broke?" I asked.

"A bird was chanting in my ear that you needed my help," Moss said.

"Help with what?" I inquired.

Moss had worked as an accountant in a county treasury office. I was not sure how he could help me now. Then I remembered what Deputy Blom said the day they picked me up at Casa Iris. Moss had connections with both my father and my father-in-law, and they wanted him to testify and enter protective custody.

"How were you involved with the Colombian narcos?" I asked.

"How do you think I supported your mother all those years? My civil servant job paid so little. I learned a few tricks, using the money the Colombians sent your mother.

Creative accounting," Moss responded.

"What have you been up to, UNCLE Moss, for the past five years?" I asked.

"A little of this, a little of that. Mostly trying to help the Sai Baba Center to rehabilitate Baba's image after that most horrific and untrue scandal. I tried my best and followed Baba's teachings; whatever you undertake, do it thoroughly or not at all," Moss said.

I thought Moss had dropped Baba, but I was wrong. He still seemed smitten with the now-dead guru.

"How would you help me, Uncle?" I asked playfully.

"A bit here and there. I can help manage your husband," Moss suggested.

"He knows nothing about the finances, and let's keep it that way," I informed him. I could use Moss as a right-hand man. We had not yet set up the full-scale money laundering, and I was far from my goal. I wanted much more.

Moss didn't want a big cut. But I felt grateful for his tender care of my dying *mami*, Azalea, so I offered him a higher percentage than he asked for.

"Too much. We're still family, and I know what you've been through," he said, touching my arm.

I had no idea what he knew. It was all supposed to be secret according to the US marshals.

I invited Moss to visit *Que Rico* so he could meet Acer. Moss and Acer hit it off and developed an odd relationship: sometimes, master and servant, and other times, guru and disciple. Acer loved all of Moss's Indian expressions and especially the Sai Baba lore. If Moss thought Acer was misbehaving, being obnoxious, or not doing his job as a restaurant manager, he would refer to him as "Dominican."

"Customers waiting too long for food, Dominican. That Cuban cook, slacking off," Moss announced.

"*Si, si*, Moss, I fix," Acer would say and then scurry into the kitchen.

Other times, Moss acted like a valet by picking up Acer's dry cleaning or getting his sports car serviced. Moss knew Acer could be a loose cannon and should be controlled. I bought a two-family house near *Que Rico* so Moss could monitor Acer.

We lived in the first-floor apartment, and Moss lived upstairs.

We kept Acer happy with a fat bank account, a fancy car, and designer clothes. We even rented an apartment in Manhattan's Chelsea neighborhood so we could enjoy the nightlife on the weekends. Acer was hanging out with a fast crowd, but I stayed away. I warned him not to have any drugs in the house and to keep any police away from our door. He agreed, but I was not sure if he would comply. The doormen mentioned "people" coming to visit Acer, so I installed surveillance cameras. At some point, someone had tampered with the cameras, and they were not working.

What I didn't know at the time was that Moss and Acer had started an escort service. They were pimping out the hot *Que Rico* waiters. I ignored the rumors that Acer was fooling around. Our sex life was always good, but he stayed out late. Many times, he talked in whispers on his mobile in the bathroom.

Moss was his "handler," and must know his secrets. One day, I asked him, "Is my husband cheating on me?"

"He's a flirtatious type, but don't think anything serious," Moss said, adding, "As my stepdaughter, I could have matched you up with an Indian doctor, lawyer, or tech billionaire. But you were in love with that artist and his family. All trouble."

I had forgotten that Moss tried to convince my mother to take me to an Indian matchmaker when I was seventeen. At the time, I was horrified and threatened suicide.

Acer started spending more time in the city at our apartment and leaving me to manage the restaurant. I surprised him on a weekday evening and found our apartment crawling with people who were clearly undesirables, *desgraciados.* The coffee table was covered in white powder, and there was no sign of Acer. I headed to the bedroom and opened the door. There was Acer, pumping away on top of another MAN while another man watched and masturbated. A fourth one was watching while shaking his *pito* that was pitifully limp. I was horrified but maintained my cool.

Acer was so involved in his sex act that he didn't even notice I was standing in the doorway. The masturbating man did see me just as he ejaculated on my designer duvet. I walked over and said, "Tell Acer his wife is here." The man didn't seem to know who Acer was, so I pointed.

"The man on top is my husband," I announced and walked out of the room.

I proceeded to throw all the partygoers out of my apartment by first whistling and then screaming, "Cops on their way," then repeating "*policía*" in case there were non-English speakers in the room.

My announcement cleared the place within minutes. I made some young girl, who looked like jailbait, clean all the white powder from the tabletops and empty the ashtrays. I also told her to gather the empty bottles and place them in the recycling bin.

I watched the young woman clean while I sat in a chair, tapping my high heel. I recalled that Acer had bought me these designer shoes. Was that a red flag he might be queer? I always took him for a metrosexual, obsessed with clothes and grooming.

As Acer and his boy ménage finished their business, I heard one of them comment, "How did she find out? I cut the wires to the camera."

The partygoers left, and it was just Acer and me. He broke down crying. My heel tapping helped me gather my thoughts and create my plan of action. The first item in the plan was that under no circumstances would I allow Acer to put his *pito* in me ever again. I would make him get tested for STDs. I probably wouldn't divorce him, as I wasn't finished using him as a front. There was also the question of him testifying against me if I was ever prosecuted.

Acer said he loved me and would never do anything to hurt me. Then he paced around the living room, complaining about the treatment of gays in the Dominican Republic. I didn't even pay attention when he told me the tortured story of suppressing his love of men. I just wanted to figure out how to deal with a homosexual husband who was also the front man of my lucrative money-laundering business. I said nothing for ten minutes and surprised myself about how calm I was.

"Say something, *coño,*" Acer insisted.

"I'm not angry. I am disgusted," I said.

Acer threw himself into my arms. I pushed him away.

"*Por favor, mi amor. Te amo tanto,*" he pleaded and sounded like phony telenovela dialogue.

"You can't help it if you like men. But no more orgies or drug fests, and no more playhouse. Canceling the lease on this place," I announced.

"Yes, OK. Stay home in New Jersey with my Dalia and be calm," Acer said.

"We will have separate bedrooms, and when the time is right, I'll move."

The words came out of my mouth involuntarily. *Good idea, moving out,* I thought. In reality, I was angrier at Moss than at Acer. It was Moss's job to keep Acer in line.

On the car ride back to New Jersey, I realized no man had ever truly loved me. I was going to have to find emotional satisfaction somewhere else.

When I arrived at *Que Rico,* I found Moss alone in the back, doing the books and counting all the money we laundered that week. Moss was snacking on leftover empanadas.

"Almost as good as our samosas," Moss said, then stopped when he saw my angry face.

"Acer has boyfriends," I commented.

"No, but he likes girls too. He's crazy about you," Moss said.

"I'm like a big sister or a mother to him. From now on, limit his allowance and track all his spending," I told him.

"So sorry, no idea that Dominican was into buggery. My God, the shame."

"Forget it. I'm working on Casa Dalia. You're in charge, so figure out how much more you want to run the business."

Moss held my hands and was in tears.

"I don't want more, dear. In fact, I'm lowering my share for the embarrassment, to make up for my failures." Moss became emotional and fell into my arms. Why did Moss feel that Acer's "buggery" was his fault?

In processing the Acer incident, I compared it to losing my business and my identity, being forced into witness protection, and having cancer and a double mastectomy.

Finding out my young, dumb husband liked boys was fairly low on my panic scale.

My gut told me to step away from the business and leave dreary New Jersey. I changed the ownership of the restaurant and the two-family house from Acer's name to Rico Enterprises. At the time, I didn't realize "RICO" was also the name for the US racketeering act. I was not sure our crimes fell into any categories of the RICO Act. We weren't killing people, only washing the money for people who probably killed.

I gave Moss temporary power of attorney for Rico Enterprises under his new name, Moss Oliver, which he changed from his birth name, Bakul Indukamal Moshayan.

I didn't want Blom or the US marshals to track me down. Not only was I in violation of the WITSEC contract, I could be exited from the witness protection program and/or arrested for new crimes.

My former self, Iris, was a good *santera* but a subservient and naïve girl. On the other hand, Dalia was a badass, street-smart woman with millions in the bank. Anything and everything felt possible.

CHAPTER TWENTY-THREE

BILBERRY LANE

What a relief that the visit to family Shaw was semi-successful and I prevented my mother Daisy from seducing my boyfriend, Olmo. By the next morning, the Dalia mourners were at it again and already at the gate clamoring to worship the tree.

I had put off Rosita and Sage for weeks about their picnic for another Dalia memorial event. After they arrived with all their picnic shit, things got out of control real fast. I ran outside and was appalled at the scene.

"What the fuck is on your face?" I asked with alarm in my voice as I approached the olive tree.

"It's a mud mask, made from dirt around Dalia's tree. It has special magical properties," Rosita said, bragging.

"You were supposed to be having a picnic, not a mud bath," I shouted.

Should I tell them 1) Dalia was no longer "in the house," and 2) the magical mud was soaked with her ex-husband Romero's piss?

"That ground and the tree are sacred. Dalia is sacred," Rosita said.

"Neighborhood dogs have been doing their business, and for all I know, the gardener has also. Suggest you stop what you're doing," I pleaded.

The Dalia devotees ignored me and took pics of themselves with mud masks, posing by the tree. They posted on the Facebook page and the WhatsApp Dalia group. There was a "Love" posting from a "Jasmin," followed by a comment, "OMG, when can I join you?" Some fans asked if they could come right over and participate. Others were in town for the six-month death anniversary party that would take place the next day.

"Could we do mud masks during the party?" Rosita yelled across the yard. I just scowled and ignored her. Eventually, Rosita and her mud-faced gang left, but only after they messed up my bathroom.

The next morning at ten a.m., I heard the chaos. I looked at the gate camera. Sage spilled out of a van with a group of saffron-robed monks. I could see her and Mu Jin helping Sage unload supplies.

While the monks arranged themselves around the tree, a seven-tiered cake by a Malibu surfer bakery dude arrived. On top of the cake was a plastic angel ascending to heaven. It was rumored it was a wedding cake for a couple that called it off at the last minute. For a discount, the surfer baker offered to repurpose it for a death anniversary. The other rumor was the bride was banging the surfer baker. The groom found out and called off the wedding.

Lily and her friend, Ginger, the social media maven, had decorated the yard earlier that morning. Ginger was an older woman, definitely an XL or maybe an XXL. In keeping with her name, she had a red-haired bob, and was wearing a muumuu. Lily emerged from the pathway, followed by Sage and her gender-fluid Buddhist monks. One was carrying a bamboo flute and another a set of singing bowls. It appeared this event would not be as noisy as the drum circle present for the Dalia birthday celebration.

As soon as Ginger saw Sage, she lunged at her.

"Sage! You were blocked and banned from the Dalia channel. What are you doing here, psycho?" Ginger shouted.

"I changed my profile, bitch! Get a grip," Sage shouted back. Ginger took her phone from her muumuu's pocket and did a search.

"Who the hell are you now, crazy girl?" Ginger asked.

"You'll never find me, old hag. My avatar is too cool," Sage responded.

One of the monks approached the bickering women. The monk tried to take Sage's hand and join it with Ginger's, but she pushed the monk away. Another monk approached and made a peace gesture. Ginger ignored them both.

"Who are these freaks?" Ginger asked angrily. Lily intervened and tried to calm Ginger down.

Sage stood on a bench with her hands on her hips and shouted, "These are holy people paid by ME. They will pray for Dalia's soul and cleanse the burial site after that nasty man desecrated it with his bodily fluids."

"What's she talking about?" Lily asked me.

"Romero, the ex-husband, peed all over the grave," I whispered in Lily's ear.

"But she's not there anymore, so it really doesn't matter," Lily said.

"Go ahead and tell these people that her remains are MIA and in the hands of the government marshals," I said.

Lily shushed me and noticed that the crime scene tape was rolled around a branch of the olive tree. She gestured to me, and I removed it. I would play along with the circus one last time. But I was determined to quit this Dalia addiction.

Ginger surveyed the yard with a group of Dalia fans sitting cross-legged in the lotus position. They formed a circle on the ground surrounding the tree and meditated with the singing bowls. Ginger interrupted the meditative music.

"Lily, I need a photo op with just mourners. Eighty-six these robed dudes," Ginger announced.

"Chill, babe. What's eighty-six?" Lily said. Ginger gestured to get rid of them.

Millennial or Gen Z, Lily, was unfamiliar with the old-school term 'eighty-six.' Ginger was showing off her advanced age. Lily eighty-sixed Ginger to the main house.

The singing bowls were hypnotic and so goddamn spiritual. I was transported to Tibet or wherever the hell these monk people came from.

I was suddenly compelled to run into the guesthouse closet. I was drawn to one of Dalia's shawls that she wore in her videos. I also put on her floppy hat and her sunglasses. Already I was being enticed back into the Dalia world. I needed serious therapy.

When I returned to the yard, the circle was bigger. Lily had left the gate open so anyone could come in and join the bizarre ceremony. Even the neighbors appeared.

I sat down in the circle. Sage crawled over to me and caressed the shawl. "One of hers?" Sage asked. I nodded.

One by one, the Dalia fanatics crawled on their knees toward me and touched the shawl. It reminded me of the pilgrims who crawl on their knees at Our Lady of Guadalupe in Mexico. It felt empowering to be worshipped. The Dalia partygoers took their turns to touch or kiss the shawl. It was the opposite of being cyberbullied over pastel foods.

I was deep in a trance and could see the Himalayas. I could hear the sound of the wind until someone tapped my shoulder.

It was Deputy Blom. I was so startled, I nearly fell back, but he caught me. His arms felt reassuring. For a moment, I forgot he was the law and invited him to sit in the circle. Blom gestured to follow him to the guesthouse and helped me stand.

Ginger appeared and stood leering at Deputy Blom. Lily, who was sitting at the other end of the circle, flashed me a "Who dat?" look. The two *buttinskies*, Ginger and Lily, followed. We left the Dalia fans, the chanting, the singing bowls, and the monks behind us.

Blom looked more serious than I had ever seen him. I introduced US Marshal Layton Blom to Ginger and Lily. Ginger hovered around Blom like a bitch in heat. She presented herself to Blom as "the Dalia expert" and guardian of the dead woman's online social media presence. Blom paid no attention to Ginger and told everyone to sit down. Blom stood in front of us as if giving a lecture. He paced and spoke as he glanced at the Dalia sketch.

"This is a bizarre and unhealthy worship of this woman you know as Dalia. It's well beyond a girl crush. You've created a cult!" Blom shouted.

I was certain he was talking only to me, so I piped up in my own defense.

"Not my fault. I knew nothing about this Dalia until I met Lily and she offered me the guesthouse. She made me organize this circus around the burial site. I just got dragged into the cult, then the clothes, and her voice. I'd admit I'm unhinged and need therapy," I said, getting emotional. Lily patted me on the back and then chimed in.

"I have my personal reasons for worshipping this woman. She overcame multiple emotional and physical calamities with courage and grace," Lily responded with eloquence.

I added tearfully, "She was everything I'm not. She was even prettier and sexier than me."

Ginger looked like she was going to explode. She jumped up and faced Blom up close. Her initial physical attraction to Blom turned into rage.

"Who the hell are you to tell us what to think and feel about this fabulous force of life?" Ginger exclaimed.

Blom paced around the room.

"I SO hate California. In my town, we'd put you all on meds and in straight-jackets. The bureau ought to have a separate manual for California." He complained.

"Everyone just calm down and listen to the deputy. He's here for a reason." I said hoping to score points with the feds.

"Thank you, Poppy. In my capacity as a US marshal, I have been dealing with Dalia and her crime family for over a decade. I was the shoulder she cried on when she lost her business and her boobs. I consoled her when her husband cheated on her. Who did she want at her hospital bedside? Me. Who did she ask to choose her new implants? Me! I protected, cajoled, reasoned with her to stay out of danger. Now it looks like she betrayed me. I mean the US government. She's no saint," Blom said as he paced the room.

There was a silence until Lily spoke up. "It was only cult like after she died."

Blom suggested Ginger leave as he had urgent business with Lily and me.

"Lily, better call your mother in too. Miss Ginger, would you mind waiting outside?" Blom asked.

"Yes, I do mind. I'm the caretaker of Dalia's image, dead or alive. Besides, I own the Casa Dalia domain and the YouTube channel."

"Since when, bitch," Lily remarked and texted, presumably Mu Jin, to get her ass down to the guesthouse.

Ginger then fiddled with her tablet. She set up a video.

"I came here to show Lily this lost-and-found Dalia video. Y'all might as well watch," Ginger announced and hit play.

Mu Jin had slipped into the room just as the Dalia video started. We heard that raspy voice from the later videos when she was ill.

"I hope I brought you all some joy, peace, and healing. This is my last video, and don't worry about me. I am in a beautiful and tranquil place with my dear sister, Lily. I wish you all good health

and happiness."

Dalia ended the video with her signature sign-off, crossing her heart and offering, *"Y siempre con mucho mucho amor."*

"WTF. You're sisters?" I screamed and turned to Lily, who turned bright red.

"Now we're going to play Who's My Daddy?" Blom said to Lily and then turned to Ginger.

"Whatever Dalia paid you, darling, it was probably with laundered money, so you'll need to pay it back," Blom warned.

Ginger grabbed her tablet and hurried out of the guesthouse. As she exited, she said, "I'm history. But you're one hot deputy."

Blom chuckled.

As Ginger left, we heard her shouting, "Party over, go the fuck home," and the sound of disgruntled Dalia mourners packing up their shit.

I was speechless and still floored by the revelation that Lily and Dalia were sisters.

Lily wanting to keep her sister spiritually alive made sense. Blom motioned for Lily and Mu Jin to sit on the sofa. Then he sat in a chair. I brought out the vodka and gestured to ask if he wanted a shot. He shook his head and approached Mu Jin.

"This must be Dr. Mu Jin Ju, mother of Lily? And who is her papa?" Blom asked.

Lily perked up and said, "Eneldo Espinoza."

I noticed Mu Jin didn't respond.

"America's most wanted," Blom informed us.

"He bad man," Mu Jin said.

"Whom are you talking about?" I asked.

"Eneldo was Dalia's father, or I should say Iris's father, who evaded capture by the DEA in Miami. But we have reports of him in Colombia and Cuba," Blom informed me.

Mu Jin stood up, waving her fist.

"Yes, get him, he do bad things for Fidel," Mu Jin reported.

"And you, Doctor, have also done bad things and have been on the CIA's radar," Blom quipped.

"I knew it," Lily muttered.

"Prove it!" Mu Jin shouted at Blom.

Mu Jin was on the CIA's radar? Just when I thought I couldn't take any more, there came a new info bomb.

"Who do you think owns this property?" Blom asked. Mu Jin perked up.

"Lily now own. Right?" Mu Jin asked and turned to Lily, who did not respond. Blom made the buzzer sound in a game show for a wrong answer.

"Dalia signed over the entire property, main and guesthouse, at 1611 Bilberry Lane, Topanga Canyon, to Poppy Shaw," Blom read from a document.

"WTF. That can't be possible," I said, then did a Poppy pause and looked at Lily. "So why does Poppy pay rent to live in her own house?" I asked in the third person. Lily did not react.

"Dalia, she owe us, big time. We take care of her. She promised the house to Lily. *Ai yah!*" Mu Jin shouted, following up with a swirl of Cantonese that sounded nasty.

"Relax, Ma," Lily said.

Lily seemed to take the information that she did not own the house in stride. "Don't get too comfortable, Poppy. The government could seize assets if they were bought with drug money. You could also be implicated in money laundering," Blom said.

"Are you fucking crazy? I did nothing except move into this place, play cemetery gatekeeper, and wear that woman's clothes, sometimes," I said.

"Interesting. Why would Iris Ortega pick Dalia Shaw as her new identity?" Blom asked.

"Lily? Mu Jin?" I asked and looked at the women, who had blank expressions.

"You ladies could all be in *mucho* trouble," Blom informed us, adding, "Let's take this from the top. Lily, you first."

"Dalia and I stalked Poppy for months online. I was finally able to meet Poppy through an acting workshop. Dalia felt she owed you. She thought you were super talented," Lily said.

"She did?" I asked in shock.

"She wanted you to be successful," Lily noted.

"Successful? WTF. She almost drove me to street drugs," I said angrily.

"Why did she owe Poppy? Is she also a relative?" Blom asked.

"No fucking idea, Deputy. Dalia just said, 'Poppy saved my life,' with no details," Lily replied.

"Dalia came to Topanga. She was so happy, then got sick. We help her," Mu Jin added.

"She was trying to heal herself with her own potions. She said there was an experimental treatment in Miami. I wanted to go with her, but she said no," Lily said tearfully.

Blom handed Lily a legal pad.

"Write down the names of all those crazy people who visit

the tree and when you last heard from her and the date when you last saw her alive," Blom instructed.

"It was a rainy day. Dalia left with some Indian. Look like that man you spend the night with, Poppy," Mu Jin noted. Blom looked at me.

Busted for screwing around, but she got the wrong guy. "That was an Uber driver," I clarified.

"A few weeks after Dalia left with her dog, Dill, an urn arrived with instructions to bury her near the guesthouse under the olive tree. There was a note. 'Let my people visit, Love, Dalia,' along with a fat check," Lily said.

"So, neither of you saw her after that?" Blom asked. The women shook their heads.

I contained my anger. I was paying rent on my own property, and Lily was getting paid for the mourner madness. Lily could see me seething and looked at me.

"I didn't know, Poppy. I assumed it was my house or her husband, Acer's," Lily said.

"We need Acer to answer some questions. Has he been here?" Blom said.

This time, I thought it best to fess up just to knowing the dude, not to having fucked him.

"Yes, Acer has been here," I said meekly.

"Ask him to come over as you need to speak to him about Dalia's assets," Blom instructed me.

"I can text him," I offered, not wanting to mention he had ghosted me. If I mentioned money, maybe he'd surface.

"Let me know when Acer will be here. In any case, ladies,

please stay nearby and shut down the circus outside," Blom demanded.

After Blom left, Lily informed me we were not shutting down the Dalia circus. Neither she nor Mu Jin acknowledged that they were living in MY house. I could charge them rent. They returned to the main house as if it were business as usual.

I sat for days in a stupor. I had to do my "I am not confused" mantra repeatedly.

If Dalia wanted me to be successful, why would she throw me into being a suspected criminal? Made no damn sense unless she did it on purpose.

I needed peace, but the Dalia mourners never slept. There were requests to visit from fans who missed the death celebration. The Facebook live event with the monks, singing bowls, and chanting didn't satiate their Dalia appetites.

I was determined to shut it all down and follow Blom's orders. It was my property.

Fuck Lily.

I replaced the crime scene tape around the tree. I dug a hole and took photos. I posted them with the message, "Dalia MIA. Nothing to worship. It's over, dudes, deal with it!"

There was a barrage of sad-face and angry emojis, and lots of WTFs and calling me a cold bitch. Too fucking bad. I was so done. It was high time to get rid of the Dalia addiction. I created a new mantra.

"I will be successful with or without your clothes."

#homeowner #monks #chant #singingbowl #hotginger #done

CHAPTER TWENTY-FOUR

—

DOGGIE DILL

After Deputy Blom's visit, I needed intense therapy. But who could I tell about this crap? And would believe me and who would think I was insane?

I was temporally distracted with an invitation to audition. I went wearing my own fucking clothes. It was a test. If I got the part, I had broken the Dalia spell. It meant I was no longer obsessed or possessed. I had started to believe that her clothes had magic powers.

Olmo drove me to the audition in Santa Monica after our lunch date. He ran lines with me at the table. It was for a recurring character in a sci-fi, TV pilot called *Hotel Lilac*.

Olmo was such a great acting coach and a great fuck buddy. I knew he still wanted more, but I was not there yet. Not even close. That awkward business at my parents' house with my mom, Daisy—he didn't even try to fight her off. Red flag?

I was apprehensive about the upcoming audition. Was I getting another crack at the "role of a lifetime" that Fig the Frog had predicted? I was rather quiet on the ride down to the studio for the audition, and Olmo noticed.

"What's goin' on, hon? Nervous?" Olmo asked.

"Stuff went down with that Dalia business. Long story. Can we talk about something else?" I answered.

"OK. But get that dead woman out of your mind so you don't blow the audition," Olmo said.

"It's all so ridiculous. We should write the screenplay. A dramedy, no, a tragedy. How an innocent actress gets dragged into a crime vortex by a dead woman. Narcos, US marshals, CIA, witness protection, sugar mamas, laundered drug money, and ..." I stopped short of the Bilberry Lane property ownership revelation.

"Whoa, Nellie. Back up," Olmo commented.

"Deputy Blom's last visit revealed it's even more fucked up than I thought. Picture all the crime shows and *telenovelas* rolled into one ball of shit, with me in the middle. I won't let it ruin my mojo for the audition," I said defiantly.

"Copy that," Olmo said and saluted.

We parked in front of the studio, and Olmo hugged me. "You know, hon, I'm here for you anytime, anywhere."

Olmo was a great guy, and I wondered if he could again be considered a Mr. Right.

The day after the audition was my meeting with Acer. He had ghosted me since the time I left the Bloom Room. Deputy Blom asked me to also invite Dalia's ex, Romero. Not sure why the US marshal wanted a Dalia husband-club gathering. I just hoped these Latin lotharios would help clear my name.

I had texted both husbands, and they agreed to meet at the guesthouse. I didn't even know if they knew about each other. Could be fireworks.

I told Lily and Mu Jin to lie low. I felt empowered by the fact that I owned the house, at least for now. If I were a true bitch, I would have thrown their asses off my property.

Acer arrived first. I hadn't seen him since our sexcapade. I met Acer at the gate, and he kissed me on both cheeks. There was no explanation of why he had ghosted me.

As we reached the yard, Acer noticed the crime scene tape and the empty hole. I told him a US marshal removed the urn. Acer asked if it was a black guy and told me he had heard about him.

"Dalia liked him a lot. I always wondered if they were fucking." Acer seemed morose and not his usual perky self.

"Are you staying at the Marigold Hotel?" I asked.

"Camellia and Juniper's sofa. My credit cards are frozen." Acer was busted out.

The gate buzzed, and I could see Romero through the camera. I let him in and decided it was a good idea to warn Acer.

"Do you know Romero Robles? Dalia's ex?" I asked.

Acer flashed me a look of angst as Romero appeared on the walkway. He headed to the olive tree and chuckled at the crime scene tape.

"Was that because of what I did?" Romero asked, and I responded by introducing the men.

"Romero, this is Acer Flores."

They looked at each other without talking, then did a light

fist bump.

I thought that was a good sign until they started talking, then arguing in Spanish.

"*Me robaste mi dinero con tu restaurante, maricón cabrón,*" Romero shouted.

He rhymed insults. Cool.

It sounded like Romero was accusing Acer of stealing his money to open the restaurant. This accusation was met with Acer calling Romero "*hijo de puta,*" for abandoning his wife in her time of need. Then he added that Romero had treated her badly.

"*Nunca la trataste bien.*" Acer announced.

"*Come mierda, maricón!*" Romero responded.

Was that comment, "Eat shit, queer," just a general Cuban insult, or did Romero think Acer was gay? That was enough Latino boy fight, although the dialogue was better than the usual *telenovela.* I had a Poppy pause, raised my hand, and took control.

"Let's go inside, guys. I think we all need a drink."

As soon as we entered the guesthouse, Romero went straight to the framed Iris/Dalia sketch and removed it from the wall.

"I'm taking this," Romero announced.

"Don't think so, *cabrón,*" Acer said. Then they argued in Spanish again, and I whistled to make them stop. I grabbed the sketch from Romero.

"Sit the fuck down. Time out. Can I speak?" I shouted.

"Yeah, why are we both here?" Acer asked.

"I think we've all been played by Dalia. Deputy Blom will explain," I announced. The gate buzzed, and I could see Blom in the camera. There were several cars and men in dark suits. Shit.

Did that mean we were all getting hauled off?

"What does that dude want from us? Can only be bad. *Carajo,*" Romero commented.

"*Quien es, mano?*" Acer asked Romero who Blom was.

"*Un negrito del gobierno, compa.* Haven't seen or heard from that guy for years. He destroyed my life and sent me to die in the desert, *hijo de puta,*" Romero said.

I felt compelled to politically correct Romero's statement and refer to Deputy Blom as an African American US marshal. It seemed that things had calmed down between the men. Romero called Acer "*compa,*" short for "friend," and Acer used "*mano,*" which meant "bro."

I was still worried about the suits and cars outside waiting to grab us. But I held it together and didn't crave vodka.

Blom knocked lightly on the door and entered. Romero seemed to change his tune and hugged Blom.

"Good to see you, bro. Been a while," Romero said in a friendly tone.

"Lookin' good, man," Blom said, giving Romero the once-over.

"Workin' with what I've got," Romero said.

"This must be Acer Flores," Blom said as he shook Acer's hand.

"Why are we here, señor?" Acer asked Blom.

Blom gestured for us to sit. He opened his leather satchel and pulled out documents and a small recording device.

"Let's start from the beginning, how each of you met Dalia and each other. In Romero's case, I know they were married, but not sure how Acer and Poppy met her."

"Hey man. I told you I only met Acer and Romero when I moved here," I said.

"I met Dalia, who was registered in the hospital as Azalea Espinoza. She was so lonely," Acer reported with a sly grin.

"That was her mother's name the marshals used for cover," Romero chimed in.

"She had cancer, and they were going to cut her . . . you know. *Tetas*. Both!" Acer said, motioning towards his chest.

This was news to me that Dalia had a double mastectomy.

"So, you hooked up with my wife in the hospital?" Romero asked.

"Amigos only! I knew in my heart, we would find each other again someday. She found me in New Jersey almost two years later," Acer informed him.

"When did you meet Poppy?" Blom asked Acer.

"Here in this house, after my wife died. She was in charge of the Facebook group," Acer replied.

I was so glad Acer left out our fuck fest. Phew.

"Many *locos* in that WhatsApp group. That Sage. *Dios mio*," Romero chimed in, remembering the Sage meltdown after he pissed on Dalia's grave.

Blom held up an eight-by-ten photo of an orderly in a white lab coat, pushing a bed down a hospital hallway.

"This must be you, Acer, rolling a bed down the hallway at Jackson hospital after Dalia's surgery. That was when we lost track of her," Blom noted.

Acer sheepishly nodded.

"I heard one of your deputies said some *sospechosos* were

looking for Dalia. She was still drugged after they cut her *tetas*. Terrible."

"We heard a Colombian hit squad had breached the hospital entrance," Blom said. Romero laughed.

"Those Colombian *asasinos* were fake. It was ME. I called one of your deputies from the Happy Homestead pay phone. I pretended to be in the hospital," Romero informed him.

Blom was visibly furious.

"It was you who phoned in a death threat?" Blom asked.

"I said in a low, scary voice, '*Vamos a matar la tracionera*, we're going to kill the traitor Iris Ortega.' Your dude didn't understand me, so I repeated, 'Iris Ortega is about to get whacked,'" Romero said.

Blom shook his head and gestured with his hands.

"Don't wanna know anymore. If I open an investigation, I'll never retire, and you'll be drawing sketches in an orange jumpsuit, Romero," Blom warned.

"You need to hire better deputies who speak Spanish, especially in Miami, bro," Romero said.

"I switched the bracelet of this woman with Dalia's in the recovery area," Acer reported.

Blom handed me a hospital bracelet, and I read it. WTF. "My name!" I shouted.

Acer grabbed the bracelet and looked at it.

"It was you? I switched your bracelet with Dalia's?" Acer said, turning to me.

"I was in the hospital in 2010 having my colon redesigned at the same time Dalia had mastectomy?" I asked. Blom nodded.

"We actually loaded you on a chopper headed to D.C. They realized you were not Dalia, so they dumped you back at Jackson. Then we grabbed Dalia, who thankfully was still in recovery," Blom informed me.

"*Que desastre.* Romero calls in with a fake threat; I switch Poppy's bracelet with Dalia's. Then your deputies take Poppy on the chopper, thinking it's Dalia," Acer recalled.

"Wait! I remember someone fiddling with my hospital I.D. and a voice saying a Colombian was after me. Was that you, Blom?"

"One of my young boys who screwed up." Blom replied

"Did Dalia know this?" Romero asked laughing.

"She knew that someone switched her bracelet with Poppy's, which saved her life," Blom replied.

"After I wheeled Dalia back to recovery, the other woman, you, Poppy, was gone. I thought they had killed you," Acer noted.

Gee, thanks, Acer. At least I know I wasn't hallucinating. I feel so fucking vindicated.

"So, the whole 'Poppy and Acer saved my life' was *mierda*, bullshit," Romero remarked.

"That's why Dalia felt Poppy saved her life and signed over the house," Blom conjectured.

"You scored this house? And Acer and me, *NADA!*" Romero shouted.

"And this house, 1611, is the same number as the Jackson hospital. I know it because I used it as my address." Acer announced.

I got the chills.

"And you weren't in on this?" Blom asked me.

"I never heard of this place until Lily brought me here." I

replied.

"*Quien es Lily?*" Romero asked but no one replied.

"*Espera.* Maybe Dalia took the name Shaw in respect for Poppy," Acer proposed.

"I gave Dalia the bracelet before she went to New Jersey. Somehow, the bracelet ended up in the urn buried outside," Blom reported.

"With her ashes?" I asked.

"Not exactly. The ashes in the urn were tested, and they are animal ashes, not human. There was a dog chip tracker for Dill," Blom said.

"All this time, they were worshipping a dead dog," I commented.

"*Madre de Dios.* I pissed on a dog," Romero said.

"So where are Dalia's ashes?" Acer asked. Blom shrugged. I was numb. TMI, and I needed vodka.

Acer and Romero paced the room. They looked at each other and asked in unison, "*Esta viva? Esta viva?*"

Blom turned to me for a translation.

They were asking if she was alive. Blom just shrugged.

"Which brings us to the next mystery," Blom announced and showed Acer a document. "Do you recognize these transactions?"

Acer shook his head.

Blom informed Acer that his beloved *Que Rico* restaurant was a money-laundering operation set up by Dalia. She did business with an impressive roster of narcos, Russian mobsters, and old Mafia crime families. Acer swore he knew nothing and cried. Romero put his arm around Acer.

"The price for marrying, *una bruja impracable*," Romero said as he consoled Acer. He told him it was the price to pay for being married to a ruthless witch.

"She owes me. It was my idea to do the Walter Mercado thing to end her videos." Acer noted.

I outstretched my arms and imitated Dalia's voice. *"Y siempre con mucho mucho amor."*

"Yeah, *amor y mentiras!*" Romero countered with "love and lies."

Both men were now sobbing in each other's arms as they realized they were both Dalia victims. I couldn't believe I had been attracted to these men and even fucked one of them. I was absolutely disgusted with myself.

"I hate when men cry," Blom mused, and I concurred with him.

Lily then texted me frantically that Mu Jin was having a meltdown in the main house.

They could see from their window the men in suits at the gate. Freak out.

I excused myself and rushed over to the main house. I watched Mu Jin packing suitcases and Lily pacing the room.

"My mom thinks those guys outside are here to arrest her," Lily said.

"No. It's me and Acer they want," I informed her.

"No matter, no taking chances, going back to China," Mu Jin said as she wrapped her joss sticks in her granny panties.

"Those are flammable, don't pack them. Airport security will flag them," I warned.

"Ma, they aren't here for you. They would have come long ago after you sold those reports to your Chinese pals," Lily said.

I put my hands over my ears and did a "la, la, la."

"I've had it with everyone's life of crime. Lily, what shit did you do?" I asked.

"I'm clean, girl," Lily said with her hands raised.

"Here's a fun fact. The ashes in the urn you buried were her dog's and not Dalia's," I announced.

"Well, fuck me," Lily said.

"I hated that dog. We eat them in China," Mu Jin informed me. I left her to continue her frantic packing.

When I returned to the guesthouse, Romero was showing Blom and Acer his new artwork on his phone. He decided to leave his teaching job and return to Miami.

Romero was ready to risk exiting WITSEC and revert to being Cardoso Ortega. He had arranged a Miami comeback exhibition for the famed Cardoso Ortega, complete with a press conference. He invited Acer to be his gallery manager. One minute, these two dudes were at each other's throats, and now, they were BFFs.

"Not so fast, boys, Acer is facing possible jail time if they don't believe he was duped by Dalia. There's also the male escort service," Blom pointed out.

"It's all Moss. That Indian *hijo de puta*!" Acer shouted.

"Moss, her stepfather?" Romero asked.

"It was all Moss. He ran the business. It was his idea of renting my stripper friends to those old ladies," Acer said and added, "Moss sent me here to Los Angeles. He told me to be nice to Poppy as she was getting money from Dalia. She could be a future wife."

"So Poppy was going to be your new sugar mama?" Blom asked.

Not only was I furious, but also so goddamn lost and confused. Moss was Dalia's stepfather, and he encouraged Acer to woo me for money?

Acer informed me that Moss disappeared a few weeks ago. Just that morning, he found out that Moss was registered under another name at the Marigold Hotel in Malibu.

"I'm glad Moss is in town. To be continued, lady and gentlemen," Blom said as he packed up his documents and recorder.

I glanced at the gate camera and noticed Mu Jin wheeling two suitcases. Blom's phone buzzed, and he took the call. I heard him say, "Let the women go for now."

I walked Acer, Romero, and Blom back to the gate and wondered if any of us would be arrested. But the agents and cars were gone.

"I've arranged a safe house for you both," Blom informed Acer and Romero. Acer and Romero exchanged whispers in Spanish.

"OK, Blom. Feed us dinner and take us to a nice hotel. Better not be like that Happy Homestead, *cabrón*," Romero warned.

"You've earned a five-star meal and hotel, Romero Robles," Blom said, rolling the *r*'s, then added, "Poppy, I'll have agents outside your gate from now on. We think Moss is after you for money and the house." Blom beeped his car doors open. The three men piled into one car and drove away.

I really didn't feel like adding any more Post-it notes to the back of my closet. But I did anyway. "Stepdaddy Moss, Jackson switch, Happy Homestead, and Mu Jin escape to China. Doggie Dill, agents."

I needed to perform a grand gesture to flush the Dalia business out of my orbit. I went to the closet and bagged the rest of Dalia's clothing. Just as I finished stacking the bags, I had a text from the casting director with a callback for *Hotel Lilac*. I had worn all MY own clothes for the audition. Score!

I looked in the mirror, held up my hand for a Poppy pause, and said, "You can do this."

Then I called Goodwill for a pickup and while on hold I chanted, "Dalia, out of my orbit."

#switchees #chopper #boyfight #tetas #poppypause
#baddaddymoss #goodwill

Chapter Twenty-Five

TOPANGA

New Jersey is known as the Garden State. For me, it was all ugly homes, old buildings, potholes, traffic and pollution. Where the fuck were the gardens? I had been here too long and needed to get out. By 2016, I had been married to Acer for three years and had made him rich with a green card. Not bad for an undocumented Dominican who left school at fourteen.

After I caught him in the boy orgy, I made him sleep in the guest room permanently. It was sad to cease marital relations with the young stud. He had a purpose as a front for the money-laundering business. There was a huge advantage being married to a naïve, uneducated Dominican.

Moss did a good job keeping Acer happy with platinum credit cards. He didn't meddle in Acer's affairs unless he thought drugs were involved. I knew Acer was stripping for fun at *Dante's Inferno*. Our housekeeper often found dollar bills in Acer's underwear when she did the laundry.

I put my energies into CasaDalia.com. All I wanted to do

was heal and help people. I published articles on using natural healing and sold products. I repackaged remedies from the FlowerPower.com with a Casa Dalia label. The products were highly rated essential oils, bath balms, and lotions. I relabeled their blends and gave them titles like Eternal Love, Friend Zone, Money Honey, Mood Boost and Perfectly Potent. Every purchase included a bonus healing mantra. Occasionally, I would get asked to perform a spell, but that was through word of mouth with VIP clients.

I needed millennial help to grow the business. Lily! I had an occasional text from her, and she had been traveling. I was anxious to reconnect with her and considered her my half-sister. When we finally spoke, Lily was totally into my identity and my website and loved my new name, Dalia Flores. She screeched, "WTF," over the phone when I told her I was still married to the Dominican hospital attendant.

"Cougar slut!" she teased me and added, "Spill the tea. Is he still hot and horny?"

"I'd rather hear if you have any hot and horny in your life," I replied. I didn't dare tell her Acer was gay and I was sleeping alone.

Lily and Mu Jin had moved to Los Angeles so Lily could pursue acting. Mu Jin had lost her job at the Alfalfa Institute. It sounded like Lily hadn't managed her modeling money well. They were on food stamps, so I started sending them money.

Lily suggested that I start a YouTube channel to plug my CasaDalia.com remedies and healing philosophies. She wanted me to go viral.

"Call Ginger. She can set up a YouTube channel," Lily suggested.

I contacted the social media consultant and YouTube guru. Ginger was bossy but knowledgeable. She upgraded my website and started my YouTube channel, Casa Dalia.

Ginger coached me on recording the videos. It took several tries to get the right tone.

She advised me to give my videos an exotic air and to play up my accent. It sounded "continental," as my mother would say, referring to the European continent and not the breakfast.

I taped my first video on healing erectile dysfunction—*pito* problems. I featured two guest couples, one straight and one gay, endorsing my sensual potion. My gay followers were thrilled that I addressed the problem. Everyone assumed that ED couldn't affect gay men. But they were wrong. I found out the night I caught Acer with his gay boys and watched one guy failing to get hard.

I sent a video link to my five-hundred-plus CasaDalia.com clients who circulated it.

My channel subscribers expanded overnight.

In my next video, I moved on to infertility and featured a lovely lesbian couple. I also did a weight-loss video, one on smoking, and one on how to flush your toxic friends from your life. I called that one "*Kill Those Emotional Vampires.*"

Ginger convinced me to pay *mucho dinero* for influencers to plug my channel and online store. Each week, my subscribers doubled. After the first month, I had twenty thousand. It was hard to keep up with the weekly videos, and sometimes, I created flippant messages. My subscribers didn't seem to care. I spoke in a low, smoky voice and recited my own version of the Cuban poet, Jose Marti's, "*I Cultivate a White Rose.*" We added soft drums for more *sabor* or flavor to the beginning. I spoke in Spanish, then in English:

Cultivo una rosa blanca,
En julio como en enero,
Para el amigo sincero
Que me da su mano franca.
Y para el cruel que me arranca
El corazón con que vivo,
Cardo ni ortiga cultivo:
Cultivo la rosa blanca

Yo soy Dalia, a sus ordenes

I have a white rose to tend
In July as in January.
I give it to the true friend
Who offers his frank hand to me.
And for the cruel one whose blows
Break the heart by which I live,
Thistle nor thorn do I give.
For you, too, I have a white rose.

I am Dalia, at your service.

I ended all my videos with a gesture ripped off from the

famous Puerto Rican astrologer, Walter Mercado. I threw my hands forward, placed them on my heart, and said, "*Y siempre con mucho mucho, amor.*" And always with much, much love.

I did note, in writing, that my sign-off was a homage to the great Walter. I already imagined some smart-asses trolling me for stealing his signature line.

Lily loved the videos and texted:

Lily: "Bewitching! You send people into a trance with your opening poem. Those drums are lit, girl!"

ME: "Glad you like the drums, they can be intoxicating."

Lily: "Luv your delivery, sistah. Normally you're a badass Latina, which I love, and then you're this motivational and inspirational healer."

ME: "Not feeling it here in dull and gray New Jersey."

Lily: "Come to California. We should live in funky boho Topanga Canyon. You'd be surrounded by woo-woos and witches."

I had a sudden epiphany and called Lily instead of continuing to text.

"I'll buy a house with a granny flat. You and I live in the main house, and Mu Jin lives in the other," I said excitedly.

"That sounds awesome: they're called guesthouses here. At the mo, we're in a one-bed efficiency in the hood. The neighbors all wear ankle bracelets," Lily reported.

"How much do you think a decent house would cost?" I asked.

"About a mil, maybe two. Is that too much?" Lily asked gently, sounding like she was preparing for a no. I hesitated to make it more suspenseful, just because I'm a Cuban bitch.

"Two mil, no problem. Let's do it. Send me some properties

and virtual tours," I proposed.

Lily texted back emojis of balloons, fireworks, and four-leaf clovers.

I felt a new energy, thinking about sunny California. I looked at images of Topanga Canyon, and it looked fabulous. My only reluctance came from wondering if Topanga was anywhere near Cardoso, my ex, now known as Romero Robles.

Occasionally, I would get a letter forwarded by the secret marshal post office. Romero wrote me about his shitty teaching job and always included a PS about what a cunt I was for stealing his money. I just hoped he would start getting laid and stop writing me letters. He was dead to me.

I needed a peaceful place to do my videos and recover. Topanga looked like a quiet, wild, and rustic area close to Los Angeles. Lily sent me photos of houses for sale, which I shared with Moss.

"Lovely garden, and looks like a good investment," Moss commented.

"Moss, I'm not looking for investment. I need a peaceful place to recover or die. My cancer is back," I announced.

Moss took my hand and kissed it. "We will not let you die," Moss said.

"No control if it's my time," I informed him. I found myself consoling Moss for my possible impending death.

"I watched your mother die and can't watch the daughter too," Moss said.

After looking at a dozen listings, I found my dream property with a guesthouse at 1611 Bilberry Lane. Oddly, it was the same number, 1611, as the Jackson hospital in Miami, where I was nearly assassinated.

I purchased the house sight unseen. Since I offered a cash deal, we were able to negotiate the price from $2 million to $1.8 million. I purchased the house with a trust that Moss controlled. I didn't want Blom or the feds to track me down. I wanted to appear as if I were living in New Jersey. I packed up a few suitcases and was ready for my new chapter in 2018. I didn't want to see that *puto,* Acer, or the garden state ever again.

Lily collected me from LAX. We made our way north to Topanga and my spectacular new home. The strong sunlight was so invigorating that I forgot I had cancer.

By the time we reached the Pacific Coast Highway, I almost felt cured. Seeing the majestic Pacific Ocean, I felt so peaceful, riding with Lily to my new home. We climbed Highway 27 up the mountain. The scenery was magnificent. Topanga Canyon Boulevard led us to Bilberry Lane. As we approached the house, I felt like a new woman.

Bilberry is such a strong and potent plant for the eyes. I could see my life clearly. There was so much space and incredible panoramic views. For most of my life, I had lived in dense cities. I felt I could breathe again.

As soon as I arrived at the house, I followed the path around the back. I was drawn to the guesthouse. As I crossed the yard, I knew the guesthouse was a sacred place. It had a large living area, an open-plan dining area, a kitchen, and a large bedroom and bathroom. The walk-in closet would be perfect for my clothes, handbags, and shoes.

"This is where I want to live. You ladies are welcome to the main house," I announced.

"Are you sure? I was kind a of hoping we could room together. My mom ... ya know she can be ..." Lily lamented.

I hugged Lily. "We'll be close, no worries. Just across the yard," I reminded her.

"I'm just happy you're here with us," Lily said.

Lily showed me the main house. It had a large living room with a vaulted ceiling. I noticed my nude sketch hanging on a wall.

"You kept it," I said as Lily took it down and handed it to me.

There was a den, a beautiful kitchen, and three bedrooms. As we returned to the kitchen for coffee, I spotted Mu Jin in the garden.

"She loves it here. But she's afraid it won't be forever," Lily said.

"Don't worry, no matter what, I'll take care of you both," I assured her.

Lily threw her arms around me.

"I believe you, big sistah. Thanks."

After our embrace I remembered something was missing.

"Where's my baby?" I asked Lily.

Lily motioned me to follow her to a door from the kitchen. She opened it and there it was. My new red jag sports car. I approached it and kissed the hood. Lily dangled the keys and we went for a drive around Topanga. It was heaven and despite my prognosis, I felt at peace. Lily didn't seem as in love with the car as me.

"It's cool, Dalia. But it's usually an old, white dude, kinda car," she said.

"Then let's make sure an old white dude gets it after I die,"
I noted.

I loved living in the guesthouse. I continued to create many
inspiring videos. The yard was always in bloom. Mu Jin insisted
the property should be *feng shui* friendly. She brought in an
authentic *feng shui* master. He made a list of changes to enhance
positive energies, good health, and prosperity. Those changes
would have meant another half million bucks. I was reluctant but
agreed to some of the changes.

"I do it for you, Dalia," Mu Jin said. She sat me down, felt my
pulse, and looked at my tongue. "Red purple, much stagnation.
I make you special tea. *Un te especial*," she repeated in Spanish.
This was a perfect segue to question her about my *papi*.

"Tell me about how you learned Spanish," I asked.

Mu Jin attended a neuroscience Chinese/Cuba exchange
program. Mu Jin said Papi Eneldo moved from Colombia to Cuba
for business. She met him and his cousins in a Havana bar. She got
pregnant. End of story. There were no details on what occurred
between meeting Eneldo, his cousins and getting knocked up.

"Very stupid girl I was," Mu Jin said.

"What was my father doing in Cuba?" I asked.

"Working for Fidel. Lily born. I got a job, and we moved to
Miami," Mu Jin reported. I was super confused with the timeline
at this point.

"We had message to find your father-in-law, Mr. Ortega, and
get money. We found him at your mom's funeral, but he no talk

to me," Mu Jin complained.

"How much money were you supposed to get?" I asked.

"About fifty thousand. Your daddy, very sexy, but bad man. Many people wanted him dead. No way he still breathing," Mu Jin conjectured.

"Could he still be alive?" I asked.

"If he not dead, I kill him. He owe me!" Mu Jin shouted.

It was difficult for my brain to take in this information. Could *Papi* Eneldo still be alive?

Lily confided she thought her mother was a Chinese spy. She expected her to be arrested by the CIA at any time. I didn't want any contact with the feds and tried hard to conceal my whereabouts.

I engaged daily online with my subscribers. They were loyal and some a little intense. One girl, Sage, sent me private messages that were unhinged and desperate. She wanted to meet me in person. I discouraged any personal contact with my followers and strictly interacted online.

Mu Jin and Lily were my only live social contacts, plus my little doggie, Dill. Lily had surprised me with a rescue dog. He was adorable, and I loved him.

For several years, I had dodged a bullet. My potions and spells were working at keeping the cancer at bay. Then they stopped working, and I became weaker each day.

Around this time, Acer and Moss wanted to visit me in California. I was reluctant to have them invade my sacred space. I arranged for them to stay at the five-star Marigold Hotel near

Malibu.

I got to know the Marigold staff. The darling Camellia, her snoring sister, Juniper, and the headwaiter, Leaf, all became my subscribers. They were so sweet to me, especially when I was sick and weak. They also adored Acer as he threw around lots of cash. For all I knew, he was fucking all three of them.

During one trip to California, Moss took me aside with some news.

"The Dominican is most taken with the Kama Sutra. I am removing the pages of the same-sex acts. He accepts that it's taboo in many religions, and we chant many times about love for women," Moss informed me. I doubted it was that easy to turn Acer completely hetero.

Acer tried to entice me to the Bloom Room at the Marigold Hotel, a kind of honeymoon suite with a large soaking tub with candles and incense. Not interested.

He caressed my neck and my cheek and approached my mouth with his. I gently pushed him away. I couldn't figure out if this was real or if he was protecting his ass and his money flow.

"We can still stay married, and you can keep your business. But it's over between us," I informed him.

"This is torture. I love you. Your body and soul." Acer sounded like a *telenovela*.

"You ruined it with your boy orgy. Keep your *pito* away from me," I instructed him.

"What happens to my restaurant?" Acer asked, showing his true colors.

"When I die, everything will be yours," I lied.

I had no intention of leaving him a dime. He collapsed in my arms, sobbing. I got the impression the tears were a show. He wanted to save his ass and his bank account.

Once the doctors and tests revealed I was sick again, it was critical to locate Poppy Shaw. I was determined to pay this woman back for saving my life. When Acer switched bracelets, she was in danger of being murdered by the *Colombianos*.

I cyberstalked Poppy for weeks.

She lived in LA and was working as an actress. I was able to see her in small roles on TV and in films. Her acting was so good, and I was jealous. I admired her abilities and courage to take on a new career in midlife. I felt a deep connection with her. I remotely channeled her. She needed healing, grounding, and focus. I often held Poppy Shaw's hospital bracelet and chanted blessings.

I was alarmed when suddenly Blom contacted me through my website and wanted to speak to me. We spoke by phone, and he told me that there was a pending investigation. Moss and Acer's illegal escort service surfaced. The feds followed the money trail and found a connection to Rico Enterprises.

Blom said I could be arrested, ejected from the WITSEC program, and have my assets seized. He wanted to see me in person, but I put him off, as I was undergoing treatments. I called Moss and told him we were in the spotlight. He was apologetic.

"My fault," he lamented.

"You really screwed up this time. I doubt Sai Baba would approve of you and *papi chulo* renting out men," I informed him, referring to Acer as a pimp.

"I never mix my personal philosophies and business," Moss

said.

"This could be the end, Moss. We need a plan," I informed him.

I had to come up with a plausible scenario for Lily and Mu Jin. I sat them down one day in the yard.

"My cancer is back. I'm returning to Miami for an experimental treatment," I announced.

"Good doctors here in Los Angeles, stay here. We take care of you," Mu Jin offered. I took Mu Jin's hand.

"I have been so happy with you both these last few years. You've been a dear, sweet stepmom. My dad chose well," I said. Mu Jin didn't respond and looked embarrassed.

"Let me go with you to Miami," Lily insisted.

"My treatment could take months. You have a career here. I'll come back," I assured her.

But I lied. I was not going to Miami and was probably never coming back to Topanga alive. I was heartbroken, as I had never been happier.

I told them they could stay in the house. I left instructions for Mu Jin and Lily to bury my urn in the guesthouse yard under an olive tree. I also told Lily to befriend Poppy Shaw and somehow get her into the guesthouse. Let Poppy stay for free until she landed a major acting role.

"I owe her my life. Be very nice to her," I demanded.

I recorded the final videos for the Casa Dalia YouTube channel, where I purposely looked frail. I really was feeling weak but somehow was determined to beat the odds and survive. After all, I was a healer.

I packed up one small suitcase and left the rest of my clothes in the closet. I thought about taking my sketch but left it on the wall for Poppy. I was on my way to fighting my illness in private and on my own terms.

I called Moss, who flew from New Jersey to California. He carried me off, along with my doggie, Dill. I disappeared myself in 2018.

CHAPTER TWENTY-SIX

WIRED

I generously tipped the Goodwill workers who picked up Dalia's clothes. I had bundled so many bags, I felt obligated to help carry them out to the truck. As they pulled away, Lily appeared at the entrance of the main house.

"No escape to China for you?" I asked. Lily beckoned me over.

"I was afraid they wouldn't let my mom leave. I'm sure she used a fake passport," Lily revealed.

Lily invited me into MY own house for coffee. There were bean buns that Mu Jin had left behind. I was gonna miss that lady: spy or no spy, she was special.

We sat at the kitchen counter. I admired the stainless-steel appliances and the designer quartz countertops that resembled an Impressionist painting. Lily said it was remodeled following a *feng shui* master's suggestions.

"You're not mad about me getting the house?" I asked as I sipped coffee.

"Don't worry, Dalia took care of me," Lily said.

"Took care of you?" I asked, trying not to spill vanilla creamer on the fancy countertops in case they were really mine.

"She knew how to hide money from the government. Dalia said she would make sure the assets would be safe and out of reach," Lily replied.

Lily pulled up a photo on her phone and showed me a McMansion. She said it was at the other end of Topanga Canyon. It looked three times bigger than the house on Bilberry Lane.

"Dalia gave me this house and an offshore bank account with a lot of cash stashed on some island. I'll never have to work again," Lily said and put her finger to her lips.

At this point, I didn't know who or what to believe. It was all smoke, mirrors and a dead woman who used to be buried in the yard. Now it turned out it was really MY yard.

As we finished our coffee, Blom texted he was coming back to the guesthouse for "further investigation," and more fun and games.

"The deputy marshal is coming over again," I said. Lily was rattled.

"I'm, like, gone," Lily said, grabbing her bag and preparing to leave.

"Do you think she's really dead?" I asked, and Lily shrugged.

"She was at death's door when she left. I doubt she's still alive," Lily responded.

After Lily left, I wandered around the main house. I imagined how I would redecorate it. I found a photo in the hallway of Dalia, Lily, and Mu Jin. It appeared doggie, Dill, photobombed, peeing on the peonies in the background.

I had a text from Acer, who was also summoned by Blom to return to Bilberry Lane. I had no idea what to expect. There were also texts from Olmo, wondering if I was OK and reminding me of our movie date. I texted.

Me: "All OK, kinda. Will explain tonight." I included heart emojis.

Olmo: "Luv you, hon."

Me: "Got a callback for the pilot."

Olmo: "Celebrate!"

Me: "Double celebration. All her shit went to Goodwill this morning."

Olmo: "Good girl and good riddance, Dalia."

If he only knew that it wasn't the last of it. What would he think about a dead woman leaving me a $2 million house for no reason?

Blom arrived with a young FBI agent, followed by Acer in an Uber.

Cute Agent Alder was a little short for me, so I wasn't tempted for any "flirty skirty." This time, Acer seemed friendlier. He squeezed my ass while Blom wasn't looking.

"Agent Alder is here to train you," Blom announced.

"Training? To be an assassin?" I asked sarcastically.

"Not killing anyone. Just wiretapping," Blom responded.

"Who are we taping and why?" I asked.

"Moss. He's at the core and may threaten or blackmail you both," Blom replied.

"He's such a spiritual guy. Don't understand," Acer said.

"The Colombian cartel is behind him, and they don't fuck

around. Once we arrest Moss, you two will have to testify. I can offer you and Acer entry into the witness protection program as your lives could be in danger," Blom warned.

"*Madre de Dios.* That's why you made me tell Moss to come here today?" Acer asked.

"Is this the only way Acer and I can save our asses?" I asked.

"Yes, ma'am. Also need to find out from Moss where Dalia died and what happened to her body," Blom noted.

"Are you both ready to be trained and coached in wiretapping for a meeting with Moss?" Agent Alder asked.

I was reluctant at first, but it was like being offered a TV role in a crime show. The idea of wiretapping someone was kind of exciting. I would be taking part in a REAL sting operation; I was being proactive, taking control. It was bold.

Blom explained the next steps. The goal was to get Moss to admit to money laundering. That would lead to his arrest and information implicating his Colombian cartel bosses. Acer and I would testify that we had no knowledge of Dalia's machinations and were innocent victims. As Acer and I could be in danger, we had the option of entering the witness protection program.

I pondered the idea of a new identity and the prospect of free plastic surgery. I could start fresh in a new place; no contact with family or my few, mostly fake friends. The family Shaw? I could take them or leave them. Frankly, the only one I would miss was Olmo.

FBI Agent Alder handed me a script. He offered Acer a copy, and he refused it. Blom made Acer take a copy of the script.

I reviewed the pages like I did with any sides or material for an audition. In an audition, I could be rejected. But this was real. I could get hurt or killed. I had no choice. If I didn't do it, I could face jail time for shit I never did.

Agent Alder wanted us to practice. I took a silent Poppy pause and excused myself to go the bathroom. I took the script with me. While standing in front of a mirror, I read the lines, using different voices and expressions.

"I have no knowledge of the hospital incident as I was still under anesthesia."

"Moss, you seemed to have been so loyal to Dalia. I am surprised as you are that she signed over this house to me. I never met the woman."

"Why do you think she signed over the house to me?"

"I would be happy to sign over the house to you or Acer."

I returned to the living room while Acer reluctantly read his lines in a monotone:

"I thought you were my friend, what changed?"

"How and where did my wife die?"

"Those ashes in the urn were not hers."

"I thought we were partners, Moss, what changed?"

Blom and Agent Alder scowled.

"Acer, can you say the lines with feeling?" Blom asked.

"Why do I care? It's all over for me. Poppy gets the house for what? All my fault. Should never have switched bracelets," Acer shouted and paced the room.

"Too late. This is for you to avoid jail time, buddy," Blom clarified.

I memorized both sets of lines in case Acer screwed up. "You can do it," I whispered to Acer.

Agent Alder attached a small microphone under my collar. He attempted to do the same with Acer, but he waved him away. They didn't insist on wiring him but placed a mic behind the Iris nude sketch.

"I just want to go back to my old life, *coño*," Acer said and slammed the coffee table with his fist.

"Somehow, I don't think anything will be the same again," I predicted.

Acer's phone dinged, and Moss was on his way. Blom and Agent Alder exited the guesthouse quickly. I watched them drive off the property in a van. Blom placed a few agents around the grounds and one in the main house. The agents could storm the guesthouse in seconds if anything went south. If Moss arrived with others, the agents would detain them and not let them enter.

Acer and I sat on the sofa like sitting ducks, waiting to be beaten up, maimed, shot, killed or kidnapped. I was contemplating having a drink when Acer's hands reached over and grabbed my pussy. WTF. Then he started unzipping my jeans and kissing my neck.

"Are you crazy?" I asked and pointed to the mic on my collar. "Forgot," Acer replied, then wrote on a pad:

"They can only hear, not see."

Acer unzipped his pants, and he was erect.

Who gets a hard-on when you're about to do a sting operation? I whispered in Acer's ear, "You need help."

Thankfully, Moss texted and interrupted Acer's pawing. Moss indicated he was fifteen minutes away and wanted to make sure we were both at the house.

Acer texted back, *"Si, señor."*

I rushed to the freezer and grabbed some ice cubes. I approached Acer and unzipped his pants. He thought I wanted to play until I stuffed a few ice cubes down his bikinis. Not sure if he was wearing a dick sock. Acer quickly removed the ice and shook his head.

"You made your point."

A few minutes later, there was a buzz from the gate. I watched Moss through the camera. I was hoping he would arrive with a hit squad so that Blom and the boys wouldn't let them in and end it all.

Through the window, we saw Moss entering the yard. It was showtime. Moss glanced at the tree and did not stop. I opened the door as he approached.

We shook hands.

"Nice to see you again, Moss," I said.

Moss kissed my hand. "It's a pleasure, Miss Poppy," he said, and then beamed when he noticed Acer.

"Dominican, my old friend," Moss said, attempting to give Acer a hug with no success.

"Old friend? You freeze my credit and my bank accounts, *hijo de puta*," Acer shouted. Acer was clearly going off script and was visibly angry.

"As Sai Baba said, anger is like an intoxicant; it reduces man and degrades him to the level of an animal," Moss said, plopping in a chair.

"You want animal?" Acer said with his fist in the air.

"Sit, I will explain," Moss said.

This conversation was not going well. I hadn't yet said any of my prepared lines.

Acer took out his wallet and lined up all his credit cards on the coffee table. "I worked hard, Moss. Where's MY MONEY?" Acer asked.

"You think you worked hard. In reality, the restaurant and bakery lost money," Moss informed him.

"What about the escort service? We had a nice profit," Acer pointed out.

"I have sold the business and owe you one hundred and twenty dollars and forty-three cents," Moss said, reaching into his wallet and peeling off six twenties and a single dollar.

"Keep the change."

"*No lo puedo creer*! Can't believe this! Fuck you, Moss. *A la mierda*!" Acer shouted. He sat down on the sofa pouting, with his arms crossed. It was my turn.

"If the *Que Rico* restaurant was not making money, how was Acer able to live so lavishly?" I asked.

"He must thank his very smart wife, Dalia," Moss said.

"For doing what, exactly?" I asked.

Moss didn't answer but looked intensely at Acer.

"Dominican, you were pushing her away from New Jersey with your buggery. Shame!" Moss said.

I hoped "buggery" didn't mean what I thought it did.

"I can't help it. I like boys and girls, sometimes," Acer confessed.

"Sometimes? You just tried to . . ." I said loudly, forgetting I was wearing a wire.

"So sorry, Miss Poppy, if you had illusions about this disturbed Dominican. You must know the truth," Moss exclaimed.

Illusions? I regretted my night with Acer. I wanted to slap my own face and say, "Bad Poppy." My phone dinged.

Blom texted, *"Stay on topic."*

"Being gay is not a crime," I noted. Thankfully, we used condoms in the Bloom Room.

"Haven't heard from you, man, in weeks. Who's running my restaurant? No one answer the phones. All my guys say they were fired," Acer said to Moss.

"No longer your business, *hermano*," Moss informed him.

I thought Acer was going to kill Moss as he stood up. "Then who does, *cabrón*?" Acer asked.

"Very mysterious. I arrived one day, and the doors were bolted. All the accounts were closed. That's why you have no money, Dominican," Moss replied.

We were clearly getting nowhere. Blom scared the shit out of me. I expected Moss would be menacing, but he was so friendly and calm.

"Why did Dalia sign over Bilberry Lane to me?" I asked Moss.

"Burning question of the day, Miss Poppy. Those were her last wishes," Moss replied. I grabbed my phone and turned on a YouTube music video to drown out our voices.

Maybe Moss wasn't a bad guy. I grabbed a pad. I took a long shot and wrote:

"Feds think Acer and I were involved in money laundering. How can we make them believe we had nothing to do with it?"

Moss wrote back on the pad, *"Don't worry. I will speak to*

them and ensure you keep the house and the money."

"What money?" Acer asked. I shushed him.

Moss continued writing: *"Dalia left offshore bank accounts. Out of reach."* He then reached into his jacket pocket and handed me two envelopes marked "Acer" and "Romero." I handed both to Acer. Then Moss ripped up the paper we were writing on into little pieces and placed the torn bits in my palm.

"Toilet?" Moss asked. I pointed towards the bedroom, thinking Moss wanted to pee. He gestured I should go, then whispered, "Flush." Smart dude.

As I headed to the bathroom, I was like, holy shit. Whose side was anybody on? Both Acer and Moss left the guesthouse.

I didn't hear back from Blom or any of the agents. They all just vanished. I wondered if Blom figured out if we had been secretly communicating. Later that night, Blom texted, *"Standby."* No idea what the hell that meant. I was so over it. I chanted, "I am not confused," multiple times.

#confused #dominican #offshorebucks #gayboner #wiretap
#cuteFBI #badMoss

CHAPTER TWENTY-SEVEN

HOTEL LILAC

Should I have been concerned, being ghosted by a deputy marshal? It was enough dealing with a dead Dalia ghost but now the government?

There was no response for several weeks from Blom to my texts. I asked for an update and hopefully closure. Moss promised to make it all go away, but did he? Would the authorities show up unannounced and arrest me?

Acer, Romero, and Moss also ghosted me. It was like they had vanished. I placed all my energy into getting prepared for my Zoom callback audition for the TV pilot *Hotel Lilac*. They asked me to prepare a two-minute monologue of my choice.

I searched through all my materials and couldn't find anything suitable. Olmo sent me a few ideas and offered to coach me. The pages I had memorized from the script for the wiretap were still in my head, as were Dalia's voice and crazy story. I wrote a two-minute, Dalia-inspired monologue.

I set up the laptop camera in front of the nude sketch. When the Zoom audition began, I was fully in character and imitated Dalia's low, raspy voice.

"I know what you're thinking. How could a thief also be a healer? It's easy. My husband, my father, my father-in-law, and my stepfather betrayed me. My identity no longer existed. My only pride and joy was a thriving business, and then I was forced to start from zero. If that wasn't bad enough, the universe gave me cancer. They removed my lady parts. But that didn't stop me from building my empire by cheating and stealing my way to earn millions. At the same time, I helped people to heal with my magic potions and soothing words. So, I ask you, dear Saint Peter, please consider it all as you decide if I, Dalia, can enter those gates."

The producer and director were super impressed. They asked what play or film the monologue was from. I proudly informed them that I wrote it after being inspired by a dead friend's complicated life. Kinda true.

A few days later, the *Hotel Lilac* producer called. They loved the Dalia character so much, they considered writing it into the show. I could get a writing credit, but there was no word about whether I would play her. That was so weird.

The producers were being very secretive about the show. All I knew was the title and that it was a sci-fi drama. I had several more auditions. I would only receive snippets of the script, and we had to sign a nondisclosure agreement. Olmo thought it could mean they hadn't fleshed out the series idea, or it was so groundbreaking that they were keeping the concept under wraps.

I was short-listed for a role in *Hotel Lilac*. I owed Olmo big time. He had coached me on the subsequent auditions and was very patient. I found his Method acting technique draining. Our sessions usually ended with me either sobbing in his arms or angry. Either way, it led to great sex.

After the fourth audition, it was down to me and another actress. Olmo came over to the guesthouse to celebrate. This time, he arrived with half pastel-colored foods and half dark. We drank a lot of wine, and I became emotional.

"Without your support, Olmo, I never would have gotten past the first audition," I said tearfully, with wineglass in hand.

"You did the work, hon. I only pulled out what was already there," Olmo said.

"I don't like it when you pull out too soon," I said. Olmo blushed.

Olmo searched on his phone and rattled off all the big names associated with the show on IMDb, the film and TV industry site. I'm glad I didn't know in advance, as I wouldn't have taken a chance on my original "Dalia" monologue. I showed the two-minute piece to Olmo.

"This is awesome, Poppy. I'm a little concerned that it feeds into your obsession with this woman. Then again, it may have landed you into the big time," Olmo commented.

"After what happened, I had to vent in the Dalia voice," I said.

I broke down and told Olmo about 80 percent of the saga. I left out banging Acer and that he was bi. I told him about the hospital bracelet switch and how Dalia thought she owed me for saving her life. For the moment, I skipped the part about the house being in my name. I described the wiretapping setup and how I asked Moss to clear my name.

Olmo refilled our glasses.

"Now I see why you had to do a Dalia monologue for the audition. If you wrote this as a screenplay, nobody would believe it was a true story," Olmo noted.

Olmo suggested we call his attorney. The one who helped him avoid jail when his wife, Violeta, was found dead. Olmo put his comforting arms around me.

"That would be a kicker if I get the part in *Hotel Lilac*, and then I get carted off to jail or thrown into witness protection," I mused.

Olmo and I had shared a mutual awkward laugh. My phone dinged with a text from Blom: *"Coming over with news."*

I showed Olmo the text. "Will you stay?" I asked.

"Absolutely. To show them there's someone looking out for you," Olmo replied. I didn't think any of my asshole ex-boyfriends had ever said or thought anything remotely like this. Olmo was a catch.

Blom arrived alone.

"Deputy US Marshal Layton Blom," Blom said while shaking Olmo's hand. "Olmo Branch," Olmo introduced himself. Blom lit up.

"Big fan of *Love and Secrets*. So sad when they killed off Mace Garland. Loved that guy," Blom said.

Olmo's demeanor changed, and he went into character. I'm sure he had played TV lawyers so many times, the lingo came naturally.

"If you don't mind, I would like to sit in and take notes," Olmo said.

"If it's OK with Poppy. Glad she has someone watching her back," Blom noted.

"I could also phone my attorney, who has experience in these matters," Olmo mentioned.

"The guy who got you off on the murder charge?" Blom asked. AWKWARD.

Olmo didn't respond or flinch. He grabbed a pad and a pen. "Sorry we didn't get much from Moss," I suggested.

"We got enough. Did he give Acer any money before he left?" Blom asked.

"Not that I'm aware of," I lied. I didn't know what exactly was in those envelopes.

Either way, those boys deserved something for being dicked around by Dalia.

"Maybe Moss slipped Acer something outside while they were leaving. Both Acer and Romero took a red-eye to Miami that night. But I've got eyes on them," Blom reported.

"Deputy, may I ask why you are investigating Poppy?" Olmo asked.

"As a possible conduit for Dalia's money-laundering scheme. It seems to have continued after her death," Blom informed him.

"I'm sure you've investigated Poppy's unremarkable tenure as an office manager, her midlife crisis, her medical drama, and her transformation to acclaimed actress," Olmo said.

"Who, me?" I asked, and Olmo continued.

"She's a victim, not a perpetrator," Olmo said as he paced the room, like he was summing up closing arguments in court to a jury.

"Yeah," I cheered him on, while Blom was silent.

"Also, did you question how an unstable and whimsical actress could navigate drug lords and money laundering?"

"I'm whimsical," I exclaimed and disregarded the "unstable." I just loved being described as "whimsical."

"Poppy is an intelligent woman. You don't give her enough credit," Blom replied.

"Surely her bank accounts and lifestyle do not point to a person engaged in suspicious activities?" Olmo asked.

"I'm flat broke with a mountain of credit card debt and student loans," I informed them.

"You do?" Olmo said with a raised eyebrow.

I was exaggerating my dire finances a little, but it may have turned Olmo off.

"Did Poppy tell you Dalia signed over this property to her, worth over two mil?" Blom asked.

Olmo pretended he knew about the house. I was really getting into being-dumped territory now. I was probably deemed too much baggage for him and not girlfriend material at this point.

"On paper, I own the house. But if Dalia bought it with her laundered money, it's seized by the feds. Right?" I asked Blom.

"Deputy, let's cut to the chase. How does Poppy exonerate herself? A quitclaim deed where she gives up her ownership of this property? Are you asking her to testify against dangerous narcos? Will you provide protective custody during the trial? And if she remains in danger?" Olmo said with authority.

"Yes, to all of the above, counselor. You're good. Moss is still a wild card with mob connections. He was very mellow at the meeting, but he could plan something sinister. We intend to apprehend him soon," Blom replied.

"Until you arrest this guy, Moss, I will stay here with her, with your team's twenty-four-hour surveillance and protection," Olmo demanded.

"You got it. Do you have a weapon in the house?" Blom asked. "Only Mace and a whistle," I replied. I forgot about Dalia's pistol.

"In the meantime, Poppy, document everything Romero and Acer told you about Dalia."

"What about Lily?" I asked.

"Oh, forgot to mention. They're not sisters," Blom said. I was now into major mental free fall.

"WTF, excuse me?" I asked.

"It was a con job by Mu Jin for money. She hooked up with Dalia's father in Cuba, but he's not Lily's father," Blom replied adding, "probably another black dude."

I was confused again, and then so was Dalia, apparently. Lily and Mu Jin conned Dalia and maybe Mu Jin conned everyone.

Olmo stood up and shook Blom's hand as he prepared to leave.

"Keep us posted on when you arrest Moss," Olmo said.

Blom nodded, then made a call ordering the surveillance and protections of 1611 Bilberry Lane.

I was so relieved that Olmo knew almost everything and there may be an end game. Then I had a text from Holly, whom I hadn't heard from in over a month. It was all caps: *YOU ROCK CALL ME!!*

I showed Olmo. "Holly probably got wind of *Hotel Lilac*. She's going to make a shitload of money off you if you get the part."

"She fired me, so can I fire her?" I asked.

"Depends on if she got you the first audition. Better call her as she may have info about the role. Not good to hold grudges if you want to keep working in this brutal town," Olmo advised me. Even before I called Holly back, there was a flurry of email with docs attached.

"Looks like you got the part, hon. So proud!" Olmo said and kissed me.

"They are offering me a creator role for the Dalia character. I'm also playing her in the show. Shit," I said nervously.

Olmo pointed out the draft press release. I was listed in the cast along with major actors. *Hotel Lilac,* a one-hour dramedy. The series was about a hotel spaceship set in the year 2500, hosting space travelers. The diverse staff are trained diplomats who attempt to resolve the many space wars and broken alliances. *Hotel Lilac* acts as an intergalactic United Nations. An ARG game would also be released along with the show. The cable channel ordered a pilot and five episodes.

"That's why they kept it under wraps. It's because of the ARG element," Olmo commented. I looked puzzled.

"Alternate reality game and probably interactive. Cutting edge," Olmo explained.

Holly called as she was desperate to have me back as a client. I avoided asking her whether she expected me to pay her a commission on the show. As she was copied on all the emails, I pointed out that I created a new role for myself.

"Oh, now I see. Dalia? That Dalia?" Holly asked.

"Kinda. Based it on her crazy world," I replied.

"We'll talk about my commission some other time. So stoked, girl," Holly said.

My excitement over *Hotel Lilac* was muted as I thought about Moss returning and causing trouble. Even with Olmo by my side, I was spooked.

I looked around, and all I wanted to do was to get out of the guesthouse, even if I owned it. But it seemed every time I wanted to get away from Dalia mania, I was pulled back in. If *Hotel Lilac* became a popular show, I could be trapped in playing the Dalia character for years.

Olmo and I broke out some champagne and made love on the sofa. Then we got a little crazy and moved to a chair and knocked over a side table, smashing a lamp. We went back to the sofa and finished up. Olmo looked worried after our mutual climaxes.

"You'll become a big star and dump the geezer," Olmo said.

I threw a pillow at him.

"Not! Hard to find a man to put up with all my nonsense, tantrums, insecurities and WHIMSICAL moods," I stated.

"And one who loves you deeply and unconditionally. We may not reach a golden-year anniversary. I can try for silver," Olmo said.

"You're assuming I'll live another twenty-five years," I noted. "Did you not get what I said, Poppy, hon?" Olmo asked. "Yeah . . . oh, was that a proposal?" I asked.

There was a loud knock at the door, which ruined the moment. Olmo and I, stark naked, leaped up from the sofa. Was it the agents or Moss?

The agents apologized for knocking, but they had heard loud noises.

"Everything's OK," Olmo shouted, adding in a whisper, "Excuse us, we were fucking."

Olmo and I spent the night in the guesthouse surrounded by armed guards. We didn't dare touch each other again, fearful the agents would storm in and find us thrashing around.

I tidied up while Olmo was making notes for his play. He grabbed my hand as I walked by and kissed it.

"You can't imagine how writing this play is helping me process. It's all because of you. You're amazing, Poppy."

"Thanks. I hope to see the end of this Dalia nightmare," I said, as Olmo took me in his arms and held me close before returning to his play.

Before going to bed, I looked in the bathroom mirror.

"Don't fuck it up" became my new mantra. I went to bed feeling unhinged and a little weepy.

"I need to move out of here, Olmo," I said.

"I know, hon, we'll make it happen," Olmo said.

"Olmo, did you really mean those things you said to Blom about me being unstable and whimsical?" I asked. He kissed me deeply with a lot of tongue and hoped it meant "no."

#scifi #newidentity #arg #fidel #notmysistah #whimsical #2500ad

CHAPTER TWENTY-EIGHT

#ENDGAME

The morning after my magical night with Olmo, I noticed my dear, departed Grandma Shaw's ring was missing. I wore it daily. It was a black onyx stone mounted on a gold band. I looked all over the guesthouse bedroom, the floor, the closet, the bathroom, and under the bed. No ring. I could feel Grandma Shaw glaring at me in disappointment from the beyond.

"Have you seen my antique ring anywhere?" I asked Olmo, who was making coffee in the kitchen.

"Haven't seen it, hon," Olmo replied. I loved it when he called me hon.

"Hate when things go missing. Enough spooky shit happens around here," I said.

I was still freaked about Blom and the Dalia business. Without warning, our twenty-four-hour posse and surveillance team had suddenly disappeared. There was no news from Blom if Moss had been arrested or if I was still under investigation.

After breakfast, Olmo and I walked over to the main house,

as we noticed activity. There were moving men carrying boxes and furniture. We entered through the opened back door. Lily was nowhere in sight.

This was Olmo's first time inspecting the main house. He nodded his approval as he walked around admiring the vaulted ceilings.

"Better digs than my modest Sherman Oaks bungalow," Olmo noted.

"I like your bungalow," I said.

"The taxes are probably triple. How did these ladies afford it?" Olmo asked. "Mu Jin sold secrets to the Chinese," I said.

"Is that on a Post-it note?" Olmo asked, raising an eyebrow.

"Along with the rest of the vortex of crime, mystery, and money. I always thought I was quirky and unique, but compared to Dalia's crowd, I'm SO boring."

"This is a beautiful home. Up to you, hon, if ya wanna fight to keep it," Olmo suggested.

"We agreed I should move away," I reminded him.

"That was before I realized the dead lady gifted you a two-million-dollar property," Olmo noted.

Lily appeared in overalls and a cap, holding a clipboard. "Gotta bounce," Lily announced.

"To your new place?" I asked. "You got it, sistah," Lily replied.

"Speaking of sistah, Blom said you and Dalia aren't really sisters," I said.

"I know," Lily noted.

"It seems Dalia didn't know either," I said.

"Maybe Mu Jin isn't even my mother. It's so fucked up. Oh

well." Lily quipped as she rushed over to manage the movers lifting a glass table.

"I'll just be down the street. We can hang out," Lily proposed.

"You're assuming I'm staying here," I said.

"Why wouldn't you, silly? You and your cute old man should enjoy. Almost forgot, my mom left you this," Lily said as she handed me a large, padded envelope.

I peeked inside, and it was one of Mu Jin's granny panties wrapped around Dalia's silver pistol. It was the gun I found in the Manolo shoebox with Iris Ortega's license.

Olmo and I headed back to the guesthouse. He looked concerned and stopped in the yard in front of the olive tree.

"This cops-and-robbers game needs to be over. I'm getting my criminal attorney involved. He'll call Blom and get it fixed," Olmo declared.

"OK," I said, impressed that Olmo was taking control. He then left for the supermarket, as he was cooking dinner that evening.

I was still holding the envelope with the pistol wrapped in Mu Jin's panties when there was a text. It was from Jasmin, who wanted to visit the Dalia tree. She had been on the VIP mourner list, and I remembered she was out of the country. I texted back:

"Did you see the last photo? The urn is no longer there."

I was also reluctant, as Blom's boys no longer guarded the house.

Jasmin insisted with a *"PLEASE."* I took a chance and gave her a thumbs-up. Within ten minutes, the gate buzzed. She must have been around the corner.

I could see Jasmin in the camera and doubted she was coming

to kill me. She looked emaciated. She wore a shawl over a long sundress, sunglasses, and a floppy hat. I swore this Jasmin was the last Dalia mourner I would ever let in.

I watched the woman as she entered. She moved slowly and seemed to float towards the yard, where I met up with her.

"Jasmin?" I asked.

"Yes, my name is now Jasmin," the woman replied in a low voice.

"Did you know Dalia?" I asked.

"You're Poppy. Much prettier in person," Jasmin said, looking at me.

When she spoke, Jasmin sounded a lot like Dalia's raspy voice. OMG, was that her standing in my yard?

She headed to the olive tree, crouched down with difficulty, and examined the hole in the ground. I joined her.

"So, you're not dead?" I asked.

"Not yet, Where's my Dill?" Jasmin/Dalia answered my question with a question.

OMG It's fucking her!

"Dalia, Deputy Blom has the ashes. Shall I call him?"

"Don't bother, I told him to meet me here."

We both sat on the bench in the yard and didn't speak for several minutes. I was still clutching the manila folder with Mu Jin's granny panties and Dalia's pistol.

I noticed she was carrying a beige, crochet handbag, a replica of one still in the closet. She was also wearing some hot, gold lame sandals.

As we sat in silence, I spotted the plastic angel that decorated her death anniversary cake. It was lying in a flower bed, so I picked it up.

"This plastic angel was on the cake for your death anniversary party. A surfer baker made it," I informed her.

"I watched the event on Facebook. Those monks were awesome. That Ginger is such a bitch and ripped me off. *Pendeja.* Should have fired her," Dalia noted.

I dared not mention Ginger owned her domain and YouTube channel. Dalia was a shadow of the figure I came to know on her videos.

"So just to be clear, you are Dalia Shaw Flores? And you're not dead?" I asked. Dalia squeezed my arm tight with her bony hand. I froze with fear.

"Does this feel like I'm dead, Poppy?" Dalia replied.

She sounded angry. I peeled her hand off my arm and stood up. I did a Wonder Woman pose still holding on to the folder in my left hand. That pose saved my ass many times during auditions. I needed more proof; given there were so many crazy Dalia mourners.

"If you're the real Dalia, what was wrong with Acer's balls?"

"He doesn't have any. Joke. They seemed normal to me," she replied.

Jasmin took off her sunglasses and there were those turquoise eyes, a little dull but it was her. But I continued my interrogation anyway.

"Who's the guru that Moss loves?" I asked.

"Sai Baba. Gratitude is our life's breath." She responded and even sounded like Moss.

"OK, it's you. But I didn't save your life. It was all a prank," I said.

"I'm listening," Dalia said.

"Romero, when he was still Cardoso, made the call to the deputies guarding you in Jackson and spoke in Spanish. Imagine having young and stupid deputies in Miami not knowing Spanish. Blom said he should have fired them," I said, and Dalia interrupted.

"Get to the point of the story, Poppy," Dalia said. She did not look happy I was rambling.

"While the stupid deputies were farting around wondering what to do, Acer switched our bracelets. Then he wheeled you into a closet. Blom said they put me on the chopper transport; then they realized I wasn't you. Imagine," I said and laughed.

"Why is that funny?" Dalia asked in an angry voice.

"I shouldn't laugh, and I know your life has not been fun. In fact, pretty shitty, but exciting in a way," I said.

"I watch you on the screen and read your social media posts. I'm so jealous. You look like you're having so much fun, Poppy," Dalia said.

"Me having fun? You monopolized, consumed me, occupied my being, my soul. Dragged me into your abyss of crime."

Jasmin/Dalia became annoyed and came up to my face.

"You got what you wanted, Poppy. *Pendeja desagradecida.*"

"Hey, I know what that means. Watch it!" I shouted.

"Ungrateful asshole," said a voice from somewhere.

"Deputy Blom, you remembered your Spanish," Dalia said and turned around as Blom approached with three agents, guns drawn.

I sat back down on the bench with Dalia, and she placed her bony hand on my arm again. Did she want to draw blood?

"Check the main house and the grounds, boys. Make sure Dalia didn't bring any friends with her," Blom ordered his men.

Blom then did a once-over of Dalia. Then they stared at each other for a while.

"Long time, Deputy. I see you're still on the job," Dalia said with a smile. Her tone changed when she was talking to Blom. It was softer and sexier.

"If I close out your new case, expel you from WITSEC, just maybe I can retire and enjoy my family," Blom said and signaled to the agents to stand down.

"Family? Surprised she didn't dump you for being away so much," Dalia said.

Blom put his gun on the bench next to Dalia, who could have easily grabbed it. He took out his phone and showed us a photo of a girl about seven years old.

"My wife, Heather, took your herbal potion for almost a year, then got pregnant. This is my daughter, Dalia," Blom said, beaming.

Holy shit. Blom named his kid after Dalia? This was beyond weird, but kinda touching. Dalia clutched my arm again. I pulled away and made a face.

"Sorry, didn't mean to hurt you," she said to me, then turned to Blom. "Glad I did something right, Papi. Where's Dill?"

"In an evidence box labeled 'US versus Iris Ortega, aka Dalia Shaw Flores aka Jasmin Thorn,'" Blom replied.

"After I staged my own, 'Dalia's' death, I changed my name

to Jasmin Thorn. I've been hanging with the Colombian black Indian Raizal tribe. They practice the purest form of Santería," Dalia informed him.

"I heard that tribe is so powerful, the narcos don't go near them," Blom said.

"Not powerful enough to cure me. I don't have long, Papi," Dalia reported.

Now she's really dying and she calls him, 'Papi?' WTF?

"Sorry to hear that. But you're being charged with racketeering under the RICO Act. Moss gave you up," Blom announced.

"Did Moss make a deal, and is he now in custody?" Dalia asked.

"Not at all. He's back at Langley, getting reassigned," Blom answered.

"Reassigned? Langley? CIA?" Dalia asked.

Moss is CIA? Double WTF! Maybe I've been played by all of these assholes. I needed a plan, so I grabbed Blom's gun and dropped the manila envelope with the loaded pistol. It could be a backup if they took Blom's gun away from me. But I had no idea who I wanted to shoot. It just made me feel empowered.

I could feel the deputies lunging for me. Blom was frozen and Dalia was calm.

"*Querida*, give the man back his gun." Dalia suggested.

Blom rises and gingerly took his gun from my hands, turned and shot the memorial tree.

"Does that make you feel better, Poppy?" He asked.

"No. I don't feel better. Now I have a dead tree in my yard."

Dalia reached up for my arm again but I pulled away.

"We're all connected, Poppy. *Calma.*" Dalia pleaded.

Blom motioned for his boys to stand down and tried to diffuse the scene.

"Ladies, I only found about Moss today. For decades, he was deep undercover for the CIA," Blom responded shaking his head.

Dalia laughed. Why is this now business as usual? Here we go again.

"So, Deputy, you got played too. I got played by my father-in-law and my husband, then I played Acer, and Moss played all of us," Dalia reported.

To make my point, I jumped on the bench and did my power pose. Then I realized the manila envelope was still on the ground. A Plan C involving the pistol was still an option.

"And I got played by all of you."

So, Dalia, you were conned by your father, Eneldo, your father-in-law, Lirio Ortega, your husband, Cardoso—he's back in Miami, BTW—then conned by Moss, your stepfather. You can also add Mu Jin and Lily," I said.

"Lily, a traitor?" Dalia asked.

"Yes, ma'am. Not your sister. Mu Jin made that shit up and by the way her panties are in that envelope with another item belonging to you, Dalia." I noted and indicated to the envelope on the ground.

Dalia looked at Blom who was eyeing the envelope.

"So, the only truly loyal person is Poppy," Dalia announced and looked at me.

"I did my best to honor and guard your clothes and to satisfy your fans," I said.

"And my husband," Dalia said in a weak voice.

"Oh, sorry," I said in a low voice and whispered, "don't worry, he's still gay."

"I forgive you for wearing my clothes. I always intended to come back and wear them," Dalia shared.

Son of a bitch. I'd have to repurchase all her stuff from Goodwill.

"All the clothes you left here are also in the evidence box with Dill's ashes," Blom said.

Saved by a US marshal.

"I came back to die in the guesthouse. I made sure Lily would move out and hoped Poppy would live in the main house," Dalia said.

I climbed down from the bench and sat. I took a moment.

"The feds may take the house away from me," I noted.

"Somehow, Moss made sure all the assets she handed out to Poppy, Lily, Acer, and Romero were clean," Blom informed me.

"You have to admit that Moss is good," Dalia said and cracked a smile.

"He's seasoned CIA. Unfortunately, Moss didn't erase all the crimes of Rico Enterprises under the RICO Act. That was so silly, calling it 'Rico.' But you're facing time, Dalia," Blom said.

"How much?" Dalia asked.

"Up to the judge. They may release you early on compassionate grounds, as it looks like you're not well," Blom observed.

I felt like I was watching a twisted crime show.

"Whatever sentence they give me, I won't last, Layton," Dalia said.

Blom seemed to melt when she called him "Layton." Oh my, can't believe these two never did it.

"No more voodoo, babe. Why not have real treatments? We can still arrange—" Blom said and was interrupted by Dalia, who touched his arm, then put a finger to her lips.

"It's too late. And for the record, the voodoo works. Just look at your daughter."

"Touché," Blom said.

Blom wiped his wet face with a handkerchief. This was so way beyond *telenovela*. "Before the love fest breaks up, a question. Why did a nobody like me, Poppy Shaw, a talented, sometimes insecure, well-meaning person, whose family is quirky and crazy but meant no harm, get ensnared with a big-time, Cuban, crime family, and put through an emotional roller-coaster ride?" I asked.

"She has a point, Dalia. Why?" Blom asked. Dalia sat motionless on the bench.

"Tell me Poppy Shaw. Since you came to live in this guest-house, aren't you in a better place with your career, love life, and finances?"

"Finances? Hope it's enough to pay for the mental recon-struction I'll need to recover from all your bullshit," I noted.

"You'll be fine. *Suerte, querida* Amapola," Dalia said.

She slowly rose from the bench after wishing me luck, using my Spanish name, Amapola.

Dalia walked over to examine the gunshot wound to the olive tree which tore into the lower trunk.

"Poppy, one last favor. Can you bury my real ashes in the yard with Dill's under the olive tree?" Dalia asked. I choked up.

"Sure, if the tree lives and as long as no visitors allowed. No more mourner management, babe." I demanded. Dalia nodded.

Blom brought out handcuffs. I backed away, as Blom was about to apprehend Dalia.

Dalia put her hand out to stop Blom. Then she beckoned for me to come over to her. She handed me her shawl, hat, and sunglasses. The deputy placed the handcuffs on Dalia. Then I raised my hand in a Poppy pause and pointed to Dalia's sandals. She would not need those in prison.

Dalia, still handcuffed, slipped her sandals off. Deputy Blom knelt, picked them up, and handed them to me. A barefoot Dalia was led out of the yard.

I slipped on the sandals and donned the floppy hat, shawl, and sunglasses.

Olmo pulled up in the red Jag as the agents were escorting a handcuffed and barefoot Dalia to a waiting black van. Dalia stopped and stared at the red Jag and Olmo as he exited the car.

"Hey old, white dude, take care of my baby." Dalia said loudly. "The Jag too."

He stared at Dalia like he knew her and asked, "Do I know you?"

WTF, is Olmo part of this shit? I nearly strangled myself with Dalia's scarf from the stress.

"Señor Branch? It's me from Casa Iris, remember. *Todo para salvar el amor.*" Dalia responded.

OMG. Olmo knew Iris, the old Dalia, and there was love involved. Help!

"This is why I hate California, everybody is six degrees from

Dalia," Blom remarked and added, "Take her away, boys."

The agents escorted Dalia into the black van which took off down Bilberry Lane.

Olmo was ashen and turned to Blom.

"Oh God, Dalia is Iris from that narco Ortega family? Does Poppy have to testify and go into hiding?"

"Let's go inside," Blom suggested.

As we walked back to the guesthouse, I wondered if I was off the hook with Moss or if he was still after me. And would I have to testify against Dalia? That woman, dead or alive, was going to blow up my life again. And what the hell is her connection with Olmo? I was on overload again and couldn't handle anymore.

Blom and Olmo sat in the living room, and I paced.

"Deputy Blom, what if after Poppy testifies, she changes her name through marriage? Would that work as well as witness protection?" Olmo asked.

It didn't register, what Olmo was saying.

"Hey, Poppy, I think the guy wants to get hitched," Blom said with a smile then added, "Go for it, bro."

Olmo looked at Blom then led me to a chair, then got down on his knees with difficulty. He pulled a ring box from his pocket. OMG, my first marriage proposal in forty-six years.

"I borrowed your ring this morning for sizing. Hope you like it, hon, 'cause I love you. Will you marry me?" Olmo asked, then opened the box, revealing a huge, shiny diamond.

"Please say yes, Poppy," Blom insisted.

Olmo suggested that instead of entering witness protection, I change my name to Violeta Branch, after his late wife.

"And give up Poppy Shaw playing Dalia on *Hotel Lilac?*" I asked.

"Not necessary, you're off the hook. Case closed. The house is yours. Say yes to the man, goddamn it," Blom insisted.

Blom was impatient, while Olmo looked nervous.

"Yes, I'll marry you, Olmo Branch," I said, then muttered under my breath, "Eventually."

Olmo slipped the bling on my ring finger and kissed me.

"We can bury Violeta's urn under the olive tree so there's a NEW dead girl in the yard," Olmo suggested.

I raised my eyebrows. Even Blom shook his head.

"Ok, I get it. *No mas muertas en tu patio,*" Olmo said quietly.

I took a Poppy pause and agreed.

"Correct. No more dead girls in MY yard."

#readOn

POPPY 2.0

SIX MONTHS LATER

Olmo and I moved into the main house and turned the guesthouse into an Airbnb. The rent pays the taxes. No crazy guests, yet. We are still engaged.

His play, *Rosemary and Juliet*, is in rehearsals, and he's playing himself.

Dalia was in prison only a few weeks. She was released under home confinement and in hospice care. She spent her final days with Deputy Blom, his wife, Heather, and their daughter, Dalia. I still have her silver pistol but threw away the granny panties.

Blom reminded me that Dalia asked to be buried in the yard. He returned to Bilberry Lane and found the traumatized tree he shot survived and thrived.

"I assume this time she's really dead," I said. Blom nodded.

We burned Mu Jin's leftover paper effigies at the tree. Then Blom, Olmo and I bowed our heads in silence. But there was unfinished business.

"Do I REALLY need to know what happened between you and

Iris?" I asked Olmo who shook his head. Blom high-fived Olmo, "Good choice dude."

I had no intention of advertising that Dalia was back in the yard buried next to the olive tree.

We shot the *Hotel Lilac* pilot. They released a trailer to great success. I play the character Dalia, the queen of Planet Rico. The planet is rich in healing powers, but Dalia weaponizes them to extort favors from other planets and galaxies. The flowers, plants, and botanicals on Planet Rico are all pastel colored and create a land of love . . . *y siempre con mucho mucho amor.*

#therealend #ornot